ACTS
OF
LOVINGKINDNESS

A NOVEL BY
NINA KENTSIS

Porter Place Publishing
Printed in the United States of America

First Edition 2025

ISBN 979-8-9926161-0-1 (paperback)
ISBN 979-8-9926161-1-8 (eBook)

This is a work of fiction. You may think it's about you, but it's not.

Cover design by Nina Kentsis. Photo from iStock.
Interior formatting by Nina Kentsis and Alex Kentsis.

Distributed worldwide by IngramSpark.

www.ninakentsis.com

For Alex, whom I met at the right time.
And for my father, who left us too soon.

ACTS
OF
LOVINGKINDNESS

I thought it was just going to be Jason and me hanging out, like we always do the night before school starts, but he has invited some of his friends over, Dave and Mike and Tracy and this girl Carly, who's only going to be a sophomore, for Lord's sake, and even though he was like, Stay, stay, it'll be fun, I decided it was time for me to walk home.

"Francie, c'mon, you'll like these guys if you get to know them," Jason says.

"Jason," I say, as I sit on the floor of his entry hall, tying up my Converse, "sweet, sweet, Jay. I do know them. That's how I know I don't like them."

Just as an example, here's why I don't like Mike. In the eighth grade, at Sammy Metzger's bar mitzvah, Mike convinced everyone that we should play seven minutes in heaven in the basement of the synagogue. Then, when he and my friend Susannah—Sooz—ended up in some closet together and she definitely did not give him a hand job, he told everyone she did. My point is, it's not like these kids are new. We've been in school together since the sixth grade, at least.

Jason has been one of my best friends since kindergarten. His house is a few blocks away from mine, and we would sit on the bus together all through elementary and middle school. When the bus dropped us off at his house, he would walk me home, and then I'd walk him home, and we'd walk back and forth between our houses, talking about everything and nothing.

But freshman year of high school, somehow Jason got cooler, and I did not. I'm not, like, a huge loser with no friends or anything, and obviously it's not like he can't be seen with me in public, I mean, this isn't a John Hughes movie. It's more like, Jason has some new friends who I don't really like that much, and I spend more time with my girl friends.

Anyway, I stand up, laces tied and open my arms to hug him goodbye. Instead, he puts on his flip flops and says, "I'll walk you home."

He leashes up his dog Roxie and grabs his beeper—Why? Who is going to beep him in the five minutes it'll take to walk to my house and back?—and tells everyone else he'll be back in a few, that he's walking me home. I wonder what they all think, like, do they wonder why Jason's friends with me?

"I can't have you walking home alone in the dark," Jason says, lighting up a cigarette. He blows the smoke sideways away from me. It's a little bit misty outside and I can feel my hair curling up.

"I've done it before," I say. We live in a very safe, suburban neighborhood on the South Shore of Long Island. I read the police blotter in our local paper because my mother is the editor there. There is really nothing for me to be worried about.

"Yeah, but..." he looks at me. "Were you wearing a tank top like that last time?"

I look down at my tank top, which is bright blue and says "Duke" on it because I'm obsessed with Duke University.

"What are you talking about?" I ask. "I've been wearing this tank top, or a tank top like this, all summer." I look at him. "By the way, I've been meaning to discuss your t-shirt." Jason is wearing a ringer tee that says "Elmhurst High Class of 1995" in bright red.

He laughs. "I was wondering when you were going to comment on it."

"Where did you even get it?"

"Well, as class vice president, I have special, early access to these items. You can buy one from the school store for the low, low price of $8."

"I guess I'm glad that we're class of '95. And we'll be class of '99 from college. Those are good numbers. Joseph would've been class of '91. That's not a great number."

Jason pauses, cigarette halfway to his mouth. "Oh," he says, "Francie. I'm sorry."

"He's not dead, Jay," I say. "He's just ... not here."

Joseph is my older brother. I haven't seen him in almost four years. He left home six years ago, when he was fifteen, to go to drug rehab. He went to a few different rehab centers, and then a halfway house in Minnesota. He ran away from the halfway house and made it back to New York City, where my mother's brother Leo took him in, against my parents' wishes.

That was a huge deal in our family. My parents were trying to use "tough love" with Joseph, to make him choose between living on the street and going back to rehab. When my aunt and uncle didn't turn Joseph away, my parents basically cut them out of our lives. And then my grandparents took sides, against my parents. We barely speak to them, and my younger sister Lola and I don't see our cousins, either. The whole thing came to a head right after my bat mitzvah.

So, Joseph is living in Brooklyn, like 40 minutes away, and working with my uncle. Lola and I have only seen him a few times. I was very angry with him for a while, for running away from rehab, going to my aunt and uncle's house instead of coming home, but now I know it's not his fault. He was only 17, the same age I am now, and trying not to have to sleep on the streets. I was angry at my aunt and uncle, for not listening to my parents, but then I think, What would I have done, in their place? I don't know.

And my parents almost never talk to Lola and me about Joseph. It's like this person who was part of our lives for all these years just vanished and there's no way to bring the subject up without my mother dissolving into tears and my father working himself up into a rage about my uncle and my grandparents.

Jason knew Joseph pretty well. Jay is an only child, and I think Joseph thought it was cute that one of my best friends was a guy. When Jay would come over, Joseph would play video games with him, or he'd let us deal him in for cards, or they'd just play catch.

Jason and I look at each other and I give a little shrug against him.

"What does vice president even do? Do you have to make up, like, little cheers for us? Like, Class of ninety-five, you're going to thrive!" I do a pretend cheer.

"No, more like, Class of ninety-five, you're learning to drive!"

"Class of ninety-five, you've arrived!"

We are both giggling uncontrollably.

"Ninety-five is alive!" he says in a robot voice.

"Oh, my god, not that movie. With the robot! I forgot how much you loved that movie."

"That was my ninth birthday party, that movie!"

We turn the corner and he puts out the cigarette under his heel on the sidewalk.

"Litterbug," I say, giving him a little push.

"You're right," he says. "Smoking is really just an excuse for me to litter."

Roxie sniffs at the cigarette, then pees on it.

"Watch out for that on the way home," I say.

My house is on a small street with only four houses. Our front porch has a little bench that no one ever sits on and on national holidays, my mother puts out an American flag in a little flag holder. There's one flying now, for Labor Day.

"Your mom is so patriotic," Jason says.

"Yeah. I think she just wants to shame the neighbors for buying foreign cars."

"Don't you have a Volvo?"

"They have German cars," I say. "Swedish cars are OK."

"Wow. That is some weird logic."

We pause in front of my house.

"It's very Long Island noir here, with all this mist," I say. Jason and I watch a lot of movies together.

I bend down to give Roxie a little pet and when I stand up, I open my arms again for a hug and Jason steps toward me and kisses me. He tastes like the popcorn we were eating before everyone else arrived and the cigarette he just smoked and he smells like Ivory soap and apple shampoo and a little bit like Roxie and I can see his green eyes even in the dark and even though this is so unexpected, I mean, Jay and I have never kissed, before I can overanalyze it, I pull him closer and kiss him back. He's not too much taller than I am, so this is really easy. Kissing Jason is so easy. Why have we never done this?

We kiss like this, my fingers in his soft dark brown hair, his hands around my back, until Roxie starts barking and I pull away. We look at each other for a long moment.

I touch my mouth. "I should go in," I say.

"Francie," he says, as I turn up the driveway. "I'll see you tomorrow."

He turns around and walks back toward his house, Roxie trotting along behind him.

What just happened? Jason kissed me—we kissed each other. I've only ever kissed two guys, one guy at each of the summer programs I did before sophomore and junior years of high school. No one from our school. And really mostly just kissing.

I stand outside for a few minutes, waiting for my heartbeat to slow down to normal. I open the front door, turning off the burglar alarm and then setting it again, and walk up the stairs to my room.

There's a little knock on the door and Lola pokes her head in. Her room is at the other end of the hall from mine, and Joseph's room is in the middle.

Lola is two years younger than I am. We look nothing alike. I am short with shoulder-length brown hair that could, on a good day, be described as wavy and, on a bad day, scraggly. I always wear my glasses because my contact lenses bother my eyes. Lola is tall and fair-skinned with freckles and very curly hair that I covet and she always wears her contact lenses except for now, when she's ready for bed.

A stranger might think I'm weirdly nice to Lola, like, are most people so nice to their younger sisters? I don't know. None of my friends have younger sisters. But most people who know my family get why it's different for Lola and me.

"Lo," I say. She comes in and flops down on my bed. "Jason just kissed me."

She gives a little squeal. "What? I knew it! I knew he would, one day. How was it?"

I think for a second. How was it? "It was nice," I say. "Weird, because it's Jason. But, like, neat."

"Neat? Like, neat-o? Like it's the 1950s?"

"No, neat, like, not messy."

"OK, kind of a strange way to describe a kiss, Francie. Do you want to kiss him again? Does this mean you're going out? Is he still driving us to school tomorrow?"

"I don't know, I don't know, and yes."

"Francie. Francie pants. Do you want more neat kisses or not?"

I smile to myself. "Maybe." Do I want more kisses from Jason? Yes.

After Lola leaves, I pick up the phone and call AJ. Alison Jacobs. We've been best friends since the third grade, when we met in a district-wide program for gifted kids. We used to sing Bon Jovi songs into our hairbrushes and put leaves in the mailbox and make risqué clothing for our Barbie dolls out of old socks. We have a similar sense of humor, we are both a little sarcastic, though I like to think we've outgrown our mean streak. There was a minor interlude in our friendship in the sixth grade, when she attempted to ingratiate herself with the popular kids. I forgave her for it when she realized they were not very smart and she came back to me, but by then, I'd already met Susannah, who is silly and fun and doesn't take herself so seriously.

"What's up, Francie?" she says when she picks up the phone. AJ has caller ID. I can hear her snacking on something. AJ is always snacking on something. She has the metabolism of a cheetah, but her mother is always warning her that one day, it will slow down and she should learn to be a healthy eater now. AJ wholeheartedly ignores this advice. "How was your back-to-school ritual with Jason?"

Historically, the night before the first day of school, Jason and I look at our old yearbooks and eat popcorn and watch his bar mitzvah video and just generally make fun of who we used to be while we make plans for the next year. Historically, there has been no making out.

"It got cut short when Mike and Dave and those guys came over."

"Why did they come over?" AJ asks.

"I don't know. But that's not why I'm calling."

"You know you don't need a reason to call me, Francie. We've been over this. I know I might not be as cool as Jason, but you don't need to make up excuses to get me on the phone."

"Ha ha, very funny. He kissed me."

I can hear her stop chewing. "What?" she says.

"Jason kissed me. He walked me home and then he kissed me and then he was like, I'll see you tomorrow, and then I walked into my house and I told Lola and then I called you."

"OK, thank you for that play-by-play. Did he say anything else?"

I sit down on the floor, my back against the bed, twirling the phone cord with my fingers.

"He said something about my tank top."

"Why? Which tank top are you wearing?"

"Just my Duke tank top." AJ, Sooz, and I know each other's wardrobes by heart.

"Oh, your boobs look huge in that tank top. You're gonna need a bigger one when you get there next year."

I've been dreaming about going to Duke since I was in the eighth grade, when I fell slightly in love with Grant Hill while watching him play basketball during his freshman season. I did get a little sad when I realized that, even if I got into Duke, we would not overlap. Not like Grant Hill would ever have looked twice at me, but still.

I look down at my chest. I guess my boobs look big, but they are big, they always look big. "Jason has been seeing me all summer in this tank top, in other tops, in my bathing suit, for Lord's sake. I can't imagine why all of a sudden, he was compelled to kiss me."

"It doesn't sound like you wanted him to." AJ does not get my thing with Jason, perhaps because she doesn't think he's cute. I don't think she even understands why we're friends, like, aren't she and Sooz enough? I also don't think she can be friends with a guy without wanting him to be totally into her in a way that's kind of embarrassing. For the guy, I mean.

"Did he do anything else, you know, while admiring your tank top?" AJ asks.

"No! We were standing in front of my house!"

"It could happen, Francie. Guys' hands sometimes do wander. It would not be terrible for you to get past first base."

It's not like AJ is so experienced, but she's hooked up with more guys than I have. So has Sooz. There's nothing holding me back, really, except I haven't had the chance.

"Very funny. I just don't know what it means that he kissed me, right before senior year."

"Maybe stop looking for meaning in it, and see what happens tomorrow."

And then we hang up and I call Sooz and have basically the exact same conversation.

The next morning, my mom makes Lola and me stand outside the front door for a picture, as she has done every first day of school for my entire life.

"Girls," she says, getting teary-eyed, "look this way." She tugs down at the hem of my skort. "This isn't too short, Francie?"

Lola rolls her eyes. "AJ picked it out."

"She did not. We picked out our outfits together."

"I thought you hated matching outfits." My mother looks confused. She knows how I feel about matching outfits, having made Lola and me wear them until I finally rebelled at age ten. Lola, meanwhile, is wearing a short-sleeve thermal shirt and long corduroy cutoffs. Why do those items exist? Who wants to wear corduroys and thermals in the summer? Lola, I guess.

"No, Mom, not matching, eew. Just so we could look our best."

"Well, you always look beautiful, whether Alison suggested this or not. Both of my girls do."

Lola and I both roll our eyes at this.

My mother puts her hand to her chest. "I can't believe this is your last first day of school, Francie."

"Mom," I say, picking up my backpack. "I am planning to go to college."

"Yes, but I probably won't be there to take a photo of you on your first day of college."

She definitely won't be there. I am not going to college anywhere near home, if I can help it. Certainly not on Long Island, and while I love New York City, and I'm sure I'll move back after I graduate, if I don't leave this area for college, I don't think I'll ever leave.

Jason pulls up in his '89 Mercury Sable.

"Good morning, Mrs. Baum," he says, getting out his car.

"Good morning, Jason," my mom says. "C'mon, you get in the picture, too."

Jason looks at me. He looks really uncomfortable, but he stands next to me and puts his arm around me and smiles for a photo for my mother, just a few feet from where we stood last night, kissing.

I get into the front seat and Lola gets into the back seat. We wave goodbye to my mother, who is brushing away tears.

"Sorry about that," I say to Jason.

He looks at me again and smiles a little, shaking his head.

Jason got his license over the summer. My birthday was only two days ago, on Rosh Hashanah, so I couldn't go for my road test, obviously. I'm going to get my license this weekend, I hope.

"Jay, are you gonna do the school play this year?" Lola asks from the back seat.

"Maybe," he says. "Have to see what Whit chooses." Mr. Whitman is the chorus and drama teacher, but everyone only calls him Whit. Lola and Jason are always in the school plays, although Lola is more of a drama queen and Jason is more of a ham.

We pull up to the school and park in the student lot, which has a lottery for spots and Jason has one for September. Lola gets out of the car and runs over to her friends, who are all standing by the stairs outside the gym hallway, smoking cigarettes and playing with a hacky sack and with, like, rain sticks.

"Whew," I say. "I can practically smell the patchouli from here." Just as I'm about to say something about our kiss, Jason turns to look at me, very serious. My stomach drops.

"Francie," Jason says.

"Jason," I say.

"I shouldn't have kissed you last night," Jason says. "I'm kind of seeing Carly, and—"

"You're what?"

"I'm kind of seeing Carly. That's why she came over last night."

"Are you joking with me? Why did you kiss me?"

He shakes his head. "I don't know," he says. "It was like, like you said, it felt like a movie, and you looked so pretty..." His voice trails off. "You must've thought about it, about us. You kissed me back."

"Yeah, I have thought about us, and every time I did, I was like, Jason is one of my best friends. I don't think I want to mess that up."

He runs a hand through his hair. "Did I mess it up?"

I take a deep sigh. "I don't know, Jay. Next time, don't kiss me."

I get out of the car and shut the door and lean against it for a minute, willing myself not to cry. I walk into the school past Lola, who gives me a look, like, Are you OK?, and I give her a look back, like, I'm fine, and I find AJ and Sooz sitting on the floor in the gym hallway, waiting for the bell to ring. Jason thinks I'm pretty. I do not want to be thinking about that. No one at Elmwood thinks I'm pretty. I don't know why I even try. I'm the smart one, the one who does all the reading, the one who already applied to Duke early decision.

I slump down next to Sooz and realize my mother was right, this skort is too short. Sooz is wearing platform clogs and a crop top and what could best be described as fancy sailor shorts. All of us have that top, we bought it together at Contempo Casuals, but I would never wear it to school. This is not the outfit we chose for Sooz.

"She went rogue," AJ says. AJ, meanwhile, is wearing a white linen tank top that has a matching cardigan and a pearl necklace and a jean skirt that she has tucked neatly under her legs. Her curly hair is pulled back into a low ponytail. She looks way too fancy for high school, but that's her thing. "What's wrong, Francie?"

I look at them and I don't want to cry, kissing Jason did not mean that much to me, except it meant a little bit, and it feels crappy not to be the one chosen. Like, why couldn't he go back to Carly after kissing me and be like, Hey, Carly, I'm into Francie?

"Apparently, Jason is kind of dating Carly. I have no idea why he kissed me."

"That tiny sophomore who looks like a pre-pubescent boy?" AJ asks.

"Yes, that's the one."

"How could he choose her over you?" Sooz asks. "You are amazing. And if Jason doesn't realize that, it's his loss."

"Thanks, guys," I say.

"He is a Cancer, isn't he? Usually, Cancer and Virgo go well together." Susannah is very into astrology.

"Sooz, please," AJ says.

"All right, all right, no sadness on the first day of school," Sooz says. She stands up and pulls AJ and me up and we do a big group hug. "Senior year is going to be the best year ever."

***

Our town is a medium-sized suburb, and some people have a lot of money and some do not. We live pretty close to New York City and very close to the beach, but it's a kind of insular place, like, a lot of my classmates' parents and grandparents grew up here, too. Not mine—they're all from Brooklyn, which they will tell you every chance they get.

Anyway, our high school is near the edge of town, near the busy street that goes out to Kennedy Airport. AJ, Sooz, and I organized our schedules so we could all have lunch together and when we go out for lunch, we have to walk down this street, one way or the other. In one direction is a pizzeria and a coffee shop. In the other direction are all the fast-food restaurants. As we walk, we count how many catcalls we get. Any less than three is almost disappointing.

"I still can't get over those shorts, Sooz," AJ says. "What was wrong with that blue baby-doll dress?"

"OK, I know they're a little weird, but I'm only gonna be 17 once, so I might as well take advantage of it," Sooz says. "At least, that's what Linda is always saying." Linda is Susannah's older sister—she's, like, ten years older and already married with a house on the North Shore of Long Island. She's also completely insufferable and is always saying things to Sooz like, Don't worry, sweetie, it'll happen for you, as if Sooz is at all interested in being married at age 24 and living in a split-level house in Syosset.

"I didn't want to be one of those people in pale colors comparing tans at the beginning of the school year," Sooz says.

AJ and I look at each other, in our white and pink shirts, and crack up.

Taco Bell was not my choice or Sooz's, but AJ argued us into it and that's how we find ourselves sitting in their weird vaguely floating chairs at lunchtime. AJ has flirted with / bullied the guy behind the counter into giving her a free drink, which happens to her all the time, partly because she's kind of argumentative and partly because she's really pretty. She was like, I'll have a Coke, and he was like, We only have Pepsi, and she's like, I'll have a Coke, and he was like, If you say you'll take a Pepsi, I'll give it to you for free. Sooz is pretty, too, but she's blonde and blue-eyed, whereas AJ and I are both brunettes with brown hair. It's like, based solely on our looks, we're forcing a guy to choose between one of us, and the guys tend to choose AJ.

"So," AJ says, as she bites into her taco, "what are we doing this weekend? We need to celebrate your birthday, Francie, and you getting your license."

"I haven't gotten it yet," I say.

"You will. If AJ can get her license, you can get yours," Sooz says.

It is true. AJ is not a great driver.

"Very funny, Susannah. I'll keep that in mind next time you ask for a ride," AJ says. "Do you think your parents will let you take the car on Saturday night?" she asks me.

"Probably not. They'll probably to want me to ease into nighttime driving," I say.

"OK, I can drive on Saturday night. What do you want to do?" Sooz asks. "You choose, Francie. It's your post-birthday celebration."

"Don't say you want to go to the movies," AJ says.

"Of course I want to go to the movies," I say. "I'll look in the paper and find a good one."

"What are you going to do about Jason?" Sooz asks.

I shrug. "There's nothing I can do. I can't make him like me."

They both groan. "You definitely can," AJ says. "But also, he does like you. He just doesn't know it yet."

Making guys like her has always been AJ's approach—flirt, flirt, flirt until the guy is madly in love with you. It tends to work, and then she gets bored. That's happened with all of the guys AJ's dated. We call it the boy disease, because usually it's the boys who seem to like you, and then suddenly, for, like, no reason, they don't.

As for Sooz, she never wants to hurt a guy's feelings, which is fine, OK, I don't want to hurt people's feelings, either, but she'll be trying to let them down so easy, for so long, that she ends up dating them.

"OK, then, I'm not going to make him like me," I say. "We'll just be friends, and it'll be fine. It's not like I've been pining away for him all this time. It's just, it would've been, I don't know...I'd have liked to see what happened."

They both nod. They get it.

***

My dad brought home a bunch of cold cuts for dinner from the Polish supermarket near the hospital where he works. Most of the time, he's the one who cooks, especially nowadays, since my mother started a new job last month. She used to teach English at Maplehurst, the other high school in town, but now she's the editor-in-chief of our local newspaper. She works crazy hours for no pay, my father says. Before she went back to work as a teacher, when I was in the fifth grade, she stayed at home, taking care of the three of us. AJ's mother works at a bank, doing something with computers. Susannah's mother works as a school nurse in one of the district elementary schools.

Often, Lola and I read books at dinnertime and my dad will read his beloved *New York* magazine or a medical journal, which my mother hates. Tonight, though, she demands that we put our reading material away so she can grill us about our first few days of school.

"We're going to read so much Hemingway this year," says Lola. "Did you have to do that sophomore year?"

"Yeah," I say, "but I like Hemingway."

"Ugh, it's all, 'This is a town in the foothills of a mountain. In the foothills, it is hot, but up the mountain, it is cool. We go up the mountain to cool off, and also because that's where the rebels are lying low.'"

My mother laughs. "That is a pretty good imitation of Hemingway, Lo."

Lola gets up and curtsies.

"What will the school play be this year?"

"I'm not sure yet. We should know in a few weeks."

My mother turns to me. "And Francie? What's going on with your classes?"

I shrug. "Not much," I say. "I need a graphing calculator for calculus."

"And that's it?"

I shrug again.

Lola tells my parents everything. Not that I'm hiding anything, at least not anything big, not like Joseph was. I just think that the less they know, the less they can pester me about. They tell us as little as possible, too. I didn't even know my grandmother was dying of cancer until she was in hospice care, and that was when I was 14. It gave Lola and me very little time to say goodbye to her, and I'm not sure if Joseph ever did.

When we're finished with dinner, Lola and I clear the table, putting everything away in the refrigerator. "What's that?" my dad asks, pointing at a deli envelope of cheese that my mom had put out.

"It's, uh, Havarti," Lola says, reading the label.

My father looks at us accusingly. "There was Havarti cheese on the table?" he asks. "Were you hiding it from me?"

Lola and I exchange a glance. "No, Dad, we were not hiding the Havarti from you. It was behind the seltzer bottle or something," she says, putting it into the fridge with all the other leftovers.

"I work all day, and I come home and just want to relax, and read a magazine, and eat dinner, and you're hiding things from me on the table." My dad's voice is escalating, like he really thinks that the three of us are conspiring to keep deli cheese away from him.

I pause in my loading of the dishwasher. Our dad can be like this sometimes, like, fixate on something small and strange, a perceived slight. He holds a grudge like nobody's business. Lola and I used to be a little scared of him because of this behavior, but this is ridiculous.

Lola looks at me again, and I can't help it, I start to laugh. Then she starts to laugh, and then our mom starts to laugh. The three of us are in hysterics, and my father just gets up and storms out of the room.

"Barry, they did not hide the cheese from you! You don't even like Havarti," our mom calls out of the kitchen, shaking her head.

***

I am six years old and Lola is four years old and Joseph is ten years old. This is the only year that Joseph and I will be in school together, when I am in the first grade and he's in the fifth grade. Lola is only going to Montessori school, which is for little kids, everyone knows that.

Our mother lines us up on the front porch for a photo, with me in the middle, because I'm the middle child. I am so excited to finally be at school with Joseph, and to take the bus with him. I've been taking the bus to kindergarten for a whole year, but first grade is a different school.

When the bus comes, Joseph gets on first. He high-fives everyone as we walk down the aisle and he takes a seat at the back of the bus with a few of his friends.

I sit next to Jason and we talk about summer camp as we ride to school. When we get there, Joseph pulls me aside as we get off the bus.

"Hey," he says, kneeling down so he can look me in the eye. "Francie pants. Here's what you tell your teacher, OK, so she knows you're really smart. I mean, she'll know anyway, but you just tell her E equals M C squared."

"E equals M C squared?" I repeat.

"Yeah, you tell Mrs. Romano that your older brother shared this information with you," he says. He stands up and jogs back over to his friends as they walk into school.

"E equals M C squared," I whisper to myself, certain that this will impress my teacher.

***

Susannah's parents have a camcorder they never use and she's decided she's going to film us all as part of her senior art project. She tells us this when she picks me up on Saturday night. She drives a Mustang convertible from the mid-1980s that used to be her older brother's car. It sucks to sit in the back, but that's where I find myself, with the top down, while AJ sits in the front seat, her hair unbothered by the wind, even though this is ostensibly a night out for my birthday. Sooz is playing the mix tape I made for her over the summer. Sooz really appreciates my mix tapes. I like to think of them as the soundtrack to our adventures.

I force my friends to go to the movies, of course. We go to see "Ed Wood," because I love Tim Burton and I know AJ loves Johnny Depp, but it is so weird that she leaves questioning her love for him. Afterwards, we have no real destination, so Sooz asks me to direct us to the Dunkin' Donuts in the next town over. Even though I was the last to get my license, I'm the only one who can navigate around our neighborhood.

As we pull into the parking lot, we see that the cute skater boys who often congregate here are inside the building. We've chatted with them a little bit before. There's one guy, with longish brown hair and dark eyes, who I think is particularly cute. I never mentioned it to Sooz and AJ, though. I don't like to draw attention to the guys I think are cute, in case they don't like me back, or worse, they like AJ more.

We sit at a booth and giggle with each other, studiously ignoring the boys, who are in the booth behind AJ and me. They all get up and hike up their sagging jeans and check their beepers and pick up their skateboards, which are propped against the window of the shop, and they head out to the parking lot to do some moves. We watch from the window until we finish our donuts, and then we feel we can't just sit there staring at the boys, so we walk out.

Susannah pulls out the video camera from her bag and starts to film us.

"Do something interesting," she says.

AJ smiles at her, fluffing up her hair. Even though she is pretty and smart, AJ is also self-conscious. She is always posing, as if she's concerned that people are watching her every move. I mean, right now, she is being filmed, so I guess it makes sense.

"AJ, it's a video camera. Do something," Sooz says.

One of the guys skates up to us.

"You want to film us?" he says to Susannah.

She smiles. Of course she wants to film them. The boys start doing more tricks for the camera, sometimes successfully, sometimes wiping out. The boy with the longish hair, who I think of secretly as my cute skater boy, comes over with a camera slung around his neck.

"I'm gonna take pictures of you filming them," he says, and he snaps a photo of Sooz and then one of me.

"What kind of film do you have that's gonna take a picture in the dark like this?" I ask. Susannah and I took photography last year, so I have some idea of what I'm talking about.

"Don't worry, I got it covered," he says. "Where do you go to school?"

"Elmwood," I say. "What about you?"

"BOCES," he says, taking another photo.

BOCES is the vocational school in Nassau County. I don't know anyone who goes there. It was always a threat, like, If you don't do well here at Elmwood, there's always BOCES!

"It was Francie's birthday last week. She just got her license," Sooz says, lowering her camera.

"Congratulations, Francie," he says.

"What's your name?" I ask.

"Wouldn't you like to know?" he says.

I laugh. "Yeah, I would! I just asked you!"

He walks back over to his friends and nods at them. They pick up their boards and wave goodbye, skating off down Sunrise Highway toward the Long Island Railroad station.

DRIVING AROUND MIX TAPE FOR SOOZ
Sorry Again, by Velocity Girl
Achin' to Be, by The Replacements
California (All the Way), by Luna
Alison's Starting to Happen, by The Lemonheads
No Myth, by Michael Penn
Ordinary World, by Duran Duran
Hey, Jealousy, by The Gin Blossoms
Authority Song, by John Cougar Mellencamp
Laid, by James

***

We get the day off from school for Yom Kippur. Usually, we'd get two days off for Rosh Hashanah, too, but it was so early this year that they just started school after the holiday. We all feel a little cheated about that, but especially the Catholic kids, because they get those days off and don't even have to go to synagogue. Our school is, like, half Jewish and half Catholic and some kids, like Sooz, are both, although, except for Christmas, she mostly celebrates Jewish holidays.

AJ goes to the same synagogue as we do, so we always try to find each other to sit together. Lola goes off with her friends, too. Sometimes, it seems like there is very little time for atoning between all the gossiping that goes on.

When I spot AJ and her family, I go over to say hello and to wish them all a happy new year. Her brother, Evan, isn't with them, since he's a junior in college. No one misses Evan, probably not even his and AJ's parents, mostly because he was awful. When we were in elementary school and I'd come home on the bus with AJ, he would hide in her closet and jump out to scare us when we walked into her room. Like, how long was he hiding in the closet, just for that purpose? He'd beat her up, make fun of her clothing and her curly hair.

AJ and I have to go to the bathroom first, so she can apply face powder and adjust her hair a million times. She's wearing a skirt suit and heels, and I'm wearing a dark purple dress and we have to compliment each other a few times, too.

As we walk down to the bathroom, we cross through the ballroom area where they hold the kiddush after services, though obviously not after Yom Kippur, and pass by the gym that the nursery school uses. We run into Mr. Fox, our former seventh and eighth grade teacher, who insists we call him Adam, as he is coming up the stairs. All of my Hebrew school friends and I used to really like Adam. He is cute, maybe he's 35 years old now. He dresses like someone who used to skateboard, but who has been forced to wear grown-up clothing. His other job is teaching math at the middle school in the town over from ours.

"Hi, AJ, Francie," he says to us. "Nice to see you. L'shana tovah u'metukah," which means, Have a good, sweet new year, in Hebrew.

"Happy new year," we say back.

We walk into the bathroom and run into Lola and her friend Starr. They are best friends, even though Lola is a sophomore and Starr is a junior. Starr hides her cigarette as we walk in, but when she sees it's just us, she goes back to smoking it.

"Ugh, Starr, that is such a nasty habit," AJ says, pulling face powder out of her purse.

"No one asked you to come in here, Alison," Starr says, blowing smoke out of the corner of her mouth.

"Where else am I supposed to use the bathroom?" AJ asks.

"Do you even need to pee? Or are you just powdering your nose in case some cute guy happens to be at services?"

AJ snaps the compact shut and is about to open her mouth when I say, "Let's start the year off being nice to each other. That's why we're here, right? To be inscribed in the book of life?"

AJ, Lola, and Starr look at me like I'm crazy, as if they don't know if I'm joking or not, and I kind of am, but also, that is why we're at synagogue for Yom Kippur.

Starr laughs, and Lola laughs, and AJ just glares at Starr and then she and I walk out of the bathroom and back to the sanctuary for services.

***

Sometimes, when we don't have anything else planned for a Friday or Saturday night, Sooz and I will sleep over at AJ's. Her parents are much more lenient about junk food and letting us stay up too late to watch TV, and since her brother is at college, one of us can stay in his room. Tonight, we're all in our pajamas and snuggled on the couch in the basement watching a movie when Sooz spies the Ouija board on the bookshelf.

"Ooh, let's do the Ouija board! We haven't done it in ages," she says. Sooz is into vaguely occult things. In addition to knowing all about astrology, she loves to visit psychics and get her palm read, and she has like three decks of tarot cards. She pulls the Ouija board from the shelf. AJ turns off the TV and we sit on the floor around the coffee table as Sooz puts the planchette in the middle of the board.

"No moving the pointer-thingy this time, Sooz, OK?" AJ says.

Sooz is indignant. "I never move the pointer!"

"It's called a planchette," I say.

"Oh my God, Francie, of course you would know that," AJ says.

Sooz clears her throat. "I'll ask the first question."

We each put two fingers on the plastic and close our eyes. We think closing our eyes is an important part of this exercise. "Spirits," Sooz says, very serious, her voice like an octave deeper, "spirits, are you here with us tonight?" The planchette swings around to "Yes."

"Jesus, Sooz, be more subtle," I say, opening my eyes.

"I swear, it was not me!"

AJ looks at me and rolls her eyes. I smile. Sooz used to be the worst board game cheater—she would cheat at Clue by just flat out lying about who was in her hand—so I totally believe she'd cheat at Ouija.

We close our eyes again. "Spirits," Sooz continues, "thank you for your presence. We'd like to ask you some questions. First, will I get into NYU?"

The planchette does not move.

"Maybe it doesn't like your question," AJ says. "Maybe it's too difficult for the spirits to know if 1150 SATs will get you into NYU." I smack AJ's arm.

"Or maybe it's saying, Yes, I will get into NYU," Sooz says.

"OK, OK, it's my turn," says AJ. "Who is speaking to us?" She is very literal.

The planchette veers all over the board, stopping at different letters, but not spelling anything out.

"I think that's too complicated, AJ. And usually it's not just one spirit, but a number of them," Sooz says.

"Usually?" AJ asks.

"Yes," Sooz says.

"Do you want to go?" AJ asks me.

"No, you can go again. I don't really have any questions to ask," I say.

"There must be something you can ask the spirits," Sooz says. "Maybe that's why it's not working; they sense that you don't believe."

"I didn't say I don't believe, I said I don't have any questions to ask. Fine. I'll ask a question." I clear my throat. "Spirits," I begin. "Spirits, can you tell me when I'll see Joseph?"

We are quiet for a few seconds, then maybe a minute, and then it feels like five minutes go by where the only thing I hear is our breathing, which is practically synchronized. Finally, I open my eyes, and of course the planchette has not moved.

"I'm sorry, Francie," Sooz says. "I know how much you miss him."

"I don't know what I was thinking," I say. "Like a game sold by Parker Brothers would be able to answer this for me?"

***

We are at the diner, Lola, AJ, and me, sharing a plate of cheese fries, checking out the other patrons, when this very cute guy slides into the booth next to Lola. AJ and I look at each other, like, What is going on?, but Lola gives him a halfhearted smile.

"Hey, Ari," she says.

"Hey, Lauren," Ari says. That is her real name, but literally no one calls her Lauren. "What's up? Haven't seen you in a while." He steals a fry from her plate. He smiles at us.

"This is my sister Francie," Lola says, gesturing to me, "and her friend AJ," she continues, gesturing to AJ.

Another guy comes up to the booth behind Ari and Lola, perhaps the cutest guy I've ever seen in my life, like, in person, and Ari turns around.

"This is Eitan," Ari says, and Eitan waves. "Eitan, this is Lola, Starr's friend, and—" I can tell he's already forgotten my name and AJ's name. He's speaking slowly, like he's a little stoned. Maybe he is. He shakes his head, which is when I notice that his dark hair is in a ponytail.

"I'm AJ, and this is Francie. Do you want to sit down?" AJ asks Eitan, flirting a little, batting her eyes. She moves over in the booth and I move over, too, to make room.

Eitan looks at AJ, then at me. He smiles at me and sits down and his left arm brushes my right arm a little as he runs a hand through his hair, which is medium brown and a little wavy, and I take a deep breath and swallow.

"How do you guys know each other?" AJ asks, thank God, because I am dying to know.

"We met at a party at Starr's house. They go to Maplehurst," Lola says.

"Are you guys sophomores, too?" Ari asks.

"No, Ari, how could my sister be a sophomore, too? They're seniors," Lola says, rolling her eyes.

"Are you sophomores?" AJ asks.

"No, we're juniors," Ari says.

"What were you up to tonight?" Eitan asks.

Lola, AJ, and I look at each other and giggle. We gave each other pedicures and made face masks out of yogurt and overripe avocados while watching "Beaches" for, like, the 37th time, but we're not going to tell them that.

"Just hung out at our house," I say, turning my head to look at him, his whole self just inches away from me. Everyone must be able to hear how loudly my heart is beating. Get it together, Francie, I think to myself. Why am I wearing my glasses? Why am I wearing these ancient Levi's and my ratty Billy Joel concert tee?

"I'm gonna go say hello to some other people," Ari says, getting up out of the booth. The diner is a total social scene for high school kids on the weekends. I don't know why anyone else would ever come here after nine PM, it's a complete zoo. The waitstaff hate us. "It was nice to run into you, Lo. Nice to meet you," he says, nodding at AJ and me.

Eitan stands up, too. He runs his hand through his hair again and looks at Ari, then back at me.

"Nice to meet you," he says, and walks through the diner to another booth on the far side. I do not want him to go.

"Those guys were really cute," AJ says. "Even if they are juniors."

Lola and I roll our eyes at AJ. She can be such a snob sometimes. She's always listing out the things she wants in a boyfriend, like, he has to be at least six feet tall, and she prefers brown hair, he should have a great body, he has to be smart, Jewish, have a decent amount of money or at least some prospects, like she's living in a Jane Austen novel.

"I don't know Eitan," Lola says, "but Ari is a total stoner."

"That makes sense. Starr's always high," I say.

"She is not!" says Lola.

AJ and I exchange a glance. Starr is always high. Maybe she needs help, like Joseph.

AJ gives Lola and me a ride home, even though she lives on the other side of town. "I can't have you taking a cab," she says, shuddering. "Plus, I know your parents freak out if you're, like, a minute late for curfew." She drives through every yellow light, touching the roof of the car each time.

We pull up to our house just at 11. "I'll call you tomorrow!" I say, as AJ drives off.

"AJ is the worst driver," Lola says, unlocking the front door and shutting off the burglar alarm. She resets it after I shut the front door.

Sometimes, we wonder if the burglar alarm is there so our parents know exactly when we get home. Their bedroom is on the first floor of the house, and our mom is a light sleeper, so there's no way she doesn't wake up every time it goes off.

As we climb the stairs to our rooms, Lola pulls off her platform sneakers, making her two inches shorter, but still four inches taller than I am.

"I didn't want to say this at the diner, but I kissed Ari, at that party at Starr's. He never even called me afterwards."

"I'm sorry, Lo. Did you want him to?"

"Kind of, but it's not a big deal. I mean, it was, like, four months ago."

She walks down the hall to her room, past Joseph's empty room.

"Good night, Francie pants," she says.

"Good night, Lo," I say, and I shut the door to my room.

I lean against the door for a minute before turning on the light, thinking about Eitan and how cute he was, and how unfortunate for me that he met both AJ and me at the same time. If she's interested in him, I don't think I would stand a chance.

***

Sooz and I edit the literary magazine at our high school. This is not necessarily a testament to our literary prowess, but rather to the fact that Susannah really likes the faculty advisor, Mr. O'Connor, who is also our English teacher this year. She had him sophomore year, too. Mostly, I handle the literary submissions and she handles the artistic submissions, because we publish photos and artwork, too. We are always trying to convince other people to hand over their deepest feelings on loose-leaf paper.

Sooz is also on the tennis team. She's hoping one of these extracurriculars will help her get into NYU and off Long Island.

Aside from the lit mag, I did an internship at a radio station over the summer, and if they need me in the school year, they'll call me for special events. My mom thinks I should keep it up because it'll look good on my college applications. I used to do ballet, but I quit in the tenth grade when I started getting nonstop foot cramps from going on pointe. I mean, I was not going to be a professional ballerina, not with this body.

My mom also somehow got Lola this after-school job at Planned Parenthood on some kind of student outreach team. They help kids learn about contraception through role-playing games and skits. She used to take Lola to Hempstead, but now that my mom has a new job, and I have my license, I'm stuck shlepping Lola to work once a week. She takes the bus home. She's, like, the only white kid on the bus. It's a little ironic that this is Lola's job, though, because our parents are absolutely not interested in talking about sex with us, or even entertaining the idea that we will, someday, have sex. But Lola has, like, a closet full of condoms, so we are prepared.

Jason does Model Congress and is always in the school plays and is in a band with his friend Dave.

AJ has literally no extracurriculars, I have no idea what she does with all her time. This is especially strange because she was oddly entrepreneurial in elementary school and brought me along with her. We started, like, three businesses together which mostly consisted of us trying to get our classmates to buy stuff from us that they didn't really want or need. Like, what nine-year-old needs sachets of potpourri? Apparently, AJ and I thought they did! We had some weird fascination with Crabtree & Evelyn. My grandfather even gave us business cards with our names and phone numbers on them, back when my parents were still talking to my grandfather. Now, AJ would probably start a business helping people choose their best hairstyle and makeup and clothing. That might actually be something our classmates would want.

In addition to clubs and after-school jobs and everything else we're doing, every senior has to complete 40 hours of community service. It doesn't have to be in one place, or with one organization. Unfortunately, working for the radio station doesn't count, even though I don't get paid, because it's not a non-profit or a government organization. I mean, I didn't think it would count, but I had to ask.

Sooz is going to do her community service hours at this art gallery that opened up in the next town over. AJ is going to volunteer with the local animal shelter. I have to think about what I'll do. I want it to be something I'll enjoy, so maybe something with movies or music, but there are not that many places for that kind of volunteering in our town.

***

On Wednesday afternoon, I'm lying on the carpet in my room, listening to a mix tape, gnawing away on the end of my Bic stic, which is a really bad habit that AJ and I share, reading *A Portrait of the Artist as a Young Man*, and finding it kind of a slog. When the phone rings, I am glad for the interruption.

"Hello, can I please talk to Francie?" says the boy on the phone. My heart flutters—who is calling for me? Did cute skater boy get my number somehow?

"This is Francie," I say, putting my pen in the book to hold my place. I pause the tape.

"Hi, it's, uh, it's Eitan. Ari's friend. We met at the diner—" he continues.

"I remember," I say, sitting up straighter. Even better than cute skater boy.

"I, uh, I got your number from the phone book."

"You got my number from the phone book," I repeat. Oh, my Lord, I sound like a moron.

"I, uh, yeah, I got your number from the phone book. Anyway. Uh. I was wondering—do you want to go out on Saturday?"

What is happening? A boy I met for, like, two minutes, is calling me up and asking me out? He looked up my number in the phone book? The cutest boy I have ever seen in person? I have to take a deep breath.

"I mean, it's OK if you don't want to, I just—"

"Are you sure you mean me? And not AJ, with the curly hair?" What am I even saying? Am I trying to talk myself out of this? But also, this never happens to me. Boys don't ask me out, especially if they've also met Alison.

"You're Lola's sister, right? I sat next to you. I'm definitely sure I wanted to call you."

"Yes," I say, before I say something else stupid. "Yes, I want to go out with you."

"Awesome!" I can hear him exhale a little sigh of relief. He was nervous to call me? He was nervous to call me. "I, uh, I don't have a car, I mean, I don't have a license yet, but we could meet somewhere, maybe?"

Even though we do live near the city, there's not much to do in our actual town. And you usually need a car or someone to drive you around. I just got my license, sure, but I don't have my own car or anything. To borrow my mom's car, I would have to tell my parents what I was doing, where I was going, who I'd be with, and hope they let me drive around at night. I'd have to tell them that a boy asked me out on a date.

I decide seeing Eitan is worth it. "I can drive," I say, and he gives me his address and directions to his house.

"What are you doing now?" he asks.

"Reading a book for school," I say. "It's not very interesting yet."

"What is interesting for you?" he asks.

"I don't know ... I liked this book I read over the summer about a woman who meets a guy who grew up, like, in the wilderness. He's never been with people before, and she brings him home and tries to, like, civilize him, but—I don't want to ruin it for you."

"The chances of me reading this book are very slim," he says. "I mostly read non-fiction, like memoirs and stuff."

"Ugh! So boring!" I say.

"No, it's not! History, true stories and stuff, can be so interesting."

"We did have this AP European History teacher, AJ and I had this teacher, who made European History fascinating. It was like it was one long story. We used to joke that maybe he was a vampire, like, maybe he was there at all of these events, and that's how he remembered everything."

"I'm not really into vampires, but I see what you mean."

"Not into vampires! I'm not sure we can continue this conversation, Eitan." I lie down on my back on the carpet, twisting the phone cord around my finger.

"How can you be into vampires? They are scary and undead and want to suck your blood."

"I don't want to be a vampire, or, like, encounter one, but I like reading vampire books and watching vampire movies. Like, 'Dracula,' or 'The Lost Boys'."

"'The Lost Boys' was all right, I guess. But mostly because it was funny. Vampire movies are too serious."

We talk for a little longer, but then Lola comes into my room and says she needs to use the phone.

"I gotta go," I say to Eitan, sitting up. "I'll see you on Saturday." I hang up the phone and look at Lola.

"Who was that?" she asks. "Was that Jason? You're blushing. You're, like, bright pink."

"Eitan," I say. "He asked me out on a date." I touch the side of my face and I am, indeed, very warm. What is happening?

"Oh," she says, sitting down on the floor next to me. "Do you think the parents will let you go?"

"I'm 17 years old," I say. "This would be literally my first real date. I think it's time, right?"

"I think so!" Lola says.

"Do you think Eitan is bad news? Like, you said Ari never called you..."

"I don't know, Francie pants. You'll just have to give him a try."

"I'm gonna tell the parents that he's a friend of Starr's, so they don't think he's, like, a totally random guy I met at the diner."

"They hate Starr," Lola says. This is not entirely true, although our parents are not huge fans of Starr's—they think Lola can do better in general when it comes to friends—but at least it's some kind of connection.

That night at dinner, I ask my parents if I can use the car on Saturday night, and they ask me why. When I tell my parents Eitan's last name, my dad says he knows Eitan's dad. They used to coach soccer together—Eitan's oldest brother is the same age as Joseph.

"I think he might still owe me money for soccer uniforms," my dad says.

"From, like, six years ago? I'll be sure to mention that to Eitan, Dad," I say.

This is a part of my dad I don't remember, the soccer-coaching dad. Lola used to play soccer, too, but Joseph is four years older than I am, six years older than Lola, so somewhere in that gap between Joseph turning 15 and Lola turning 15, my dad lost the urge to be involved in traveling soccer. Maybe because Joseph left the house when he turned 15.

My parents ask where Eitan and I are going, and I tell them we're going to the movies. They're like, Well, can we meet him first? But I'm like, I'm picking him up because he's a junior, he doesn't have his license yet.

My dad does not seem inclined to let me go. "We don't know anything about this Eitan character," he says. "I don't want you driving around with some strange guy."

"That's the point of Francie going on a date, Dad," Lola says. "To make him not a stranger anymore."

When I'm in my room after dinner, my mom knocks lightly on the door and pokes her head inside. She comes in and sits down on the edge of my bed.

"Francie, why are you on the floor?" she asks.

"Mom," I say from the floor, where I am finishing my math homework, which is much easier now that I have a graphing calculator. My mother hates that Lola and I do our homework on the floor when we both have, as she puts it, "perfectly good desks." I only use my desk to write letters and to organize all of my pens and pencils.

"Francie, sweetheart," my mom begins, "I talked to your father and we're going to let you borrow the car on Saturday night."

"Really? Thank you!" I jump up to give her a hug.

She pulls away and locks eyes with me. She clears her throat. "Look, Francie," she says, and I know she's going to talk about something she thinks is serious, because she starts all of her serious conversations with the word, "Look."

"Just because you're going out on a date with a boy doesn't mean...anything." She clears her throat again. "I mean, it means that you're going on a date, which is great, I'm sure you're looking forward to it. But it doesn't mean you have to ... do anything ... that you're not comfortable doing."

I am sort of enjoying how nervous she is about this conversation, especially when Lola literally works for Planned Parenthood, like, it's not a secret. My parents have no idea that I've kissed anyone, not that I'm so experienced, I mean, I've barely gotten to second base. I'm sure my mom would not understand how I could have kissed anyone, though, since I've never been on a real date, like, she would definitely not understand kissing someone if you were not on a real date. She is so 1950s like that.

"I know, Mom," I say.

"All right," she says, standing up and adjusting my comforter. I never make my bed. "I trust you."

RANDOM MIX TAPE #1
Here's Where the Story Ends, by The Sundays
Bluebeard, by the Cocteau Twins
Coming Up Close, by Til Tuesday
Hit, by The Sugarcubes
Alex Chilton, by The Replacements
Sometimes Always, by The Jesus and Mary Chain
A Murder of One, by The Counting Crows
Country Feedback, by REM

***

We're planning to go into the city on Saturday so I stay overnight at AJ's house on Friday to make it easier, since she and Sooz live near each other. AJ has two cats and this is the main reason I get allergy shots, because I'm allergic to cats. One of the cats hides, always, but the other one must know that I want nothing to do with her, because she is always winding herself through my legs. In addition to being allergic to them, I really dislike cats.

AJ's room is a normal size, but you would not know it from all of the furniture crammed in there. It feels small and crowded, which isn't helped by the fact that it's always a complete mess—clothing, shoes, books, makeup, everywhere. We clear some space on the floor and pull out the trundle bed and set it up for me before we go into the bathroom to wash up.

In the bathroom, AJ sits on the long counter, examining her pores. She has a number of face washes that she uses, including some weird bean scrub that is a powder you add water to. I am game to try any of these, although most of the time, I just use soap. She also makes this weird blubbering noise when she washes her face, so she doesn't get water in her mouth.

When we are tucked up into bed, we watch a little TV before we start to fall asleep. On Friday nights, sometimes there's a late movie, but nothing good tonight. AJ turns off the TV.

"Francie?" she asks. "Are you still up?"

"Mmm hmmm," I say.

"Are you excited for your date with Eitan?"

"Yeah," I say. "I mean, it's a little—is it a little weird that he asked me out? We barely even talked to each other."

"I think it's cool! Like, he thought you were pretty, he looked you up in the phone book, and he asked you out. That's a lot for a 16-year-old boy. Many steps were taken. He had to put some thought into it. And you talked to him on the phone, right? He didn't seem like an axe murderer?"

She rolls over to look at me, and I roll over to look at her. "I guess I'm a little nervous," I say.

"It'll be fine. It's, like, two, maybe three hours of your life. With a boy who is at least very cute."

We laugh.

"If he turns out to be normal, will you ask him if he knows any cute guys for me?"

"Even though they might be juniors?" I ask.

"Yeah. I thought we knew all the cute guys at Maplehurst, but I wasn't thinking about the juniors."

We used to hang out with these guys from Maplehurst who were a year older. We met them freshman year of high school at the outdoor ice-skating rink. We would go every Friday night, sometimes Friday and Saturday nights, and we'd see the same three guys over and over again, and we got to be friends. I had a huge unrequited crush on one of them, and Sooz dated one of them. But we only stayed friends with the third guy, Ross. He's a year older, but was old even for his grade, so he started driving way before any of us, which was very convenient. He graduated from high school and started at Nassau Community College. I haven't seen him a while, and I wonder if it has something to do with AJ, if they had an argument.

"Hey, AJ," I say. "Why aren't you talking to Ross anymore?"

"What made you think about Ross?"

"I don't know," I say. "I haven't seen him in a few months, you never talk about him anymore..."

AJ swallows. "I don't know," she says. "He just—he just stopped calling me, stopped calling me back. It's like we broke up, like he broke up with me without telling me, even though we were just friends. It's really sad, you know?"

"Yeah," I say. "It is really sad."

She rolls back over onto her back because she read in Seventeen magazine that sleeping that way will give you fewer wrinkles. I stay on my side, thinking about my upcoming date as I drift off to sleep.

***

My parents started letting me take the Long Island Railroad into Manhattan without them when I was a sophomore, but my friends' parents only let them go into the city with me. This is probably because my parents grew up in Brooklyn, and they only moved to our town because it was the closest place to Brooklyn, where my dad works, where they could afford to buy a house. So they don't think the city is a scary place. All through my childhood, we would go into Brooklyn or Manhattan almost every weekend. When I was younger, it was a pain, because it cut short my sleepovers if I had to go visit my aunt and uncle or go to Chinatown for dim sum or something like that, but now that I'm older, it means I'm once again the only one who knows how to get anywhere.

On our first unsupervised trip to the city, we went to the Metropolitan Museum of Art, because that's the kind of kids we are, and AJ spent most of the time posing in front of the art, flipping her hair, hoping some cute teenage boy would talk to her. As if most cute teenage boys spend their Saturdays at the Met. Sooz and I were actually there for the art. She is always looking for new ideas and inspiration for art projects, and I just like seeing interesting paintings.

Today, we take the subway downtown from Penn Station and get off at Eighth Street and walk west. West Eighth Street is nearly nothing but shoe stores. We walk in and out of, like, ten stores until Susannah finally finds the perfect pair of platform oxblood oxfords—she is very excited about this alliteration. She pays for them with her babysitting money and we walk out of the store and back east.

Sometimes, Sooz's art projects include designing clothing for herself. She made these pants that have bell bottoms—she sewed fabric in the shape of a bell to the bottom of a pair of black leggings. Even though AJ is a little taller and skinnier than me, we share a lot of clothes. Sometimes I'll wonder where a certain article of my clothing is, only to see AJ wear it to school the next day. I never borrow Sooz's clothing.

We wander into a few more stores—the Body Shop, where I buy some Dewberry perfume and AJ buys her weird face scrub; a bookstore, where I write down the names of like five books that I want to read; my favorite used record store, where Sooz gets some British import of a band we've never heard of, but the CD cover looks cool.

There are a lot of homeless people and a lot of grubby-looking teenagers who are maybe also homeless, I don't know. When we go into this pizzeria, a few of them are sitting outside on the street with a sad-looking dog.

"That poor dog," says AJ. She really loves animals.

"Those poor kids," I say.

"Ugh, Francie, they probably ran away from home in Scarsdale to try out life on the streets for a few weeks."

I think about my brother and look back out at the kids.

We take the subway to Penn Station, which is full of overflowing trash bins and floors that look as though they have not been mopped in twenty years. God forbid you have to pee in Penn Station. The bathrooms are nothing but wet paper towels all over the floor and no toilet paper. We always plan it so we spend as little time there as possible before our train. We stand under the board that lists the tracks for each train and as soon as it flips over with our track information, we rush to that platform. Our train never goes direct, though. We always have to change trains at Jamaica station, in Queens, to get the train out to our town.

"What are you gonna wear tonight?" Sooz asks.

"I was thinking of that maroon dress from Express with the white flowers, the one that ties in the back," I say.

"That's a good dress," AJ says. "It gives you, like, just the right amount of cleavage. And definitely wear your contacts. You look much prettier without glasses."

"You look very pretty either way," says Sooz.

"Of course," says AJ, "but if you want to kiss him? Have you ever kissed someone when you're wearing glasses?"

"I mean, I kissed Jason when I was wearing my glasses. Or he kissed me. But I'm not sure I'm gonna kiss him on the first date," I say. Usually, AJ and Sooz are very opposed to kissing on the first date. I don't really have an opinion on it, probably because I've never been on a real first date.

"He's very cute," AJ says. "I would totally get it if you kissed him on the first date."

"That would mean I kissed Jay, like, two weeks ago, and Eitan this weekend—"

"There's nothing wrong with being a kissing slut," says Sooz. "Kiss whoever you want. You know, within reason. And forget about Jason. That kiss doesn't even count."

***

I wear the Express dress and my contact lenses and these black oxfords without socks and I guess I look OK. My mother approves of my ensemble and hugs me as I leave, slipping me some cash.

"Remember what we talked about," she whispers to me. I roll my eyes a little.

"Mom."

"OK, OK, have fun, sweetie. Drive carefully."

My parents don't let Lola and me wear any makeup, so that just means we wait till we leave the house to put on our eyeliner and our Toast of New York lipstick. Eitan lives in what we call "back Maplehurst," where the fanciest houses are, right on the water. Even so, when I pull into his driveway from the quiet street, I'm a little surprised at how big the house is.

Before I can even get out of the car, the front door opens and Eitan bounds out. He's in the passenger seat a moment later. He turns to look at me. He is still adorable, I am glad to see.

"Hey," he says.

"Hey," I say. I realize I'm in a car with a near-total stranger. What if my dad was right? Or what if AJ was psychic, what if he is an axe murderer? Deep breath, Francie.

"I love this song," Eitan says as "You Can't Always Get What You Want" comes on the classic rock station, and he turns the radio up.

"Make yourself comfortable," I say, laughing.

"Oh, I will," he says, smiling, and I feel a butterfly right behind my heart at that smile.

I'm not very tall, so as I put the car in reverse, I have to sling my arm around the back of the passenger seat and hike myself up a little to see out the rear window. I never noticed this as a strange thing until right now, with Eitan sitting next to me, watching me. His face is very close. I can see a few freckles on his cheeks and that his eyes aren't as dark brown as I'd thought, but more of a golden color, and Jesus Christ, this is a distraction from driving.

"I like your car," Eitan says.

"Thanks," I say, "it's my mom's." Duh. What teenager would choose a station wagon?

We drive to the small movie theatre in town. Next door is a pizzeria and a coffee shop. This town is full of pizzerias and coffee shops.

We go to see a movie called "The Last Seduction." Based on the title alone, I'm not sure it's a great first date movie. Then, as soon as we sit down with popcorn, I realize that going to the movies on a first date is a terrible idea. We can't talk at all, obviously, but what if he wants to, like, make out in the theatre? I'm not into kissing in public, no matter how cute he is.

As the previews start, Eitan leans in to whisper something in my ear, but I can't hear him. His breath is warm on the side of my neck, and a shiver runs down my spine. What is going on? That has never happened to me before.

I turn to him, not sure of what's going on in my own body, and I must look as confused as I feel because he leans in closer—shivers again—and whispers, "We are the youngest people in this theatre by, like, thirty years."

I giggle, I actually giggle, and someone shushes me, which of course makes both of us giggle. "Everyone is wearing a beret," I whisper to him, and we giggle again. What is happening to me? I'm turning into a girl who giggles in a movie theatre with a boy.

The movie itself is good, it's fine, it's whatever, I can barely concentrate because my senses are so heightened by being so close to Eitan. Our arms touch on the seat rest between us, our fingers graze in the popcorn. It is so cheesy, cheesy, cheesy, I'm horrified with myself, but I can't help it, either. I sneak a look at him in the dark and he is looking at me. We smile at each other. I can feel the heat of my blush moving up my cheeks, and there's nothing I can do about it.

After the movie, we get ice cream at the Carvel in the same little shopping plaza. I offer to pay for the ice cream, since Eitan bought the movie tickets, but he won't let me. My friends will be pleased when I share this detail. We sit on the bench outside. My cone is chocolate with chocolate crunch, of course, why would you bother with anything else, but Eitan has gotten vanilla, and seems to be regretting it as he watches me eat mine.

"Do you want some?" I offer him my cone. He shakes his head.

"What did you think of the movie?" he asks. I see a lot of movies, both in the theatre and on VHS tapes at home. It was a banner day in my house when I realized I could rent movies for free from the public library. I know I'm a big dork, but I really like the public library. Lola is always making fun of me for it. We also used to do Sunday night movie nights in our house. Lola and I ended up watching a lot of movies that were definitely not age appropriate because Joseph chose them or they were "classics" according to my dad, who is really into

Turner Classic Movies. I definitely love movies because he loves them.

"I liked it," I say. "I didn't expect all the twists. It's fun when a movie surprises you."

"Do you like surprises?" he asks.

I think about it a minute. "I mean, I like to plan things, so I wouldn't want, like, a surprise party. But if a movie didn't surprise me, I think I'd be disappointed. What about you?" I ask.

"Oh, I love surprises," he says. "But I don't think this is my kind of movie. I think I like more, I don't know, mainstream types of movies," he says.

"How could you tell this is not a mainstream type of movie?" I ask.

"It's dark, like, literally, I couldn't see things, and it's moody and there are no famous people in it."

"What? That guy was in 'Singles'! And 'Spaceballs'!"

"You've seen 'Spaceballs'?" Eitan is doubtful.

"I saw 'Spaceballs' in the theatre with my whole family. My older brother wanted to go."

We look at each other and start to talk at the same time, each of us telling the other that our dads used to coach soccer together. We stop talking and crack up. I briefly wonder if maybe we had met some time before, little Francie and little Eitan, at a soccer game, handing out orange slices to our siblings and their teammates. But I don't think so. I think I would remember.

I drive Eitan home because it's getting close to my curfew. When we get to his house, he gets out of the car, and then I get out of the car. It feels weird to be walking a guy to his door. We stand there for a moment, looking at each other, and as Eitan runs a hand through his hair, I think about what it would feel like to do that myself. His hair looks so soft. My stomach flips over. Oh my Lord, are we going to kiss after all? And then the door opens, and there's Eitan's mother. She smiles at me.

"Francie?" she says. "It's so nice to meet you! Eitan has been talking about you." She has a Hebrew accent. "Did you tell Francie that Abba used to coach with her father?"

Eitan looks completely mortified and I try not to smile.

"Yes, Eema, I told her," Eitan says.

He looks pointedly at his mother, who shuts the door.

"So, uh, yeah, that was my mom," he says. He leans in to give me a hug. "I'll call you."

We look at each other and then he disappears into his huge house.

Eitan has been talking about me to his mom.

When I get home, Lola is waiting up for me. She comes down the stairs as I'm turning off the alarm.

"So? How was it?" she asks.

"The movie was interesting," I say.

"FRANCIE! I don't care about the movie," she whisper-yells at me.

We walk upstairs to my room and shut the door.

"It was ... it was really good," I say, smiling. "He's sweet. And so cute."

"You never like anyone," she says.

I smack her a little with one of my pillows. "That's not true."

"Yes, it is. You always say the boys at Elmwood are boring and dumb. Did you kiss him?"

"No," I say. "Hopefully next time."

***

Eitan calls me again on Monday night. My heart has been fluttering every time the phone rings. One more day and I'd've looked up his number to call him. How did I not get his number?

"Hi, this is Eitan. Can I please speak to Francie?" he says. He's so polite, I nearly swoon.

"Hey," I say.

"Hey," he says, and I can almost hear him relaxing a little. "So, uh, I had a really great time with you on Saturday. Sorry about my mom interrupting..."

"That's OK." We are not winning any awards for conversation here.

"Do you want to go out again? Maybe not to a movie with a bunch of old people?" he says.

I laugh. "Yeah. What do you want to do?"

"I really don't care."

"Well, my friends AJ and Susannah were going to play pool on Saturday night. Do you want to do that?"

"You want to go out with your friends?"

"Well, you could bring a friend or two. Like Ari?"

"Oh. Do—do you want to hang out with Ari?"

I realize immediately what he thinks, and my heart flutters again. Don't mess this up, Francie.

"No. I want to hang out with you. But maybe Ari would like Susannah. Or AJ. Or bring someone else. It doesn't matter to me."

I hear him sigh in relief on the other end of the line.

"Yeah, we can play pool. I'll ask Ari."

***

On Saturday night, AJ and Susannah pick me up in AJ's Jeep, and we go to pick Eitan and Ari up from Ari's house. Ari lives close to me, even though he goes to a different school. I offer to sit in the middle because I'm the smallest, but Eitan takes it.

"I like to sit in the middle," he says. "It makes me feel like I'm in on all the conversations."

Our thighs touch in the dark backseat, and he leans back and puts his arm around my shoulder. The whole right side of my body tingles where his hand sits. The silence in the car is a little awkward until Susannah turns up the radio and she and AJ start singing along to the Counting Crows. They both have bad voices, but then Eitan leans forward and starts singing at the chorus, getting really into it, and his voice is just as bad. Ari and I look at each other behind Eitan's back and crack up.

"Hey, how's your sister?" Ari asks me.

"She's good," I say.

"Say hello to her for me," he says. I nod.

The pool hall is all ages, which is kind of nuts, since everyone is drinking and smoking like crazy. Even though there are five of us, they let us take one table since it's still so early. Eitan and I team up against Ari, Susannah, and AJ.

We are all awful, but AJ is definitely the worst, and even though she's usually really competitive, she absolutely does not care, which drives Ari crazy. He really wants to win this no-stakes game of pool. When it's just us girls, we play for fun. No one cares who wins, so we have not gotten very good. We're also not that tall, any of us, so when Sooz takes out the bridge from under the table, both of the guys groan.

"You can't use the bridge!" says Eitan.

"I need to use the bridge or I can't make the shot," says Sooz.

"Susannah, you can't make the shot anyway," says Ari.

"Hey, I'm on your team! Have some faith!" says Sooz, lining up the shot. She perches on the side of the pool table.

"One foot on the floor, please," says Eitan. She gives him a look.

Sooz calls the shot, takes it, and sinks the ball. She pops off the table and puts the bridge back. "And that is why I use the bridge," says Sooz. She high-fives AJ and then Ari.

"You have to go again," Ari says.

"Oh, right!" says Sooz. She misses the next shot.

Eitan is a decent pool player, but the best part is him leaning over me to show me a better way to hold the cue. As if I care about holding the cue properly. Every time he touches my hand, I feel a shiver again, and I can tell I'm blushing and I really have to learn how to control it, but I'm not sure how because it never happened to me before I met Eitan.

When the game is over, and Eitan and I have won, we leave the pool hall and go to the TGI Fridays next door. The waiters definitely hate us because we are five people at a table for six, on a Saturday night, and we order, like, sodas and cheese fries and chicken fingers.

Susannah has brought her camcorder again. "So, Eitan, tell me more about your family. Francie said you have brothers. Are they single?" Susannah swings the camera around the table before it ends up with Eitan.

"You are gonna need some Dramamine to watch this video," Ari says. AJ snickers. Maybe there is hope for them yet.

"My oldest brother just graduated from Cornell, and my middle brother is at Michigan," Eitan says.

"So your family is smart and good-looking," Susannah says. She lowers the camera and gives me an entirely unsubtle thumbs-up.

"And when's your birthday?" Susannah asks.

"June 26."

"Also a Cancer!" Sooz says.

I turn to Eitan, ignoring Sooz. "What are you doing tomorrow?" I ask him.

"We're going to the Gunks to go climbing," he says.

"The what?" I say.

"You go rock climbing?" AJ says. "I used to do that at camp! It was so much fun."

One of the weirder things about AJ is that, even though she is so put together here, on Long Island, and seems like she would not hike farther than Bloomingdale's, she went to this crazy outdoorsy sleepaway camp where they had no electricity in the cabins and they climbed all the peaks of the Adirondacks.

"Yeah, we're all really into it. Climbing, camping, hiking...my parents used to do a lot of that in Israel," Eitan says. He turns to me. "Maybe you'd want to come some time." I do not climb, camp, or hike, at least not historically, but I am willing to learn.

"Sure," I say.

AJ laughs, laughs, laughs. "You are going to go camping?" she says. "With your Care Bears sleeping bag?"

"It's very soft!" I say. "But we have a real camping sleeping bag somewhere. It was Joseph's."

"It doesn't matter, Francie. I'd share my sleeping bag with you," Eitan says. I blush so pink that I think I might, briefly, have a fever. We have not even kissed yet, and he's offering to share his sleeping bag with me.

At the end of the evening, AJ is like a taxi. She drops Ari home first, leaving Eitan and me alone in the back seat. Instead of scooting over, he stays in the middle seat and he puts his hand palm-up on his thigh, and looks at me and I put my hand into his and interlace our fingers. When we pull up to my house, I have to take my hand away from his to get out of the car and Eitan gets out to walk me to the front door.

"Is it gonna be weird for you to hang out with AJ and Sooz?" I ask as we walk up the front steps, practically spot lit by AJ's headlights.

He shakes his head. "We'll just sing along together to the popular hits of the day," he says, and I laugh.

"Hey," he says. He swallows. "I, uh..." He looks at me, then back at AJ's Jeep, where we can see AJ and Sooz talking in the front seat and hear the sounds of Z100 wafting out through the open windows. "Next time, can it be just the two of us?"

Next time. I have flutters in my stomach. I nod.

I stand on my tiptoes to hug him goodbye and he wraps his arms around me and I can feel his breath on my ear and I shiver.

"Good night, Eitan," I say, opening the front door. "I'll talk to you."

"Good night, Francie," he says.

***

I am eight years old and Lola is six years old and Joseph is twelve years old. We are driving to a hotel in the Catskills to spend Memorial Day weekend with my Nana and Pop Pop and Uncle Leo and Aunt Jenny and our cousin Georgia. Joseph is reading comic books in the back seat of the car, so I decide to read my book, too.

"What are you reading?" Lola asks, looking over my shoulder.

"A Wrinkle in Time," I say. It was Joseph's book, which is why I'm reading it. I want to be like Joseph.

"That was a good book," Joseph says. "Too bad you can't read yet, Lola. Did you get to the part where—"

Suddenly, I throw up all over Joseph.

"Ugh, Francie, that's so nasty!" he says, his hand over his nose and mouth. My mother turns around and says, "Barry, pull the car over. Pull the car over!"

My dad pulls over on the side of the highway and my mom and my siblings and I get out of the car and my mother gets clean clothing out for Joseph and me and makes us change on the side of the road.

"What happened, Francie pants?" Lola asks.

"I don't know," I say, crying a little as my mother wipes puke off my hands.

"You got carsick, Francie. Don't read in the car," my mom says.

"Joseph reads in the car," I sniffle.

"Joseph doesn't get carsick," she says. She crawls into the back seat and, with one of the sheets that's always in the trunk of the station wagon, one hand pinching her nose, cleans everything off the vinyl seats of the Datsun. She wraps all our dirty, pukey clothing in the sheet and leaves it on the side of the road. She puts a fresh sheet down for us and Joseph gets back in the car. As I follow him, he shakes his head.

"No way. What if you get sick again? Lola, you come sit next to me."

Lola smiles as though she has won a prize.

My father starts the engine again and we roll down the windows, even though we're on the highway, because the car smells awful.

"Jesus, Francie," Joseph says, "that was my new X-Men."

***

Without even asking me, my mother signs me up to do my senior year community service at our synagogue. We aren't very religious, like, we go for the High Holidays and maybe a few other times a year. Joseph, Lola, and I all had bar and bat mitzvahs, but I haven't been to Hebrew school since the eighth grade. I'm taking Hebrew in high school, but only because it's a fun class and I'm good at languages.

The first time I go, Dr. Simon, the principal, asks me to help out with this soup kitchen in Far Rockaway. Adam, Mr. Fox, leads a group of people from the synagogue who go there every Sunday to make and serve dinner. To me, this is more like volunteering at the soup kitchen, and not at the synagogue, but it doesn't really matter to me one way or the other.

So, I go to talk to Adam after his class is over and he asks me if I can meet up with everyone at the synagogue on Sunday around 4 so that we can gather everything up and bring it over to the soup kitchen.

"What do you want to get out of volunteering, Francie?" he asks me. "Don't tell me it's just about community service credit."

I don't want to tell him that my mom volunteered me for this volunteering. "I'm not really sure," I say. "Shouldn't it just be about helping people?"

"I like to think of it as *g'milut chasadim*, or acts of lovingkindness. It's about getting involved, about being part of your community, giving back to your community," he says. "But it should be valuable to you, too. The idea of *chesed*, it's something that should be a part of you every day. You can do *chesed*, you can do good works, acts of lovingkindness, but you should also be full of lovingkindness."

Jesus Christ, this is going to be a long 40 hours. I forgot how self-righteous Adam could be. I nod. "I'll think about it," I tell him.

***

On Friday night, AJ, Susannah, and I go out, and find ourselves at the Dunkin' Donuts again. The same skater boys are there, but there's a new guy with them.

The new guy approaches AJ as she's eating a Bavarian cream donut. She has sugar on her hands and lips and even a little on her nose. This is the worst situation for AJ, because she always likes to look perfect. "Hey," he says. "You got a little something—" he motions to his nose.

AJ wipes at her mouth and her cheeks and her nose. He laughs.

"I'm Alex," he says.

"Alison," AJ says. It is always weird when she uses her actual name. "This is Francie and Susannah."

"You ladies come here often?" Alex asks. We don't know how to answer that. It's a Dunkin' Donuts, so lots of people must frequent it, but is he asking if we come to see his skateboarding friends? "I'm just messing with you. These guys said they've seen you here before. You skate?"

AJ, who is literally wearing a pearl necklace and pearl earrings and a cashmere sweater set, shakes her head. Alex looks at Sooz and me, and we shake our heads, too.

"C'mon," he says, and we follow him and his friends outside.

The cute guy who's into photography is outside, smoking a cigarette. He stubs it out against the wall of the Dunkin' Donuts. "Hey," he says, looking at me. "It's Francie."

"Hey," I say, looking at him. "It's 'wouldn't you like to know.'" He laughs.

Alex gets AJ on his skateboard and she is not half bad—maybe because she is a good snowboarder, despite her lack of athleticism or even any coordination, really. This time, Susannah films AJ zipping around the parking lot.

She nearly wipes out against her car, but she kicks the board up and passes it back to Alex, flipping her hair over her shoulder.

"That was awesome," says Alex. "Hey, Ali. Give me your number. I'm gonna give you a call." And she actually gives it to him, this random skateboarder who calls her Ali, who meets maybe half of her criteria, just writes it on the back of a Dunkin' Donuts napkin. I mean, I guess that's what we were always hoping would happen, that one of these guys would ask for our number, but it hadn't happened yet. Of course it happens to AJ.

The photographer turns to me. "You wanna give me your number?" he asks. Jesus Christ, what is going on? I am shocked that these boys are showing so much interest. This is not their first opportunity to ask for phone numbers. My heart sinks a tiny bit. Why couldn't he have asked a few weeks ago? Because he is so cute, and I am intrigued. But I also really like Eitan.

"Sorry, I only give my number to people who give me their names," I say.

He opens his mouth as if to tell me, and Sooz says, "Francie's kind of dating someone." I'm not sure I am, we haven't even kissed yet, but I feel like I am. He said, Next time, can it be just the two of us.

The photographer shakes his head. "That's too bad," he says.

"Yeah, for you," Sooz says. We look at each other and laugh.

***

On Sunday afternoon, my parents drop me at the synagogue and Adam gives a few of us a ride over to the soup kitchen. The neighborhood changes as you go over the expressway, just a few blocks away, from big houses, almost mansions, to run-down apartment buildings and two-family homes that look like they've seen better days.

My job is to assemble bagged lunches during dinner and then, as the guests—that's what the people who work at the soup kitchen call the people who eat there, guests—as they leave, they take a bagged lunch with them, a sandwich and an apple and a cookie, so they'll have at least one other meal to tide them over until the soup kitchen opens again for dinner the next night. It's crazy to think this is just ten minutes, fifteen minutes, from my house, from my neighborhood, where it seems like almost everyone is at least middle class, if not upper middle class or flat out rich.

When the guests start to trickle out, some of them thank me for the sandwiches, some just take the bags and leave.

One of the men stops and looks at me as he's taking the bagged lunch. He looks only a few years older than me, and his hands are cracked and he has an Ace bandage wrapped around his left palm. What led him to this place in life, that he's a few years out of high school, getting his meals from a soup kitchen? Maybe he never even finished high school, who knows.

"What's your name?" he asks as he takes the bag from me. "Haven't seen you here before."

I clear my throat. "Francie," I say.

"Well, thanks for the lunch, Francie," he says. He takes another bag. "For my lady friend."

"Here," I say, handing him two more bags. "Take another."

Adam gives me and a few other volunteers a ride home from the soup kitchen. I'm the last person he drops off, so I get into the front seat and direct him to my house. The radio is tuned to NPR, which is so boring. Why would I want to listen to someone tell me the news?

He pushes in the cigarette lighter and a moment later, lights a cigarette, rolling down his window. I had no idea he smoked.

"What did you think?" he asks, blowing the smoke out the window.

"Of the soup kitchen?" I ask.

"Yeah, you know, of the whole thing. Have you ever worked at a place like that before?"

"No," I say, shaking my head. "It's a big difference from our neighborhood."

"I'm sure there are people in your neighborhood who could benefit from these services, but maybe don't know about them, or are too ashamed or embarrassed to take advantage of them. Looks can be deceiving, Francie." He stubs out the cigarette in the ashtray.

"Believe me, I know," I say.

We pull up in front of my house and I unbuckle my seat belt. For a moment, it feels really awkward between us, like are we supposed to hug goodbye?, and then I say, "Thank you for the ride. I'll see you next week," and get out of the car and walk into my house.

When I get upstairs, I flop onto one of the beds in Lola's room. Lola's room is bigger than mine and much darker. Like, really dark. She loves that, though, because she will sleep till, like, 1 PM on the weekends. Her room has two twin beds, but over the summer, one of the bedframes broke on one of the beds, and now Lola sleeps on the mattress and box spring on the floor. Is that odd? Probably, but my parents don't come upstairs all that often, so they don't have to see how messy it is.

On the wall is a framed poster from the musical Damn Yankees that says, "Whatever Lola Wants, Lola Gets!" It is very Lola. She's very much the youngest child. Technically I'm the middle child, but with Joseph gone for so long, I feel like the oldest.

"What's up, Francie?" she asks. She's lying on the bed on the floor, reading *The Great Gatsby*. My Lord, Gatsby. I'd much rather be reading about him than Stephen Dedalus. "How was your volunteering?"

"It was OK," I say. "Lo, do you think Joseph ever went to soup kitchens or anything? When he was running away, back to New York?"

"I don't know. Maybe. But that's what they're there for, right?"

I look up at the ceiling. "Yeah."

***

I am nine years old and Lola is seven years old and Joseph is 13 years old. He's been practicing for his bar mitzvah all year and it's finally here. It's a special day for Lola and me, too, because we have new dresses to wear. Even though Lola and I aren't twins, we have matching dresses. They are kind of white and kind of clear, with shiny blue polka dots and puffy sleeves and I have new black patent leather shoes without any strap, but Lola still has to wear Mary Janes.

The bar mitzvah service is very serious and Joseph has to say a lot of things in Hebrew, but afterwards is the fun part, which is the party. My mom's hair is big and poufy and my dad wears a suit and we take a lot of family photos with the five of us and my Nana and Pop Pop, my mom's parents, and my Grandma, my dad's mother. My other grandfather, my dad's father, died when I was a baby. Lola is named after him.

At the party, my dad takes turns dancing with Lola and me. We put our feet on top of his and bop around. Otherwise, Lola and I dance with each other and our younger cousin, Georgia, who is eight. Iris is only a baby. We can't dance with her. Lola and I usually fight over who gets to sit next to Georgia, because she is pretty and fun, but tonight, we don't fight about anything.

In the bathroom, there is a special basket on the long counter with hair spray and bobby pins and some long white things that I don't know what they are. There's also some perfume, and I spritz some on my wrists and rub them together like my mother does.

When I leave the bathroom, I hear a few kids in the stairway. I start down the stairs to see what's going on, and I see Joseph and a few of his friends. The boys have taken their suit jackets off and the girls have taken their heels off and put on fluffy white socks or ballet slippers. They sit on the stairs and they pass a few bottles of wine and a cigarette between them. The smoke rises into my eyes and my nose and I cough, and they all look up.

"Oh, shit," someone says, "is that your little sister?"

Joseph looks up at me and smiles. "Yeah, that's Francie. She won't tell anyone, though, will you, Francie pants? She's my cool sister."

I look back at Joseph and his friends and they look back at me, and I nod, and I walk back up the stairs to the party.

***

I get a call from the radio station that they're promoting a concert at Nassau Coliseum and since I live on Long Island, they want to know if I can work the show. It's not really that close to where I live, but my parents will definitely let me use the car for something work-related, or, really, internship-related. They are convinced this kind of stuff is what's going to get me into Duke, when it's probably going to be my nearly 4.0 GPA and 1500 SATs. But the best thing about the concert is that I can bring someone with me, so I ask Eitan if he wants to go, and he says yes.

We drive out to the Coliseum to help set up merchandise and promotional stuff for the radio station, which takes like half an hour, I have no idea why we needed to get there at six o'clock. The concert is like a showcase of a bunch of different disco acts from the 1970s that Eitan and I have never heard of, but it's still kind of cool to see how everything comes together.

As we walk through backstage and see the green rooms and the costumes, my hand grazes his, and he catches it, and then, just like that, we're holding hands. We don't have seats, but my boss from the summer, this guy Steven who is like 20 years old—he went straight into radio from high school, which my parents would kill me if I did—Steven is like, This show will absolutely not sell out, so by 8:30, take any seats open.

There's food set up for the staff, and Eitan and I grab some sandwiches and sit in this makeshift break room with all the stagehands, who are smoking like crazy.

We talk quietly to one another, not wanting to draw attention to ourselves.

"So, what would be your favorite song to hear tonight?" Eitan asks me.

"I don't know a lot of disco songs," I say. "Do you have a favorite?"

Eitan scoffs. "They're all my favorites," he says. "Anything with that, uh, that awesome disco beat. Why do you think I'm here? Did you think it was to hang out with you?" he asks, taking my hand again, smiling at me.

One of the stagehands walks over to our table, and we look up at him.

"Hey," he says to Eitan, "you in the union?"

"Uh, the stagehand union?" Eitan says.

"Yeah, the stagehand union," he says, like, Duh, what other union would he be asking about.

"No, sir, I'm not," Eitan says, then looks at me. I mouth the word "sir" at him.

"That's too bad. We're down a few guys, could've used you."

They all get up and put out their cigarettes and go off to do stagehand stuff, I guess, and Eitan and I look at each other and crack up.

When the first act goes on, we watch it on the TV in the break room and then we head out to find a place to sit. Steven was right, and we snag two seats not far from the stage.

"I was not telling the truth earlier," Eitan says. "I don't know any of these songs." He cups his hand around my ear so I can hear him. I hope I never stop getting that shiver down my spine when he touches any part of me.

I cup my hand around his ear and say, "What? That's a shocker! Don't worry about it. Just feel the disco grooves." I do silly dance moves, like the shopping cart and the disco finger thing and I hold my nose and shimmy down to the floor and Eitan starts laughing and then makes up his own silly moves and we do them together. We tire ourselves out and sit down for the third act, slouching so we can rest our heads on the seat backs.

"How many acts are there?" Eitan asks.

"Five," I say.

"Five?" He turns his head to look at me, and I turn my head to look at him, and my heart races a little. He's so close. I want him to kiss me, or really, I want to be kissing him, it doesn't matter who kisses who first, but not here. This isn't where our first kiss should be.

"Is that too much disco? Are you regretting coming with me?" I ask.

He shakes his head. "No," he says. "I wish there were, like, eight acts." He stands up and pulls me to my feet and we dance in the space between our seats and the seats in front of us, practically touching, but not.

After the concert, Eitan and I pack up the unsold merchandise and he and Steven lug it to the radio station van. I guess that's not a union job.

We get into my mom's car and when the radio turns on, Eitan spins through the dial. "I want more disco," he says. "I'm not gonna listen to anything but disco from now on. Everything else just sounds so dull. We can't dance to the Eagles."

"We shouldn't do anything to the Eagles," I say.

"You don't like the Eagles?"

"God, no, they're terrible. Though I do like Don Henley's solo work."

Eitan laughs for like five minutes straight. "I do like Don Henley's solo work," he says to himself.

When we get to his house, I get out of the car with him.

"Can I use your bathroom?" I ask. I have what must be the tiniest bladder in the Northeast, it's embarrassing how often I have to pee.

"Of course," he says, and leads me in through the side door near the garage. This is the first time I'm inside his house, obviously, and I'm only in, like, the foyer. I can see the kitchen—it is big and white and clean, and there is one light on.

He points out the powder room. I shut the door and thankfully there is a fan so I don't have to think about him out there, listening to me go. When I walk back out, Eitan has taken off his sweater, so he's standing there in a plain white t-shirt, which just about does me in. I can see his bicep flex as he absentmindedly scratches the back of his neck and my stomach flips over. Rock climbing.

"Thanks for coming with me," I say.

"Thanks for inviting me tonight," he says. "Ari was like, I can't believe you're going to a disco concert. And I was like, I'm going to a disco concert with Francie."

He takes a step closer to me.

"Do you have to leave?" he asks. "I know you, uh, you have a curfew..."

"My parents said I could stay out till 12:30 because of the concert, because it's, like, for the internship."

"Mmm hmm," he says. "Disco songs for the internship."

I giggle a little, my heart racing.

He takes both of my hands and does a little disco dance and then twirls me so my back is to his chest and then he pulls me closer and wraps his arms around me and I turn myself around and pull my hands out from his and put them on his shoulders and look up into his golden-brown eyes and he tucks my hair behind my ears and cups his hands around my face and kisses me.

His hands are warm and a little rough, and his lips are so soft. I stand on my tiptoes and almost lose my balance, but he takes me by the waist and I put my hands behind his head, pulling him closer. I finally get to run my hands through his hair.

In between kisses, Eitan says, "I wanted to kiss you when we went to the movies, as soon as you picked me up. And when you sat on that bench, licking that ice cream cone, like it was no big deal. And when we were playing pool and when we were standing in front of your house and when we were dancing at the concert..."

"Why didn't you?" I ask.

He looks at me, like, really looks into my eyes.

"Did you want me to? Did you want to kiss me all those times?"

"Well, maybe not when I was eating ice cream, because it was a really tasty cone..."

He laughs. "Well, from now on, you can assume that I'm gonna want to kiss you. So, if you feel like being kissed, you can, uh, give me a sign..."

"A sign? Like a secret code? Like this?" I kiss him.

"Yeah," he says, in between little kisses. "Yeah, that's a good secret code."

We kiss for what feels like forever, in the best way possible.

When I pull away, I take his hand and look at his palms, tracing the little bumps on them. Rock climbing.

"I should go," I say. "I don't want to be late for my late curfew." I kiss him again.

He walks me back to the car and kisses me against it. He puts his pinky finger in the middle of my right cheek, where I have a little dimple.

"Does this get deeper the more you smile?" he asks.

"I guess you'll have to wait to find out," I say, trying not to smile, failing. "I'll talk to you tomorrow." I turn around to open the door.

"Francie," he says, as I turn back to him, "it's already tomorrow."

***

The next night, AJ is going out on her first date with Alex so I pick Susannah up and we drive over to AJ's house to help her get ready. Her room is even more of a disaster than usual, with all of her fancy tops strewn all across the floor and the bed. Her mother is always threatening to stop buying her nice things since she doesn't take very good care of them, but we all know it is an empty threat.

"What are you guys doing?" Sooz asks as AJ pulls on yet another sweater.

"Playing mini-golf," AJ says. "There's a place near his house."

Alex goes to high school maybe fifteen minutes away from us, with no mutual friends, so no one can do any recon on him.

"What's up with you and Eitan?" AJ asks me as I lie on her bed, trying to avoid the one cat who loves me.

"Yeah, did you guys finally kiss last night?" Sooz asks me as I turn pink, pink, pink.

"Oh, you totally did!" AJ smacks me with a small stuffed animal. "When were you gonna tell us?"

"I didn't want to take away from your exciting getting-ready-for-a-date time," I say, throwing the stuffed animal back at AJ.

"Hey, you're gonna mess up my hair!" She blow-dried it straight yesterday, which means that she won't wash it for like three days. She says day two is always the best day. Sometimes, we have to encourage her to shampoo, like, it's too many days gone.

"Speaking of which," she says, and kneels in front of the full-length mirror on the back of her door, "should I wear it up," and she pulls her hair up a little on the sides, "or down?" and she lets it go. She makes her weird mirror face, which consists of widening her eyes and turning her head slowly from side to side.

"You look like a weirdo when you do that," I say. "Please don't make that face in front of Alex, at least not until, like, the third date."

"Wear it up," Sooz says, "and then if you're, like, Oh, I want to be more mysterious, you can take it down."

"Why is hair down more mysterious?" I ask, pulling my own shoulder-length hair up into a clip.

"Ooh, your hair looks nice like that, too," Sooz says.

"It really does," AJ agrees. "But, OK, back to me! So, up?" She pins her hair back with a clip, and does her mirror face again.

"Yes, up," I say. "You look great."

She meets my eyes in the mirror. "You're not getting off the hook, France," she says. "We need details about Eitan."

"Yeah," says Sooz. "Where did it happen?"

"Who cares? Was it good?" AJ says.

"After the concert, when I dropped him off at his house, I went in to use the bathroom."

"Of course you did," AJ says.

"And then when I came out, it just, I don't know, happened."

"Did you kiss him or did he kiss you?" Sooz asks.

"He kissed me, but if it had been, like, one more second, I would've kissed him," I say.

"C'mon," says AJ. "When do you kiss guys first?"

"When they look like Eitan," Sooz says.

The three of us giggle.

"So, how did you leave it?" AJ asks. She is very practical.

"I said I'd talk to him tomorrow, which is actually today."

"And did he call you?" Sooz asks.

"He did, and he's gonna come over to my house tomorrow."

Sooz screeches. "What? That's huge!"

"Totally huge," AJ says, finally done with her makeup. She turns around to look at us. "OK, time to go," she says. We walk her down to her car and hug her and off she goes, and then Sooz and I go back to her house and play, like, two hours of Tetris. Sooz is so good that it's almost more fun to watch her play than to play myself.

The next morning, I talk to AJ about her date. "Francie, I had so much fun. Mini-golf was whatever, but we had a lot to talk about, and ...," she takes a breath, "we made out in my car for like an hour! We only went to second base, but I really like him."

I'm a little surprised that AJ made out with Alex. Usually, she doesn't even kiss on the first date. But it's been a while since she kissed anyone, so it's understandable. "That great, AJ," I say. "When are you gonna see him again?"

"Next weekend." I can hear her flop down onto her bed. "He's so cute. His hair is, like, River Phoenix from 'Running on Empty.'"

We both sigh. Goddamn River Phoenix.

"OK, I have to finish my homework, but call me later after Eitan leaves," she says.

***

Aside from the fact that I want to see Eitan again, as soon as possible, we've been talking and hanging out for, like, a month and my parents insist on meeting him. When he gets to my house, he's really polite. My dad is in the kitchen, and Eitan calls him Dr. Baum, which my father definitely appreciates. The kitchen has a big butcher block island in the middle. Maybe it's not an island because it's connected to a wall. A peninsula? Anyway, my dad is prepping something for dinner that involves cutting lots of vegetables into very small pieces and he's a whiz at it. It's a little mesmerizing, and Eitan and I just watch him for a minute.

"How's your brother? Jonathan?" my dad asks without looking up from his chopping.

"He's good. He graduated from college in May and he's working for a bank."

I wonder what my father is thinking, like, in a parallel world, did Joseph graduate from college? Is Joseph working for a bank? I can't imagine him doing that, but I don't even know him anymore, really.

"That's great," is all my dad says. "Give my best to your parents." He does not mention the soccer uniforms, thank the Lord.

We go upstairs to hang out. I leave the door to my room open. My parents almost never come up to the second floor, but with Eitan here, there is no way they won't be just popping in to check on the state of Lola's room or something. Her room is always a mess, so it's an evergreen topic of conversation for them.

My room is smaller than Lola's or Joseph's, but I like it best because it has a little nook where my desk and bookshelf fit, under the eaves of the house. The wallpaper has flowers on it and pink carpet that's faded after ten years. Everything has flowers to match the wallpaper, even the doorknobs. Each of our bedrooms has its own bathroom, which is quite a luxury. I'm a little nervous for Eitan to see my things, but this is part of getting to know someone, right? You check out their stuff, their art and their books and their music collection, and make judgments about them based on those things.

I watch as Eitan runs his fingers over the books on the shelf. "Big Sweet Valley High fan, huh?" he says, pulling one of those titles off the shelf.

"Ha, ha. I read those in elementary school. AJ and I were obsessed," I say. I take it from him and shelve it. They must remain in order.

"Elementary school! Weren't you precocious!" he says.

"How do you know about Sweet Valley High, anyway?" I ask.

"I have girl cousins," he says. He looks at some of the things I have tacked up on my bulletin board—photos I've taken, poems Lola's written, articles from *Sassy* magazine that I like. There's a Duke pennant there, and he touches the edge of it.

"You want to go to Duke?" he asks.

"Yeah," I say.

"My brother Ori really wanted to go there, but he didn't get in."

"Why are you telling me that?" I laugh.

"It's really hard to get in."

"I know that!" I say. "But I'm very smart."

"Oh, yeah?" he says, taking a step closer to me.

We are standing in the middle of the little nook, where he won't bonk his head on the eaves, and I touch his wrist and he takes my hand and traces his fingers on my palm and I stand on my tiptoes and kiss him. He wraps his arms around me to pull me close.

And then, of course, I hear my mother coming up the stairs.

I sigh and pull away and Eitan sits down in my desk chair and I take three steps across the room to sit on my bed. It's a double bed with two stuffed animals on it. One is a dog that a friend got me as a bat mitzvah gift. It was a strange bat mitzvah gift, yes, but I snuggle with it every night, which is more I can say for a pair of silver candlesticks. The other is a tiny little beanbag creature, maybe he is a bear, who is called Peaches. The dog has no name.

My mother pokes her head in.

"Hi, Mom," I say.

"Just came up to check in on Lola's room," she says, and she walks down the hall. Eitan and I look at each other and suppress giggles.

"I'm a little jealous of that dog," Eitan says in a low voice. "You sleep with it every night?" He makes eyes at me, and I am glad that I left the door open because there is too much temptation otherwise.

"I really want to kiss you again," I whisper to him.

"I really want you to kiss me again," he whispers.

My mom goes back downstairs and Lola comes in to say hello as Eitan and I are just about to play a game of Spit on the floor of my room.

"Francie is very good at Spit," Lola says. "She honed her skills at her nerdy summer camp."

"Lola!" I say.

"What kind of nerdy summer camp?" Eitan asks.

I sigh. Thanks, Lo. "I lived on a college campus and took writing classes. And you're one to talk, Lola. You went to drama camp."

"That sounds like it was perfect for each of you," Eitan says.

"Did you go to sleepaway camp?" Lola asks Eitan as she watches us play Spit. Eitan is somehow squeaking out a victory.

"Yeah, just your basic Jewish summer camp in the Berkshires," Eitan says, shuffling the deck for another round with Lola.

"No rock climbing, camping, hiking sleepaway camp?" I ask.

"A little. I did that last summer, though, in Colorado, with Ari."

Lola makes a little face.

"What's up with you and him?" Eitan asks her.

"There's nothing up with me and Ari," Lola says, furiously playing her cards. "We hung out, like, twice, last year, and he was kind of weird," Lola says.

"He is kind of weird," Eitan says. "Anyway, he says hello," Eitan says. Lola looks pleased with this information.

That night after dinner, my dad and I play some basketball in our driveway. Usually, we just play HORSE or something. I am not Grant Hill or Christian Laettner or Carmen Wallace. The only reason I know who those players are is because of my father. He loves basketball, mostly NBA, but he'll watch college ball, too. He has a friend who can get him Knicks tickets, and he used to take Joseph and me sometimes. Once I started liking Duke basketball, he took me to see them at Madison Square Garden.

My dad took me down to visit Duke this past April. I'd already done a bunch of research into the classes they offer and the clubs they have—it's not like I wanted to go only because of their basketball team. I knew I wanted to take creative writing and documentary photography and study abroad in France. This girl Amelia I'd known since elementary school was a freshman. I got her name from the Duke directory and called her up and stayed with her for a night. We weren't good friends, but she was very welcoming and took me to one of her classes and to a fraternity party. She was pledging a sorority, which I could tell wouldn't be my scene if I went to Duke—when I go to Duke!— but everyone was incredibly nice.

The next day, as I was walking down this long, ugly concrete pathway to the student union building to meet my dad—truly, it was the only blight on an otherwise beautiful campus—I had this incredible sense of déjà vu, like, I felt as though I'd been in this exact location before, or maybe it was in a dream, I don't know. But that's how I knew that I was meant to go to school there. I hope the admissions office agrees.

"So, Eitan," my dad says, taking a shot from the edge of the driveway, near our neighbor's honeysuckle bushes. "Seems like a nice enough kid." Swish. This is high praise from my father, who barely likes any of our friends.

I get the rebound and line myself up for the same shot. Swish.

"Yeah, I think so," I say, smiling.

My dad holds the ball.

"You want to go watch a movie?" he asks, and we head inside to watch "Casablanca" for, like, the nine-hundredth time.

***

I'm taking calculus this year, as is Jason. Last year, in pre-calc, we sat next to each other and whispered to each other throughout every class. It was a miracle that I passed.

We have these graphing calculators and Jason likes to try to get them to graph weird things, or spell out words with the numbers, probably because the class is otherwise too easy for him. Our teacher, Dr. Choi, is not amused.

"Hey," Jason says to me before class starts. "Dave told me you have a boyfriend."

"How does Dave know that?"

"Starr told him. He drives her to school every morning."

Jesus Christ, this town is too small sometimes.

"I don't know if he's my boyfriend," I say. Jason sneaks a pretzel from the little snack bag I've brought.

"Why didn't you tell me about him?" he asks. "Aren't we still friends?"

"You don't tell me about all your girls," I say. "Are you still with Carly?"

"You make it sound like I have a harem. Do you want to know about all the—any of the girls I'm hooking up with?" he asks.

I turn to look at him. "No, truly, I do not," I say.

Dr. Choi, our math teacher starts writing on the board as the bell rings.

"But seriously," Jason whispers, turning to me, taking another pretzel, "we haven't hung out in a while. I miss you."

I look at him. "I miss you, too," I whisper. "But I'm still a little annoyed at you."

He nods. "I'm sorry."

"Thank you for apologizing for kissing me," I whisper.

"Well, I'm not sorry I kissed you," he whispers.

"Oh my God, Jay, you should be," I whisper. "You can't just go around kissing me for no reason."

"Jason, Francine," says Dr. Choi. "Can you two stop whispering back there? Unless you are whispering about properties of limits."

Jason and I stop whispering, but he picks up my pencil, which also has some bite marks on it, then thinks better of it, fishing around in his bag. That's how easy this class is for him, he doesn't even have a pencil ready. He writes me a note on my loose-leaf: *I'm sorry I hurt your feelings, but I'm not sorry I kissed you.*

I glare at him. He writes: *You're a good kisser.* I am getting annoyed. I cross out what he's written and write: *Stop.* He writes: *What's his name?* I sigh and write: *Eitan.* Jason writes: *Nice Jewish boy?* I nod. Jason writes: *Nicer than me?* I look at him and write: *I hope so.* Jason laughs and Dr. Choi looks over at us again and Jason shuts up.

***

Eitan and I sit on the train going into Manhattan. We sit so close to each other that we are almost in the same seat. Eitan drapes his arm around me, pulling me even closer. We're going to the Guggenheim Museum. My Aunt Darla, my father's sister, has taken me to the Guggenheim many times. She used to take me to many galleries and museums. She'd always be like, Francine, don't just look at the art, look at the space! She calls me by my full name because it is French and she and my uncle Gerald are big Francophiles.

We get to the museum and I feel old, because I am here with a boyfriend for the first time, and very young, because everyone else is much older than we are.

"Why are we always going to places where we are the youngest people?" Eitan asks me. We start at the top of the museum and walk down, looking at the art, but also at each other, looking at the art.

"I don't know if I get it," Eitan says.

"Then this art is not for you," I say.

"Maybe art in general is not for me. I don't think I ever get it. You're a photographer," he says. "What do you think?"

I have, in fact, brought my camera with me into the city. It's my dad's old single-lens reflex camera; he gave it to me last year to use for my photography class. "Just because I like to take pictures doesn't make me an expert in all forms of artistic expression," I say. I uncap the lens and take a photo of him and then he takes one of me and some stranger offers to take one of the two of us, so we pose together with the rotunda of the Guggenheim in the background.

We hold hands, our hips bump each other. What we want is a place we can be alone, but that's not possible in this city.

On the train on the way home, Eitan asks me about my brother, and I tell him the story.

"That must be really hard for your parents," he says. "I don't know what my parents would do if they didn't see one of us for so many years."

"It's like they're trying to prove something, that they want to see him when he's doing what they want him to do. Like, they think he should be in rehab, or a halfway house, or something."

"How is that working out for them, though? They've lost their son, and your mom has lost her brother and her parents, and you and Lola have lost your brother and your cousins and your grandparents."

"It sucks," I say, agreeing with him.

"Do you miss him?" Eitan asks.

"I don't even know him anymore. I wrote him a bunch of letters, but he never wrote me back."

"That's tough," Eitan says. I nod. "Do your friends know about it?" Eitan asks.

I nod again. "I told them at the beginning of high school. I was, like, I don't know, ashamed about it. All of my friends have older brothers—you have two!—and none of them have drug problems."

"Thank you for telling me," Eitan says. He kisses the top of my head.

***

Sunday evening, instead of going to the soup kitchen, a few of us sort food for the food pantry. There was a food drive during Yom Kippur and people brought in all sorts of canned goods, and only now, a few weeks later, are they dealing with it. We sort the cans into types of food and organize them into boxes so the food pantry can come and pick everything up the next day.

When I'm finished, Adam pulls me aside and asks me if I've thought more about what I want to get out of volunteering. I can't tell him that I haven't thought about it at all, that I'm just coming because I have to. Am I a bad person? Maybe, but also, I've only been doing this for, like, three hours.

"Why do you volunteer at the soup kitchen?" I ask, turning the tables on him.

"I think it's the right thing to do," he says. "I don't have a lot of money, but I have some time, and this seems like a good way to spend that time. I like the people at the soup kitchen. I've gotten to know some of them over the past few years, and I like thinking that what I'm doing is helping them, at least a little bit. Food is really important, obviously, but feeding people can be really nourishing."

Wow. If Susannah were here, she'd ask Adam when his birthday is. I bet he's a Sagittarius. I have definitely been listening too much to Sooz's horoscope talk.

"Francie, I want you to take a look at the Book of Ruth. Do you still have that Tanakh you were given at your bat mitzvah?"

I nod.

"Maybe it will give you some ideas about why people do *g'milut chasadim*."

So now I have homework, too.

"I'll read it," I say.

"Great. We can talk about it in a few weeks."

When I get home, I pull the Tanakh off the shelf. It has a nameplate in it with my name and the date of my bat mitzvah. Lola and Joseph each have one, too. I flip to the back, to the Book of Ruth, which is very short, as it turns out, only a few pages, but it does tell a whole story. It's about Ruth, who is not even Jewish, deciding to make her way in a new land, Bethlehem, with her mother-in-law, Naomi, and all the things that Ruth does to improve life for Naomi, and all the ways that Naomi tries to improve life for Ruth.

I think about the decisions that the characters make. Maybe they were real people, I don't know, but I think of them as characters in a short story. What will Adam want to ask me about this next week?

***

For Lola's birthday in October, my parents have invited a few of her friends to a Spanish restaurant for a surprise party. Lola loves surprises, and she loves to be the center of attention. She is also whatever the Spanish version of a Francophile is.

We get to the restaurant after her friends have all arrived, and she is so confused, she's like, What are Amanda and Jamie and Penny doing here? They all yell, Surprise! Starr is late, of course. And I think, this is another celebration we are having without Joseph.

We order lots of food and when the musicians in the restaurant stroll over, my mother asks them to play happy birthday for Lola and also some song Lola and her friends must've learned in Spanish class because they know all the words.

Usually, Lola's friends are always running off to pay phones because people are always beeping them, but that doesn't happen at her party, probably because they're all in one place. I know Lola really wanted a beeper for her birthday, but my parents would never get her one. They think they're only for drug dealers. I guess they don't realize that a beeper is also kind of a leash—they could get in touch with Lola, or me, if I had one—much more easily. That's part of why I have no interest in one. I don't need my parents to be able to get in touch with me all the time.

We never open presents in front of guests, so back at our house after the party, I lounge on the bed on the floor of Lola's room, flipping through a book of poems that she put together in her poetry class last year, while Lola opens her gifts.

I got her a pair of earrings at the gift shop in the Guggenheim and I made her a mix tape. She models the earrings for me, along with a scarf from Amanda and a pair of sunglasses from Starr, which are shaped like, duh, stars.

"Will you submit some of these to the lit mag?" I ask her, pointing at the poetry book.

"No way," she says. "I don't need guidance counselors worrying about me and calling the parents."

I laugh. "You can submit them anonymously," I say.

"I'll think about it," she says. I mean, the lit mag can't be all stuff that Sooz and I have written.

15th BIRTHDAY MIX TAPE FOR LOLA
Summer of Drugs, by Soul Asylum
Sowing the Seeds of Love, by Tears for Fears
Pulling Mussels from the Shell, by Squeeze
Thirteen, by Big Star
Sweet Virginia, by The Rolling Stones
The Best of What's Around, by Dave Matthews Band
These are Days, by 10000 Maniacs
Silent in the Morning, by Phish

***

Ari is having a party at his house while his parents are in Israel. Susannah and AJ pick Lola and me up. Lola has decided that she does not dislike Ari anymore, but also, Starr will be at the party.

It turns out that Ari's mother is an artist, and the house is full of her paintings. It's also full of kids I don't know, so I am glad that Sooz and AJ are with me. Lola disappears somewhere with Starr. I hope she doesn't smoke too much pot, because it could get awkward when we get home if my parents are still awake. After everything that happened with Joseph, is still happening with Joseph, my parents think they are, like, the DEA when it comes to drug detection, but they are pretty clueless. Anyway, it's only pot.

Sooz walks around the living room just absorbing the artwork, while AJ walks around looking for cute boys. Eitan is here, I know, but I don't see him yet. I haven't seen him all week, which isn't unusual, we don't go to the same school, but I also haven't talked to him, because of homework and after-school stuff. He's become part of my life so quickly. What was I doing before? What filled that Eitan-shaped hole that I didn't even know was there?

I see Ari and he walks over to say hello. "You guys need anything? I might order some pizza," he says. We shake our heads. "Most people are outside in the backyard." He points the way through the house. "I think Eitan is out there, Francie. I mean, he's here somewhere."

We walk out to the backyard, where we can still hear Phish blaring over the stereo from the living room because Ari put the speakers in the window. Eitan spots me immediately and it feels like a flurry of butterflies rushes into my chest as he hurries over. He takes my hand and swings it up to kiss it and I laugh and blush at the same time.

"You guys are so cute," Sooz says. She sounds a little wistful.

AJ grabs Susannah to walk around the party, scoping out the boy situation. She and Alex have only gone on two dates, and she said she's not pinning herself down yet until they have some kind of conversation.

Eitan turns to me. "You wanna go inside? Let's go inside," he says. Still holding my hand, he leads me through the house and up the stairs to what looks like an office or guest room. He shuts the door behind him.

"Is this OK?" he asks. I nod, and he locks the door. He smiles at me, and I pull him in for a kiss.

"I missed you this week," I say. "I don't want to go a whole week without seeing you or talking to you." Missing him tugs at my heart. How can you miss someone you've only known for a few weeks?

"I missed you, too," he says.

He sits down on the couch and I sit next to him, and we kind of turn to face each other and we kiss. I also missed this. Kissing him is the best. He runs his hands under the back of my shirt, between my sweater and my tank top, his fingers cool from being outside, and I shiver. He lies down, pulling me on top of him.

"You're—you're so pretty," he breathes into my ear. I give a laugh that is really like a snort. He sits up a little on his elbows.

"You don't think so?" he says.

I shake my head. "What girl thinks she's pretty? You're the one that's—I bet people are like, What's Eitan doing hooking up with her?"

He sits up all the way now, his hands around my waist, his face, his mouth, just a few inches from mine. "Francie, that's crazy. You're beautiful. I think you're beautiful. Look at you—and that dimple." He clutches his heart. I giggle. "And your body is—" His hands slide down my back, his thumbs grazing the side of my breasts. I shiver again.

"Thank you," I say. He kisses me. "Thank you," I say again. He kisses me again and I kiss him back.

"It's my pleasure, and I really mean that," he says. "And I don't—I mean, uh—are we 'hooking up'?" He looks nervous. "Is that what you want? To just be hooking up? And, uh, hook up with other people, too?"

I shake my head vehemently. "No," I say. "I don't want to be with anyone else."

"Oh, good," he sighs. "Me, neither."

Later in the night, most people have left, and we hang out in Ari's room—Eitan and me, Ari, Lola, Starr, AJ, and Susannah. AJ is probably like, How did it happen that we are hanging out with all underclassmen? It's a little weird to me that I'm seeing Ari's room before I've seen Eitan's. Some of Ari's mom's art is on the walls, and the lights are low. There are glow-in-the-dark stickers on the ceiling. Starr, Ari, and Lola are definitely high, but not in an annoying way. They eat pretzels and cheddar Goldfish. Neil Young is on the stereo, and he's asking why it's hard to make arrangements with yourself. My head is on Eitan's stomach as he lies on the floor, and he's running his hands through my hair. I'm trying to live in this moment, but I'm also thinking about how it's going to end, because Lola and I have to be home by 11 o'clock.

Starr says, "What do you think he's talking about, with the silver spaceships?" She is asking about the next song.

"I think it's about how we're fucking up the environment," Ari says. "And then we have to leave Earth with the aliens, because we can't live here anymore. But not everyone can go. That's why some people are the chosen ones."

I think about this with my eyes closed, my head rising and falling with Eitan's breaths, and wonder who would get to be the chosen ones, and then I think about how sometimes, the Jews are called the chosen people, and then I think about Ruth, the Book of Ruth, and how she wasn't even Jewish and she was able to start this chain of *g'milut chasadim*, of acts of lovingkindness, and then I wonder if, somehow, I, too, am high.

Lola says, "We need to go soon, Francie pants." I open my eyes and turn to her and nod.

"Are you OK?" she asks. "Are you getting a headache?" I shake my head, not trusting my voice.

The first time I got a migraine headache, I was nine years old. We were in the city with my Aunt Darla and all of a sudden, I couldn't see anything. When I told my dad that, he freaked out a little, because he's a doctor and knows all about the terrible things that could make a person lose her vision. The aura went away maybe ten minutes later, and then I got the worst headache I'd ever had in my life.

Now, I get them every couple of months, usually a few days before I get my period. Sometimes, the migraine is so bad that I have to stay home from school, lying in bed in the dark with a cold washcloth across my forehead, fighting down nausea. It only lasts a few hours, a day at most, but I can't talk to anyone or do anything. Lola will always joke that I've taken to my bed, like I'm a Southern belle or something, but she knows it's not really funny.

"Do you guys need to leave?" Susannah asks. She stands up.

"Let me walk you out," Eitan says.

"Thanks for the party, Ari," I say. He stands up to flip the record over and waves goodbye.

Susannah walks ahead of us down the stairs and then out the front door with AJ and Lola and they get into Sooz's car. I stand in the doorway and give Eitan a little kiss and I am very aware of my friends and my sister right there, maybe watching.

"I'll call you tomorrow," I say as I shut the door behind me.

It's cool out, but Susannah takes the top down on the Mustang anyway and turns the heat on, and this is a great way to drive around. Ari's house is off a bigger street that goes across the train tracks and right past the turnoff to my house, but if you take it all the way to the end, you wind up at the docks, which is just a parking lot on the water, but people hang out there, smoking cigarettes or pot or making out or just looking for other people. I guess that, during the day, people fish there, but I've never been there during the day. If the cops are there, everyone drives away quickly, and they flash their brights at people who are approaching, to let them know not to bother heading down that way.

Sooz wants to do a drive-by of the docks to see if anyone we know is there before she drops Lola and me back at our house. When we get there, it's mostly empty. We sit in Sooz's car, listening to the music for a few minutes.

"What's up with you and Eitan?" Sooz asks.

"Yeah, you disappeared with him for like an hour," AJ says, learning forward into the front seat.

"You did? Eeew," says Lola.

"We were talking," I say, looking out the window so maybe they won't see how much I'm blushing.

"Talking?" Sooz says.

"You know," I say. "We were, fine, we were making out, but also talking. We decided we're not going to date other people. Not that there are, like, so many other people I could be dating, but you know what I mean. He's officially my boyfriend."

Sooz squeals. "Your first official boyfriend!"

"Look at you, Francie. You are so pink and smiley," AJ says. It's true, I cannot stop smiling.

"No boy disease, please, Francie pants," Lola says. "I like Eitan."

"No boy disease, Lola," I say, as Sooz pulls out of the docks to take us home. "I like Eitan, too."

***

Eitan invites me to his house for dinner. I'm a little nervous about meeting his parents, so Susannah gives me a pep talk. We are in my room as I'm getting ready. She lies on my bed, picking at her split ends. Susannah always has split ends.

"Look," she says. She is like my mother in that she thinks all serious conversations need to start with the word, "Look." "Look, Francie, you are a catch. You are pretty and smart and funny. Why wouldn't his parents like you?"

"Um, maybe because I am an older woman, preying on their beloved youngest child?"

"Please. I'm the youngest child, and my parents could not care less. Why do you think they let me date whoever I want? Plus, you're only, like, nine months older than Eitan." Susannah's siblings are eight and ten years older than she is. She jokes that she was a change-of-life baby, but really, her mother was only, like, 35, when Sooz was born, which is the same age my mother was when she had Lola. They are the oldest moms of all our friends, though.

Susannah sighs theatrically. "If only I were dating someone," she says.

I sit down next to her. "We will find someone for you, Sooz-ster."

I turn up the volume on the mix tape I'm playing, and it's "Kiss Off" by the Violent Femmes, and the two of us absolutely have to jump around like crazy to this song. "I have to stop," I say, panting. "I'm gonna get all sweaty." We flop back down onto the floor.

"You should wear the other dress," Sooz says. "It's a little sexy, but still appropriate." Sooz is the expert on what is appropriate. "Maybe you should wear your glasses," she says. "They make you look smarter, but also, less of a threat."

"Right, because no one in glasses does anything inappropriate, ever."

"Well, I hope you get up to some inappropriate stuff tonight. Somebody should," Sooz says.

I change my dress and we walk downstairs and my mother inspects me. "You look very pretty," she says.

"Remember to thank them." She hands me a Bundt cake. "You shouldn't show up empty-handed."

"I can't bring them a whole Bundt cake!"

"Well, you can't bring them half a cake, Francie," my mother says, which is, of course, true.

"Fine," I say. "Thank you."

Susannah and I walk outside together. She gets into her car and waves. "Have fun," she says. "Call me later."

As I drive over to Eitan's, I listen to a mix tape I made with tapes I found in Joseph's room. Lola and I almost never went into Joseph's room when he lived at home, especially in the year or two before he left, when everything was kind of unravelling. We were a little scared of him in the end, and scared to go into his room when he wasn't there in case he suddenly came home and found us there, but after all these years, it's hard to think of it as his room. When I was a lot younger, I totally revered him. I wanted to read by myself, because Joseph read by himself. I wanted to ride a bike, because Joseph rode a bike. Sometimes, we would gang up on Lola a little, this eleven-year-old and seven-year-old messing around with a five-year-old, trying to convince her that it would be a good idea to roll down the stairs in a bath towel.

I pull into Eitan's driveway and flip down the visor for the mirror and put on a little lipstick.

As I walk up to the house holding the stupid cake, Eitan opens the front door and walks down the path. He kisses me and takes my hand and then, inside, takes my coat. I slip out of my shoes and follow him through the house into the kitchen. His mother is putting together a salad.

"Francie," she says, smiling at me. "Welcome!" I put the cake on the cake on the counter and she gives me a hug and a kiss on each cheek, which I was not expecting.

"Thank you," I say. "Thank you for inviting me. I brought a cake." Duh.

"That's so sweet of you! Thank you. Dinner will be ready in fifteen minutes, maybe twenty. Eitan, you want to show her the house? Your room?"

Eitan makes eyes at me—in front of his mother!—and says, "Sure."

We walk upstairs. This house is enormous, and as he leads me down one hallway, and then another, I am certain that I would get lost if left alone. He opens a door at the end of the hall, and steps inside.

I pause, drawing in my breath. I'm about to see where Eitan sleeps and dreams and walks around naked after the shower—oh my Lord. I follow him into his room and he shuts the door behind him. No concerns for him that his parents are going to check in on him and his girlfriend (girlfriend!).

His room, like the rest of the house, is modern and minimal. The bed, in the corner, looks like it was made up by someone in the military. The walls are white, and he has a framed poster of Zion National Park hanging next to his desk. The room faces the back of the house, with a view of the water. There is a little dock with a motorboat moored to it. I look around at his things—his backpack on the floor, a few books on a shelf.

"Where's all your stuff?" I ask.

"What do you mean?"

"Like, all your, I don't know, your stuff. My room has a lot of stuff."

"I know," he says. "I don't like a lot of stuff out. I put it in the closet." He opens the closet to reveal a dresser whose top is, indeed, covered with random trinkets and trophies and things.

He takes a pink book off the shelf and holds it very close to his heart. "I want to lend this to you," he says. "but only if you think you'll read it. It's one of my favorite books." I take it from him and look up, skeptical.

"*Zen and the Art of Motorcycle Maintenance*?" I ask.

"It may change your life," he says.

"All right," I say, "I'll read it," and put it in my bag.

He sits down on the bed and looks up at me. I walk over to him and he pulls me closer so I'm standing between his legs. "Hey," he says. I run my hands down his arms.

"Hey," I say to him. I tuck my hair behind my ears.

"I've had a lot of thoughts about you in here," he says.

I smile. "Oh, really?"

"Yeah. They have not been very pure." He pulls me down to kiss me. My knees buckle, and I sit on his lap. I take off my glasses and put them on his bedside table.

"Can you see anything without those?" he asks.

"Not really," I say.

"So, I could be anyone right now, kissing you?"

I close my eyes and run my hands over his hair, his cheeks, his nose, his mouth. He kisses my thumbs. I run my hands over his shoulders and lean in to smell his neck.

"You are definitely Eitan," I say, kissing his jaw right below his ear, my eyes still closed.

"Did you just sniff me?" he says, laughing.

"You smell like, I don't know, boy and wool," I say.

"Boy and wool, a new scent from Calvin Klein," he says. He kisses my closed eyelids.

I open my eyes. "I would not mistake someone else for you, even without my glasses," I say.

"That's a relief," he says.

He closes his eyes and gently runs his hands over my face, my ears, my mouth, leaning in to smell me. His fingers and the palm of his hand are calloused and raise goosebumps on my skin. He whispers into my neck, "You smell like berries and flowers."

I close my eyes and then we are kissing again. His hands wander down my back and slide underneath my dress. I gasp a little as his hands move in between my legs.

"Is that too much?" he asks.

"No, it's just—we can't do this now."

"We can't do what now?" he asks, his mouth on my collarbone, his hands running up my back, fumbling for the zipper on my dress.

"Your mother is going to call us for dinner any second."

"Yeah..." Another kiss on my neck.

"And she could come into the room at any time, right?" I keep kissing him, too.

"No, I locked the door."

Smart.

"Do you want me to stop?" he asks, pulling away.

"I mean, no, but..." I shift my weight on his lap, and he moans. "Sorry," I giggle.

"Don't laugh—it's real pain," he says, also laughing. "Look what you're doing to me," he says, and I look down at his jeans.

"Jesus," I say. I reposition myself and start to unbuckle his belt. I've never seen a penis in real life— I've never seen one in movies or anything, either, because I don't watch X-rated films. Just, like, anatomical drawings in health class. I'm not sure I'll know what to do, but I'm willing to go for it. Now Eitan gasps, lying down on the bed.

"Eitan! Time for dinner!" we hear his mother call from downstairs.

"Shit," Eitan says, closing his eyes, breathing heavily. "Shit, shit, shit." He sits up and looks at me. "I'm gonna be honest, I gotta go deal with this in the bathroom," he says.

"You're gonna go..." my voice trails off.

"It'll only take a minute, believe me," he says.

He opens the door, holding his jeans up with one hand, and calls down to his mother. "We'll be down in a second, Eema." He looks at me again, then crosses the hall to the bathroom. It is really weird to think he's in there, like, taking care of himself.

I hear the toilet flush, the sink run, and then Eitan opens the door, a big smile on his face. "Good as new," he says. He gives me a kiss, and then we walk downstairs for dinner.

"How is your brother? Joseph?" Eitan's father asks me. Eitan and I exchange a glance.

I clear my throat. "Um, he's all right," I lie. Or maybe it's not a lie, maybe he is all right. I don't know the real answer, and I'm certainly not going to get into the details now with Eitan's father.

After dinner, Eitan walks me to my car. "I think my parents really like you. Especially my mom," he says.

"How can you tell?" I ask.

"To be honest, she's easy to please. She just wants me to be happy. And, she really wanted a girl," Eitan says. "She was pregnant a few years ago, and it was going to be a girl, but then she had a miscarriage."

"Oh, no," I say.

"Yeah, it was hard."

"But you're saying that, as long as you bring home a girl, your mother will be happy with her? That's not a very high bar to clear," I tease him.

"Well, I'm sure if I brought home a guy, she'd get used to it." He leans in to kiss me, pushing me up against the door of the car. "But that's not very likely."

In bed that night, I replay my time with Eitan in his room in my head. I think about his hands between my legs, and I run my hands up my inner thighs, touching myself while thinking of what it will feel like when he touches me.

JOSEPH'S TAPES MIXTAPE
In the Evening, by Led Zeppelin
Talk Dirty to Me, by Poison
Jump, by Van Halen
Hysteria, by Def Leppard
Is This Love, by Whitesnake
Over the Hills and Far Away, by Led Zeppelin
Patience, by Guns N'Roses

***

Jason is in this band with Dave and a few other guys from school and they have a gig at this coffee shop in the next town over. He drops many hints during math class that it would be nice if I came, and I do like to support my friends.

Eitan and I sit on one of the mismatched coffee shop couches and AJ and Alex sit on the loveseat next to us. Jason comes over to say hello before they start to play, and AJ introduces him to Alex, and I introduce him to Eitan. The guys all shake hands, like, is that a thing most teenagers do?

AJ and Alex have been dating for a few weeks now. Sooz met him once, but this is the first time I've met him since we all met him, at the Dunkin' Donuts. His hands are all over AJ, which she doesn't seem to mind. AJ and I order hot cocoa and Eitan orders a Coke and

Alex tries to order an Irish coffee, but the waitress asks for his ID, so he changes it to just a regular coffee.

"What's in an Irish coffee anyway?" I ask.

"Whiskey, Kahlua, coffee. Sometimes they put whipped cream on top," Alex says.

"And usually you can just order it, no problem?" I ask.

"Well, yeah. I have a fake ID, but I didn't feel like using it tonight. It's not that good and I don't need some stupid waitress confiscating it. My buddy is going to get me a better one, from California. He can get you guys one, too. They're, like, $150."

"I'm gonna get one," says AJ.

"For all of your barhopping?" I say, joking. "I don't think I need one. Plus, I don't have an extra $150 hanging around."

"You might want one next year, when you're in college," Alex says.

Next year, when I'm in college. I look at Eitan, who will still be in high school next year. I can't plan that far ahead.

"So, what's this band like?" Alex asks.

"They're pretty good," says AJ. "They're a rock band. Jason's one of Francie's best friends."

"Jason's one of your best friends?" Eitan asks.

"Yes," I say. He's probably wondering why he hasn't met him yet, or even heard of him.

"What kind of rock music?" Alex asks.

"They play covers, and they have a few of their own songs," I say. "They're, like, Van Halen or Def Leppard."

"David Lee Roth or Sammy Hagar?" Alex asks.

"David Lee Roth," I say. Everybody knows David Lee Roth is better than Sammy Hagar.

"I'm kind of a metal guy myself," Alex says. "You know, Sabbath and Ozzy and Metallica."

"Hmm," I say. I cannot stand those bands.

When the lights dim, Eitan puts his arm around me and pulls me in closer. I weave my fingers through his other hand. By the time the set is over, Alex and AJ have left. I guess the band wasn't metal enough for him.

Eitan leans into me. "So who's Jason?" he asks.

"The lead singer. I introduced you to him," I say, pointing across the café.

"No, I mean, who is he to you? Why haven't you ever mentioned him?"

I look at Eitan, wondering how he knows that anything ever happened between Jason and me. "I don't know," I say. "We've been friends forever. He lives around the corner from me."

"You guys never went out?" he asks.

I shake my head, but I don't want to lie to Eitan. "No, we never went out, but we did, I mean, he did kiss me, we kissed, once. He's dating Carly." I point to her, sitting on another couch. Eitan nods. How would I feel if I met anyone Eitan had kissed or worse, more than kissed? A fire of jealousy flares in my stomach and I blush, turning away.

"Why are you blushing?" Eitan asks, touching my cheek. Apparently, my skin is my enemy. "You're not, uh, interested in Jason, are you?"

"What? No. I was thinking how I would feel if I met someone you kissed, or dated, or something."

"How would you feel?" he whispers in my ear, which is extremely distracting because of the shivers down my spine. I turn to him and our faces are very close.

"I would feel really jealous," I whisper. "But you shouldn't be."

He leans in to kiss me and I pull away before I even realize I'm doing it.

"What was that?" he asks, hurt.

"I'm—I'm not into kissing in public."

"Francie, we're not gonna make out here. I just want to give you a kiss. I—you're my girlfriend. It's not weird to kiss in front of other people every now and then."

"I know, it's this thing I have. It makes me uncomfortable. I don't want people I know, I dunno, watching..."

"You'd rather have strangers watching? I would not have expected that." He makes eyes at me.

I swat at him lightly with a napkin. "No, silly. I don't want anyone watching. I just want it to be you and me."

***

I used to babysit for all my neighbors, but I don't want to give up my Friday and Saturday nights anymore, so I get a job at a 30-minute photo developing shop. The owner is maybe Turkish, I don't know. He is tall and bald and smokes incessantly and pays me $8 an hour under the table. I work there three afternoons a week and some weekend mornings. My parents give Lola and me an allowance, which we mostly use to buy lunch during the week at school. This job will help pay for my weekends.

The woman I work with most of the time, Michelle, is in her early 20s and is taking classes at Nassau Community College. She also smokes, but she usually goes outside to do it. There's a machine for making prints, but the owner doesn't think I need to learn how to use it; I'll be leaving for college within a year. Instead, he shows me how to use the machine that make enlargements from negatives. If she develops racy photos, Michelle shows them to me. And I always take a look if there are photos of people I know, which is probably wrong, but I just can't help it.

Jason works at a sneaker store along with, like, half of the senior class. Susannah works in her father's office, answering the phones and filing. AJ gets a job working at a housewares store in our town. She folds towels and organizes things, which is ironic, because she does not do any of that at home. She must have gotten the job by arguing her way into it.

***

Because Eitan goes to a different school, we don't get to see each other during the day, so I've started going to his house every Wednesday after school. There's no way he could come to mine, even if he had his driver's license. My parents would not let him hang out there if they weren't home. His mom doesn't work, so she's always home, which makes my parents feel like there's some parental supervision. Little do they know how little we are supervised.

I get there around three and we have a snack, like we're in elementary school or something, sitting around the kitchen counter on bar stools. Then, we go up to his room to do our homework, ostensibly. I mean, we do have to get homework done. Usually, he sits at his desk and I'll sit on the floor or on his bed. He was very concerned about my posture, but I was a ballerina for ten years, so I think my posture is fine.

One day, after I've finished AP chem, AP government, AP French and I've put off James Joyce as long as possible, I pick up *A Portrait of the Artist as a Young Man*, which I am thankfully almost done with. Mr. O'Connor has had to teach us years of Irish and English history so we can understand all of the references. Then, I realize I have not finished my Hebrew homework yet.

"Eitan," I say. He looks up from his desk, where he's working on math. "Do you want to help me with my Hebrew homework?"

"Your school has Hebrew?" he asks. "How did I not know this?"

"Yeah," I say. "We do three years of Hebrew in two years, and then we take the Regents exam."

"I thought you took French," he says, as he puts down his pencil and comes to sit next to me on the bed. I'm more like lounging in the corner, with all of my papers and books spread out. I've really made myself comfortable.

"I take both," I say.

"Show me what you're working on," he says. I show him my textbook, where I'm supposed to read a short essay in Hebrew and answer some questions about it. I absolutely do not need help with it, but why not get some additional insight from someone who's practically a native speaker?

He skims the passage and looks at me. "This is what you're reading? It's so basic."

"Hey," I say. "This is only my second year!"

"What do you need help with?"

"Umm, maybe you could read it to me. Sometimes, it's easier when I hear it out loud."

So Eitan reads the passage to me in Hebrew. Obviously, it sounds much better when he reads it versus my Hebrew teacher or the tapes we listen to at the language lab. When he's done, he looks at me again. "You don't need help with this at all, do you?" He smiles at me.

"*Lo*," I say, which means "No" in Hebrew. "I can read it," I say, also in Hebrew.

"I like your Hebrew accent," he says.

"*Lo*," I say, "*B'Ivrit*."

So he repeats it in Hebrew. "What else have you learned?" he asks. "Days of the week? Months of the year? Parts of the body? How to ask where the library is?"

I giggle. "*Ken*," I say, which means Yes in Hebrew.

"*Lamah at yoshevet kol kach karav ee-lee vi lo m'nashek eetee?*"

I have no idea what he's saying. "*Ahnee lo m'veenah*," I say, which means, "I don't understand."

He leans in to whisper in my ear. "Why are you sitting so close to me and not kissing me?" he says in English.

"*Ahnee lo yoda-at*," I say, which means, "I don't know," and I kiss him. Slowly, we make a mess of my homework on the bed.

***

Starr throws a big Halloween party and it honestly seems like half of the junior and senior classes are there. I go with Lola, AJ, and Sooz. Eitan can't come because his parents took him on an overnight camping trip to the Pocono mountains.

I'm dressed up as Strawberry Shortcake, with a white apron over a red skirt and a red long-sleeved tee shirt. I've drawn green lines on my white tights and I have a white shower cap that I've sewn a little strawberry button into, and I've put little freckles on my cheeks with my mother's eye liner. I even put some strawberry-scented lotion all over my arms. My costume is amazing.

Sooz is dressed up as Betsey Johnson, which is very Sooz, although no one knows who she is. AJ is wearing very tight, all black clothing, with cat ears and a tail.

Lola is a skater girl in huge wide-legged pants and Vans and a ribbed henley, so, basically, her own normal clothing.

When we get to Starr's, the house is already packed. There are maybe twelve girls from my class dressed up like dwarves. Why so many? Then, I see Starr, dressed up as a gypsy, and Ari, dressed up as a male gypsy, maybe? I don't know how else to describe it. He has a mustache and a beard and a shirt half unbuttoned and old bell-bottomed jeans and a scarf around his neck. Ari waves at us, and we go over to say hello.

"Who are you dressed up as?" I ask her.

"I'm Stevie Nicks, and he's Lindsey Buckingham." Are they dating? Isn't that a couples costume?

This girl Tammy from my French class is at the party, too, dressed up like Holly Golightly from "Breakfast at Tiffany's." She even has a long cigarette holder.

"Are you smoking that?" I ask her.

"Oh, no, it's a candy cigarette. I would never smoke. It would totally ruin my voice," she says, puffing on it, powdered sugar coming out of the end. Tammy is in all the school plays.

"Your sister is amazing, by the way," she says. Lola is Rosaline in Romeo and Juliet. "She'll totally be the lead when she's a senior, maybe even next year." She leans in to sniff me. "We should get lunch some time."

"Sure," I say.

"Really? You can peel yourself away from AJ to have lunch with moi?" She takes off her enormous sunglasses.

"Of course," I say, annoyed. "Let's go on Wednesday. It's two for one pizza slices at the pizzeria."

Jason is at the party, too, and he is dressed like Vincent Vega from "Pulp Fiction," which works especially well because he has, unfortunately, grown his hair kind of long. When I saw that movie a few weeks ago with Sooz, I was like, Jason is going to love this, and I wish I had seen it with him. It's just the kind of thing we used to do together, but now I think it would be weird.

He comes over to me and gives me a hug and I hug him back.

"Who are you?" he asks. "You smell like strawberries."

"That's because I'm Strawberry Shortcake," I say. I lean into him and say, "I guess you saw 'Pulp Fiction.'"

His eyes light up. "You saw it, too? So fucking good, right?"

I nod.

"I knew you'd love it," he says. "I thought of you especially because of the soundtrack. It made me think—I'm gonna start writing a movie this year," he says.

"About the mean streets of Elmwood?" I say.

"Why not?" he says. "All sorts of crazy shit happens here."

This is maybe true. Or at least, there is very believable gossip: the sophomore having an affair with a teacher; the prostitution ring that was run out of the third floor girls bathroom, which is allegedly why they closed the third floor girls bathroom; the PTA president running off with the superintendent of schools; all the mob rumors.

"Jay," I say, "when you write your movie, I would love to be the first to read it. And when it gets made, you have to let me choose the music."

"Deal," he says.

He reaches out to touch one of the fake freckles on my cheek and I pull away from him ever so slightly.

"You smell like strawberries," he says.

"You said that already," I say, and I look at his eyes and realize he's probably high.

He sighs. "I really fucked it up between us," he says. He and Carly broke up, of course.

"You didn't fuck it up because you kissed me, Jay," I say.

"Did you just curse?" he asks, his eyes wide. I really almost never curse.

"Yes," I say, "I was quoting you. You didn't fuck it up because you kissed me. You fucked it up because you didn't think about how I'd feel when you kissed me. Like, my feelings didn't matter. But it's OK. We'll be friends again." I pat him on the shoulder.

Sometimes I wonder what would've happened if we had gotten together, if I would be dating him instead of Eitan, but I'm really happy with Eitan. Just thinking about him makes my stomach flip over a tiny bit, and I blush. And then I go dance around to Deee-Lite with my friends in the living room.

DANCE MIX FOR STARR
Groove is in the Heart, by Deee-Lite
Into the Groove, by Madonna
I Wanna Dance With Somebody, by Whitney Houston
Girls Just Wanna Have Fun, by Cyndi Lauper
Stand, by REM
I'm Free, by The Soup Dragons

***

I'm reading on the couch in the TV room while my mother edits a story for her newspaper. My father is lying on his stomach on the carpet, reading medical journals and taking notes, snacking on something, while also watching the Knicks. Lola is up in her room playing music, we can practically hear every word of Ani DiFranco from here, but it's just quiet enough that my parents don't feel a need to trek up there to ask her to turn it down.

"Francie, do you have my copy of *The Grapes of Wrath*?" my mother asks, putting down her papers.

"Definitely not," I say.

"Well, can you go see if Lola has it? One of my writers is reviewing a stage production of it and I want to check a few things in the novel."

I head upstairs and check my shelves just in case, but I don't have it. I read *East of Eden* in, like, one weekend freshman year, but *The Grapes of Wrath* was so boring.

I knock on Lola's door and of course she doesn't hear me, her music is so loud, so I open the door a little. She's lying on the mattress on the floor, reading *Romeo and Juliet*.

"What's up, Francie pants?" she asks, turning the music down. Her stereo has a little remote control. It's very cool.

"Mom wants to know if you have her copy of *The Grapes of Wrath*."

Lola wrinkles her nose. "Eew, no."

I close her door again and she turns the music up and I stand outside Joseph's room. I open the door.

While my room and Lola's room have eaves and nooks, his is a square with flat ceilings. I turn on the light. My parents haven't made any changes to the room since he left, so it still has the same weird leopard-print carpet that came with the house, and the wallpaper is, like, football players and baseball players, which is also weird, because Joseph only ever played soccer. His room is cold and it smells a little odd, not the way he used to smell, but just kind of, I don't know, empty.

The bookshelf is behind the door, so I close the door and scan the shelves. There are a lot of books—Joseph loved to read as much as I did. Maybe he still loves to read. I used to read some of his books way before I was ready for them, like, they were too scary or too mature, but I read them anyway, because I wanted to be like him. That's how I ended up reading *The Shining* and *Less Than Zero* when I was 12.

His shelves are a mess. The books aren't in any particular order, and some are piled on top of others, with notebooks stuck in there, too. I find *The Grapes of Wrath* and pull it down along with a few spiral notebooks. Some pages fall out and as I tuck them back inside a green notebook, I see that it's a diary. Do boys keep diaries? It's a journal, maybe. I know I shouldn't open it, but I can't help myself. I sit on the floor, my back against the door, and flip through the pages.

The first entry is from about five years ago. Joseph would have been almost the same age that I am now. This was over the summer before I started seventh grade. Lola and I had spent the summer with our mother on the beach and then we had gone to California for a few weeks for a family wedding and while we were there, Joseph had run away from the halfway house in Minnesota and I remember there were a few weeks where we didn't know where he was, whether he was OK, whether he was even still alive.

We came back from California and Joseph eventually got in touch with our parents. He had hitchhiked from Minnesota to Santa Cruz. We were probably there at the same time. I remember my parents wiring him a bus ticket and then my dad went to pick him up at the bus station and he was dirty and his hair was long and matted and all he wanted to do was sleep. He was home for a few weeks, while my parents decided what they should do next. I was only eleven, and my parents never tell Lola and me anything more than we need to know, so we didn't know how long Joseph was going to be at home. I remember the two of us being shy around him.

Another fucking day on this fucking bus. Why couldn't they buy me a plane ticket? They have the money. Just another punishment for me, I guess. Everyone on this bus is old and they look depressed and I don't know what I'm gonna do when I get home. They'll probably force me back to rehab. Kevin is lucky—he stayed in California.

I flip ahead a few pages.

I've been home for six hours and I can't wait to get out of here. It's OK seeing Francie and Lola, but the parents are driving me crazy. Dad wants to test my piss and Mom can't stop crying and they've already got Patrick coming tomorrow and I know it's just a matter of time before I'm back in fucking Minnesota.

Patrick is Joseph's sponsor. He's a monk and lives in a monastery in upstate New York. I have absolutely no idea how my parents found him. How do you find a sponsor? I flip ahead again.

... lucky it was Dad who found me, and not Mom or Lola or Francie. At least he's a doctor. I don't think it was too messy, just a lot of puke. I guess I'm glad that it didn't work, that I failed even at trying to kill myself, but

*now they're definitely gonna ship me off again, probably
to some mental institution.*

The pages end there. My heart is racing. What did
I just read about? Joseph tried to kill himself? In a
trance, I close the notebooks and put them back on the
shelf. I go to my room and lie down on my bed and I
have no idea who I can talk to about what I've just
learned. Does Lola know? Should I tell her? No, there's
no way Lola knows—she would have told me.

I hear my mother coming up the stairs. She pokes
her head into my room.

"Did you find the book?" she asks.

"What?" I ask.

"Francie. I asked you to come up and see if Lola had
The Grapes of Wrath."

I sit up and struggle to swallow. She knows about
this, she knows that Joseph tried to kill himself, of
course she does, and she and Dad didn't say anything
about it.

I hand her the book and she thumbs through the
pages absentmindedly. I stare at her, wondering how
she can keep all of this from Lola and me. What else
aren't they telling us?

"It was in Joseph's room," I say.

"Oh," she says.

"Mom?" I ask. "When are we going to see Joseph
again?"

My mother sits at the foot of my bed. "I really don't
know, Francie. It's up to him. When will he go back to
rehab and get the help he needs?"

"Do you think Uncle Leo and Aunt Jenny are
making him go to meetings and stuff?"

"I don't think they have any idea what they're
dealing with," my mother says.

"But he's been living there for four years," I say.

She closes her eyes. "I know, Francie." She pats my foot, then gets up and leaves the room.

I pick up the phone to call Eitan. I'm not going to tell him what I just read about Joseph, I don't think. I just want to hear his voice. No, what I really want is for him to appear in my room and lie down next to me and wrap his arms around me and for me to be able to cry, cry, cry on his shoulder.

***

I am ten years old and Lola is eight years old and Joseph is fourteen years old. I'm asleep and then, suddenly, I'm awake and I don't know why. I roll over and look at my alarm clock—it is just after midnight. The light is on in the hallway and it seeps under the door of my room. That's a little weird, but I ignore it.

I close my eyes and try to fall back to sleep and then I hear my father yelling. That must've been what woke me up. I can't quite hear what he's saying, but I get up and open the door to my room a tiny bit. I can hear him yelling again, he must be in the back of the house, in the kitchen, and I hear another sound, and look up, and there is Lola at my door, holding her little stuffed bear, looking terrified.

We sit at the top of the stairs.

"What's going on, Francie pants?" Lola whispers.

"Shh," I whisper. "I don't know." I put my arm around her.

We listen as my father's voice gets louder—he's walking from the kitchen into the dining room and I look down the hall and see that Joseph's door is open and my father is yelling at Joseph.

"What the hell did you think you were doing?" my father yells. "I really want to know."

I can't hear Joseph's response, just some mumbling.

"Speak up, Joseph. Did you think you and Brett would get away with it? Or what did you think would happen when the police found the two of you drunk driving the golf carts at the country club in the middle of the night?"

I gasp and Lola looks at me. She is near tears from all the yelling.

"What does that mean?" she whispers.

"It means Joseph did something ... bad," I say.

"I don't know," I hear Joseph say.

"Of course you didn't know, you didn't think, you didn't care. What's going to happen next time, huh? You think I want phone calls in the middle of the night from the cops, telling me to collect my son from the station? Maybe next time, I won't come. You can stay there overnight."

"Barry," I hear my mother say.

"Ellie, he has to learn a lesson from this," my father says.

"He will," she says. "He won't do anything like this again, right Joseph?"

I can't hear my brother's response, but a minute later, I hear him walking toward the stairs and Lola and I hurry back into my room and shut the door.

We get into my bed together. It's a big bed. Lola snuggles up to her bear.

"Francie pants?" she says. "Will Joseph be OK?"

I look at her in the dark. I pause. "Yes, Lola. Joseph will be OK."

***

AJ's parents have a house in Vermont that they bought when we were in the sixth grade since they go skiing so often. I was a terrible skier the one time I tried it, and was very glad to switch to snowboarding in the ninth grade. The guys were much cuter, too. In the spring and the fall, her parents go up to Vermont just to get off Long Island. They used to make AJ come, too, but now that she's 17, they trust her to stay behind.

One Saturday night in November, she totally abuses that trust and invites me over, and says I should bring Eitan, too. When we get there, we order a pizza and AJ raids her parents' liquor cabinet. It's as if they knew what AJ had planned, though, because they literally have nothing but cinnamon-flavored Schnapps, which tastes like someone soaked Red-Hots in rubbing alcohol. It is disgusting, but each of us takes a shot, and Alex takes a few more. I've brought my camera again, and I'm taking photos of us, for posterity. I'm going to develop them myself, so it doesn't matter if everyone is drinking.

As we eat pizza and the huge stash of sugary cereal that AJ's family always has on hand, Alex talks about baseball. He plays on his high school team, and even though it's the off-season, he's still in training, although he is drinking like he is not.

"You play any sports?" he asks Eitan.

"I used to play soccer," he says, "but I wasn't very good."

"So you just don't do anything now?" Alex seems incredulous that a teenage boy could be uninterested in playing sports.

"Well, uh, I hike and camp and stuff," Eitan says.

"That's not a sport," Alex says. Eitan shrugs. He does not care to classify his activities.

"What about you, Francie?" Alex asks. "You play any sports?"

AJ laughs.

"I dance," I say. "Or I used to."

"Dancing's not a sport," he says. Who made him the judge? I mean, sure, it's not a sport, but it's not nothing.

We move downstairs to watch a movie, and Alex and AJ start to make out, which is super-uncomfortable for me. This is part of why I don't like kissing in public—it makes other people uncomfortable, which makes me doubly uncomfortable. I look over at Eitan, and he looks like he'd rather be anywhere but here, listening to Alex and AJ kiss. I mean, are Eitan and I supposed to just start making out here, too?

"Do you want me to take you home?" I whisper to Eitan. I was planning to stay over at AJ's, but not if she's just gonna be hooking up with Alex.

AJ pulls out of her lip lock long enough to turn to me. "I thought you were staying over," she says. "Both of you. Alex is."

The prospect of a co-ed sleepover here, at AJ's, had not even occurred to me. So far, Eitan and I have done a lot of what someone might call "heavy petting." I wonder if AJ is planning to sleep with Alex tonight, even though it's only been a few months. Oh, God, what if they do? What if we can hear them? These thoughts rush through my head, but when I look at Eitan, I can tell he has none of these concerns.

"I can tell my parents I'm staying at Ari's," he says. "They won't care. It's one of the benefits of being the youngest kid."

I nod. I'm a little nervous.

"You can have Evan's room," AJ says, leading Alex up the stairs to her room.

I take Eitan's hand and walk up the stairs.

We shut the door. Her brother Evan has a twin bed with a trundle, too, but I'm not about to pull out the trundle right now. His room is bigger than AJ's, with less crap, but more nerdy stuff on the walls, like Star

Trek posters. I do not plan to have sex with Eitan tonight, but I certainly don't plan to have sex, ever, with Captain Spock watching over me. Eitan picks up the phone to call his parents.

"Hi, Eema. Yeah, it's me. Sorry for calling so late. I'm just gonna stay at Ari's, OK?" As he's talking to his mother, I take off my glasses and pop up onto the desk, my feet dangling. I hook my finger into one of Eitan's belt loops and pull him closer. He puts his hand on my knee and I stifle a giggle and he gives me a mock stern look, pointing to the phone. "Yeah, I'll get a ride home in the morning," he says. "Good night." He hangs up the phone and I pull him in for a kiss.

I take off his sweater—another white t-shirt, slight swoon—and he takes off mine.

"Oh," he says. "I wasn't expecting another layer." I am always wearing tank tops under my sweaters, because I have a hard time adjusting my body temperature.

"Trying to keep you on your toes," I say. We are speaking in quiet voices, just above a whisper.

He picks me up from the desk like it's no big deal and lays me down on the bed. We rearrange ourselves so that I am on top of him and he brushes my hair out of my face. I run my hands down his chest and then he sits up a little and I pull off his t-shirt. I am a sucker for a skinny but somehow also well-built guy in a white tee-shirt, but I'm more interested to see what he looks like without a shirt at all. And I am not disappointed. All that rock climbing is good for something. I run my hands down his torso and can feel his muscles flex.

"Your turn," he says, and I lift my arms and he pulls the tank top off over my head. I am instantly self-conscious, which makes sense because now I'm nearly half-naked. I cross my arms almost automatically, but he gently uncrosses them.

"Wow," he says. He runs his hands down my sides and over my breasts. I shiver a little. All my bras are boring beige minimizer bras, but now I think, maybe I should get some in other colors. Black? And oh my Lord, my underwear is faded pink Jockey for Her. Why don't I have any cute underwear?

"Are you cold?" Eitan whispers, rolling over to pull me closer to him. I realize I have no idea how many girlfriends he's had, whether he's had sex before. It's not impossible.

"I don't want to have sex," I blurt out. "Sorry, I just—we never talked about it, and I'm not ready yet." He props himself up on one arm.

"I don't want to have sex yet, either," he whispers, running his other hand down my stomach. I shiver again. "I just want to—you know—explore."

"Exploring sounds good," I whisper.

Eitan stands up and pulls me up so we can pull the covers down. I take a step closer to him, touching his chest again, and then I get on the bed, kneeling so I am taller. I pull him closer to me and start to undo his belt buckle, as he fumbles with mine. His jeans drop to the floor, leaving him in just boxer briefs. I can see his erection through the thin material. I sit back and wriggle out of my jeans.

He reaches around to undo my bra and slides the straps off my shoulders and I shrug it off and this is the least amount clothing I've ever worn in front of someone who's not my doctor or related to me.

"Jesus," he whispers. He cups my breasts, then picks me up and I wrap my legs around his waist and he sits down on the bed and then I push him down, almost toppling over him. We look at each other and giggle.

We get under the covers and he wraps an arm around me, pulling me close. It feels strange and amazing to have my breasts pressed up against his chest. We kiss—on the mouth, on the face, on the neck, on the chest. I feel him hard against my hip, and it's oddly gratifying, to know that my body did this. I'm still not sure I'll know what to do when his boxers come off.

Before I can even think about that too much, Eitan slides his hands down and slides off my underwear. So much for caring about what it looks like. I am now completely naked in AJ's brother's bed. "Is this OK?" he whispers, his breath hot against my neck.

I nod. "Mmm hmmm. More than OK," I say. I can barely breathe.

He touches me between my legs, and he definitely knows what to do, and I come, shaking, and I feel him, now wet, against me.

"Jesus," he says again. He swallows, and I kiss him. We lie there for a few minutes, breathing hard.

I pull on my tank top and underwear and tiptoe into the bathroom to pee and brush my teeth. Eitan comes in after me.

"Do you need some privacy?" I whisper, as he stands in front of the toilet.

"Uh, I just had my fingers inside you," he whispers. "I think I'm OK to pee in front of you."

I look at him for a second, and we both crack up.

We get back into bed and, I mean, it's a twin-sized bed, so it's very cozy, and Eitan is backed up against the wall, and I snuggle my back into him. "Please don't do that," he says, "don't wriggle around like that. It'll be very uncomfortable for me." I turn around so I'm facing him, and I prop my head up on my hand.

"Who was your girlfriend before me?" I ask him.

He says, "I only had one real girlfriend before you. We went to camp together. What about you? Who was your boyfriend before me?"

"You're the first," I say.

"How is that possible?" he asks. "You're amazing."

I blush and hope he can't see it in the dark.

"Did you have sex with her?" I ask. I trace some of the little freckles on his cheeks.

He shakes his head. "Have you? Had sex with anyone?" he asks.

I laugh. "I just told you you're my first real boyfriend."

"I know, but—"

"No, Eitan, I have not had sex with anyone. I don't think it's the biggest deal in the world, but I want it to be with the right person, you know?"

He kisses me. "I know," he says.

We fall asleep with me cuddled practically on top of him, my head on his chest, his arm around my shoulder.

***

AJ thinks it's weird that I'm going to have lunch with Tammy, but she doesn't want to invite herself along, and Sooz doesn't really care one way or the other, so she and AJ go to Taco Bell. Instead of pizza, Tammy and I drive to this Italian sandwich shop that everyone loves, but which I almost never go to because I don't like to drive at lunchtime since it's impossible to find parking around our high school. Tammy has a spot in the student lot this month, though. Her car is a beat-up Oldsmobile and all she has to listen to are showtunes, so we belt out songs from *Joseph and the Amazing Technicolor Dreamcoat* as we drive.

"You should come hang out at the beach this summer, Francie," Tammy says, peeling the tomatoes off her sandwich.

"Why didn't you just order it without tomatoes?" I ask, picking one up and eating it.

"I don't like to get in the way of their flow, you know? Like, this is their job, making sandwiches. Who am I to interfere with that?"

She takes a swig of her soda.

"Anyway, when it gets warmer, you can come to my house and we can get on the public beach. My parents are putting in a pool, too."

"Sure," I say.

"What are you doing next year?" she asks.

"I'm going to college. I mean, I don't know where yet, but I'll hear from Duke in December. What about you?"

"Yeah, I might go to college. My older brother didn't go to college right away, he wanted to be a chef, but then he realized that it's like really hard work, and he's lazy, so he came back home and now he's going to Stony Brook."

"My older brother didn't go to college, either," I say.

"Well, my brother's there now, and I'm sure I'll go eventually. I was thinking of going to LA for a year and trying to be an actress."

I nearly choke on my peach Snapple.

"Really?"

She rolls her eyes at me.

"Yes, really. Don't worry, everyone thinks I'm crazy, but maybe I'll be lucky!"

Tammy is really talented—she has been the lead in every school play since sophomore year, which made many seniors very angry. If Tammy wants to try to be an actress, who am I to do anything but encourage her?

"I promise that when you make it big, Tammy, I won't show anyone from *People* magazine embarrassing photos of you from middle school."

"Thank you, Francie. I promise I will never forget the little people who made me who I am today." We giggle.

She peels the tomatoes off the other half of her sandwich and drops them on my plate.

"Ugh, you're right, next time, I'll just ask for no tomatoes."

***

I'm sitting on a bench in the lobby of the synagogue, waiting for Adam, reading the book that Eitan lent me. If I thought James Joyce was a slog, this is a slog and a half. I have no idea what this guy is writing about, either the philosophy stuff or the motorcycle maintenance stuff.

Adam walks down the hall.

"Hey, Francie," he says, sitting down on the bench next to me. "Is that part of a class assignment?" he asks.

"This book?" I say. "No, my—my boyfriend lent it to me. He said it's one of his favorite books."

"You must really like him if you're actually reading it."

I feel myself starting to blush. "Have you read it?"

"Yeah, a long time ago."

"Really?"

"Yeah, it's a famous book. What do you think of it?"

"Um, it's weird. Like, he had a mental breakdown, right? And maybe he is having one now, on this trip? I'm worried for his son. And I keep expecting him to, like, have an affair with the other woman."

"It's not that kind of book," Adam says. "I'll tell you that what I took from it was this idea of trying to welcome people who are on the margins. And that you never know what people are going through when you meet them, so you should be kind and open-minded."

He stands up as other people arrive and we head outside to drive to the soup kitchen.

This time, I'm helping to serve the food. I set up the plates and cutlery and cups and at one end of the long table we use to serve, and then I haul out the large pots, they are almost like cauldrons, of various things we are serving. A few things are in aluminum trays and we keep them warm by lighting Sterno underneath. Today is some kind of turkey chili and corn bread, and it smells really good.

When the guests start to come in, it's pretty much non-stop serving for two hours. Around seven o'clock, the line dies down a bit, and some of the volunteers take a break from serving to eat dinner. I join them at a table with a few of the guests and Adam sits down with us, too. He seems to know everyone here, asking them questions about their families, their kids, their health, their jobs.

He introduces a few people around, and when he gets to me, he says, "This is Francie, our high school volunteer. We've been talking about doing good works, and I asked her to take a look at the Book of Ruth." Adam turns to me and says, "We have a Bible study group here on Wednesdays."

I pause with a forkful of chili halfway to my mouth and smile at everyone. "Hey," I say.

One of the women, maybe she is around my mother's age, says, "The Book of Ruth, huh? That's a good one."

"What do you think about it, Francie?" Adam asks.

"Well, I guess it seems like a short story to me. Like, someone wrote it to illustrate all these acts of lovingkindness, as Adam puts it."

"Why do you think someone would do that?" Adam asks.

"I don't know. Maybe to show, or, like, demonstrate ways to be better. Nicer."

"Interesting," Adam says. "Anything else?"

"Well, like, most of the characters, the people in the story, didn't have to be nice. Ruth could have stayed in Moab, but she went with Naomi and took care of her. Boaz didn't have to be kind to Ruth. But also, these things they're doing, they're not selfless. It's better for Ruth to leave with Naomi. It's better for Boaz to marry Ruth."

"Why is it better for Ruth to leave with Naomi? Why couldn't she just go back to her family? The other woman did," Adam says.

"I don't know why she did. But maybe Ruth's family didn't want her back after she married Naomi's son, even after he died, especially because Naomi's family was Jewish. Maybe they looked at her as someone else's problem now."

Adam nods slowly. "Someone else's problem."

"Yeah," I say.

"Do you think parents do that, families do that?" Adam asks.

I laugh. "They do it all the time," I say. "In the Bible and in real life." This seems like it should be especially obvious here, in a soup kitchen, that maybe families don't always take care of each other.

"Why do you think they were selfish, Ruth and Naomi and Boaz?" one of the men asks.

"I didn't say they were selfish," I say. "I said that they weren't selfless. Like, Boaz could have just given some wheat or whatever to Ruth, but instead he tells his workers to leave more for her to pick up on her own."

"Why would he do that?" he asks.

"Maybe because he doesn't want Ruth to feel like she's in his debt," I say. "That way, when she decides to marry him, it's because she really wants to, and not because she feels like she has to."

He looks at Adam. "Your girl is smart," he says. Adam smiles. I am not his girl.

***

My parents and Lola and I spend Thanksgiving with my Aunt Darla and Uncle Gerald. They both teach at NYU and live in faculty housing in Greenwich Village.

We get there early and Lola and I help Aunt Darla make the sweet potatoes and whip the cream for the desserts. She always give us an ice cold copper bowl and a whisk, like she has not discovered a handheld electric mixer yet. My cousins, Jack and Matt—really, Jacques and Matthieu; Francophiles—are closer to Joseph's age and tend to ignore Lola and me. Sometimes, they will bring a girlfriend or friend from high school or college. There are typically some foreign grad students from the Physics department as well, because that is where Uncle Gerald teaches.

Uncle Gerald likes to control the situation. There are three tables: the main dining table, and then what Lola and I call the "small, intellectual tables." Uncle Gerald will sit at one of those along with the grad students. My mother usually makes the cut for one of the small, intellectual tables as well.

The reason I take French is because of Aunt Darla. She was always my favorite aunt, even before we stopped talking to my other aunt. When we are in the tiny kitchen together, cleaning up after the meal, she says, "Your dad tells me you have a boyfriend."

"Yes," I say, feeling the pink creeping up my cheeks.

"Well, I'd love to meet him," she says, "if you come into the city."

The next morning, my father and my aunt have to discuss everything that happened the night before. He sits on the floor in the kitchen with his back up against one of the cabinets, drinking coffee and gossiping with his sister. Before we had a cordless phone, he would carry that old, heavy, AT&T model to the floor with the cord dragging across the kitchen so that half the time, we would trip on it coming into the room.

I go shopping for Hanukkah presents with Sooz and Lola and Starr. AJ is in Vermont. There are no malls in our town, which is a little weird for Long Island, I know, but I drive us all to the fancy new mall that opened up last year, maybe 30 minutes away. Lola and Starr separate from us. This is fine because I have to get a present for Lola anyway. We walk into the Tower Records, which we don't love because it's so mainstream, but it's the only record store here, I mean, we are in a mall. On Long Island.

As I'm flipping through the latest CDs, looking for something interesting for Lola that would be better than a book, someone covers my eyes with their hands. I am wearing glasses, so this is a little more annoying than it might be for someone not wearing glasses. I turn around to find Ari there.

"Hey," I say, surprised to see him. Shopping malls don't really seem like his thing, although, admittedly, I don't know him that well.

"What's up? What're you looking for here?" he asks, flipping through CDs next to me. I pull off my glasses and clean them on my shirt.

"Something for Lola," I say. He walks around to the other side of the aisle and pulls out a bumpy, bright orange CD.

"I don't know about Lola, but I think you'd really like this," he says.

"Why do you think I'd like this?" I ask, taking it from him—it's a Pet Shop Boys album.

"Because you like disco," he says.

"Why do you like this?" I ask. "You don't like disco."

"Oh, I've been known to get down to a disco number every now and then," he says, looking up at me from under what I'm now realizing are very long eyelashes. Is Ari flirting with me? That seems highly unlikely.

Sooz comes over and says hello. "Hey, Susannah," Ari says. "What did you find?"

She holds up some obscure Bruce Springsteen import. Sooz loves the Boss.

"I didn't find anything for Lola. I think we should go to the bookstore," I say. We head to the cash register and Sooz buys the Springsteen and I buy the orange CD, along with a Leonard Cohen album for my dad.

"Who are you here with?" I ask Ari. "Lola and Starr are somewhere in this mall."

"Interesting," he says. "I'm here with my sister, but I'm just gonna meet up with her in a few hours."

"You have a sister? I don't know why I thought you were an only child," I say.

"Nope. I have two half-sisters. Half-sister," he says. "That's a weird expression, right? Like, could I put the two of them together to make one full sister?" Oh, my Lord, is he high again?

We walk out of the record store and say goodbye to Ari as we head toward the bookstore.

"What was that?" Sooz asks.

"What are you talking about?" I say.

"Uh, he was definitely flirting with you." She thought so, too! So weird.

In the bookstore, we run into this guy Mark who graduated from Elmwood two years ago and who Sooz used to have a little thing with. Guys get kind of obsessed with Sooz, and she's so nice that she can't turn them away, and so that's how she gets almost stuck with guys like Mark, who is not ugly, just not interesting. I think she underestimates herself. Mark is working at the bookstore now, going to Hofstra. She chats him up while I look for gifts. God forbid Susannah buy some books that aren't, like, Anne Rice. Although, man, we do both really like Anne Rice.

When Sooz and I are ready to go, I beep Starr from the pay phone with Lola's beeper code—516, so Long Island—and we meet up at the exit. Lola and Starr look as though they smoked up as soon as we got to the mall. They've been hanging out mostly in the food court this whole time. "We saw Ari," Lola says.

"Yeah, we saw him, too, at the record store," I say as we walk out.

"He said he recommended an album to you," Lola says, almost accusingly. I show it to her—it is not a secret. She pets the bumpy cover. "I wish we could listen to it in the car," she says.

When we get back to our house, we put the new CD on in my room and turn it up really loud. My dad yells at me to turn it down, so I do, but only a little. And the four of us dance around to the Pet Shop Boys in my room. Ari was right. It is a really good album.

Joseph's birthday is in November, and this year, it's the Sunday after Thanksgiving. I've been thinking about him a lot more lately, especially after I read his journal, and this is his 21st birthday. I decide to write him a letter, even though all of the other letters I sent were never answered. I write:

Dear Joseph,

Happy birthday. I don't know what's going on in your life, but I can tell you about what's going on in mine, if you're interested. I'm a senior in high school, and I'm waiting to hear about colleges. I applied early to Duke, so I'm crossing my fingers. I've been working on the literary magazine with my friend Susannah, who maybe you remember. And I'm still making mix tapes. I'm thinking maybe when I graduate from college, I want to work in the music industry, or whatever industry you work in when you choose the music for soundtracks.

I've been dating this guy Eitan. You used to play soccer with his older brother, Jonathan, when Dad coached the team. I like him a lot. I think you would, too.

Lola is doing well. She's in all the school plays. I'm sure she'll be the lead once she's a senior. Mom and Dad are OK, too. Mom got a new job as the editor of the Elmwood Gazette, so she's been busy with that. And Dad's still at the same hospital, complaining about the same nurses.

It's hard to sum up what's been going on over the past four years. Maybe you could write me back and tell me how you are and what you've been doing. I miss you.

Love, Francie

It's a weird and awkward letter, but I decide to send it anyway. Maybe this time, he'll write back. What is he thinking about, all this time? The last time I saw him, I was 13. I'm not the same person. I'm sure he's not, either. I don't know what I'd say. And forget about talking to my aunt and uncle. My parents definitely don't want that. They were like, you can have a relationship with your cousins, but how is that possible? They're all younger than we are. Lola invited them to her bat mitzvah, but it's not like they were going to come without their parents. Even our grandparents weren't at Lola's bat mitzvah. And the less said about my bat mitzvah, the better.

***

Every Wednesday, I try to get through the day as fast as possible so I can get to Eitan's house immediately after school is over. And I try to do all my homework for Thursday either earlier in the week, if possible, or during other classes, so we have time to talk to each other and fool around when I'm at his house.

I'm not ready to sleep with Eitan yet, but I'm very interested in fooling around with him. By now, we've been going out for nearly four months, and I have no idea what is normal for four months of dating, like, how far we should go. I'm not like AJ, I don't plan all my hooking up. With her last boyfriend, Rob, who she dated for, like, six months, she was always scheming about how far she would go with him, like it was all for practice. Like, should she give him a hand job? What about a blow job? Like, how would that set her up in terms of experience for her next boyfriend? And I was always like, Do you want to do these things with Rob? Do you enjoy doing these things with Rob? Or to Rob?

The answers to those questions didn't seem to be important to AJ. Maybe it's different for her with Alex. I'm really enjoying everything with Eitan, and I'm pretty sure he is, too.

It's starting to get darker earlier, so even though it's only, like, 4:30 in the afternoon, it feels much later, and Eitan wants to knock off homework early, too, so we lock the door to his room and he closes the shades and then we fall into the bed.

This time, we take off all of each other's clothing under the covers and we are both completely naked together for the first time, and it's amazing. Maybe I use that word too often, but I am amazed at how great it feels. That sounds weird, like, of course it would feel great. Think of all those nerve endings, right up against someone else's warm body. We continue to explore with our hands, with our mouths, and we are not having actual sex, but we are so close, I understand how it could happen so easily.

***

Sooz invites us all to a tree-trimming party at her house. She lives in the house that her father grew up in. It's on the border with Queens, not all that far from the soup kitchen, actually. When her dad was young, there was a grassy expanse next to the house. Then, at the end of middle school, New York State finally finished a stretch of highway that goes from Kennedy Airport to the beach, running right past the house. Goddamn Robert Moses, her father is always saying, even though he was dead for like ten years by the time the highway extension opened. Anyway, the only real change since her father grew up there, besides the highway, is that they added a pool when Sooz's brother was little.

Sooz's mom is Jewish, and she was raised mostly Jewish, but her dad just couldn't give up Christmas. Her family has a big tree set up in the corner of the living room, and her mother has made little sandwiches and Christmas cookies for us all.

There are a lot of ornaments that she and her older siblings made and an absurd quantity of tinsel. Eitan and I start to decorate the tree with Sooz and Mark, our former Elmwood classmate, the one Sooz ran into at the bookstore in the mall. This decoration mostly consists of flinging the tinsel at the tree and hoping that it sticks, but also the four of us end up tossing a lot of tinsel at each other.

When AJ and Alex arrive, we see that Alex has a black eye. "I don't want to talk about it," he says. Sooz and I exchange a look. When I try to take photos of him and AJ, he's puts his hands over his face, like, the paparazzi are everywhere.

AJ corners me in the kitchen. "He said he wasn't going to fight anymore—"

"Anymore?" I say.

"He gets into fights at school sometimes," she says. "If someone picks a fight with him, it's really hard for him to walk away. He always wants to fight back." Maybe now is the time to mention that Alex is not a very big guy. He's, like, 5'9" and probably 140 pounds soaking wet.

"AJ, that is not good," I say, Little Miss Obvious. I know I'm not supposed to criticize my friends' choice in love interests, especially if they're not, like, being abusive, or something, but Alex does not seem like the right person for AJ. I don't know who would be—we all thought it was Ross, from the skating rink, but he stopped calling her, and anyway, they never even kissed. It seems like it would be an act of lovingkindness to get AJ to realize that Alex is bad news.

"He got suspended from school for three days, too."

"Alison!" I whisper-yell. This calls for use of her full name.

"I know, I know. But I really like him." She looks over at the living room, where Alex, Mark, and Sooz are trying to get the star on the top of the tree. Eitan plucks it from Sooz's hands and just pops it up there.

After the party, I drive Eitan home and give him his Hanukkah present, which is a scarf that I found at a little store in our town. Does he need another scarf? I don't know, but I saw it and thought of him. It's soft and green, and when I drape it around his neck, his eyes look a little more hazel. He gives me a silver bracelet with my name on it, which he fastens around my wrist. I hold it out, admiring it.

"Now you'll have something that reminds you of me," he says. I laugh, but he looks really serious.

"Eitan," I say, turning to him. "This bracelet is beautiful, but I don't need anything to remind me of you. Will that scarf help you think of me?"

He wraps it around his neck, tucking it into his coat. "It's close to my heart," he says, patting his chest. He is looking at me in a funny way. I don't know what's happening between us right now, but it feels strange and awkward.

Eitan touches the bracelet on my wrist, then circles my wrist with his fingers. I wonder if he can feel my pulse speeding up.

"You're really important to me, Francie. That's why I want to know you're thinking about me."

"I think about you all the time," I whisper. "Like, it might be a problem."

He shakes his head. "Don't joke."

"I'm not," I say, reaching out for his hand.

The front door to Eitan's house opens and his mother pokes her head out.

"Do you want to come in, Francie? It's cold. Eitan, invite Francie in."

"Francie has to get home for her curfew," Eitan says, looking at his mother. She shuts the door.

I swallow, a lump in my throat. I'm trying to suppress tears. What is going on? Eitan gave me a gift, and I gave him a gift, and now it feels like we're fighting.

"Eitan—" I don't know what to say.

He shakes his head. "It's OK, Francie. Thank you for the scarf. Get home safely."

He walks into the house. I'm not going to see him for, like, two weeks and we didn't even kiss each other goodbye.

Get home safely?

***

I've been checking the mail like a maniac, racing to the mailbox when we get home from school. The mail gets delivered every day around 10 AM, so on the first day of Christmas vacation, I am sitting on the steps in the front hall, waiting for the mailman. When I see him come up the front path, I open the door and say, "Happy holidays," and take the mail and rifle through it and there is a very thin envelope for me from Duke and I sit back down on the stairs and I can feel my heart plummet into my stomach. A thin envelope is not a good thing.

I open it up and scan the letter quickly.

Dear Francine Elizabeth Baum, Blah blah blah, outstanding students, blah blah blah, many qualified applicants, blah blah blah, welcome to the class of 1999.

A sticker for the back windshield of the car flutters out of the envelope and I pick it up before I sit back down on the stairs and take a few deep breaths and my heart rate goes back to normal. I can't believe I got in. I mean, I've been telling everyone else I was sure I would, but I wasn't sure I believed it. And now that I'm dating Eitan, maybe it would have been OK to apply to schools in New York City. Maybe I don't want to be 500 miles away. Maybe I want to be like Tammy, but instead of going to LA to be an actress, I want to go to Manhattan and, I don't know, work for the radio station, make mix tapes on an epic scale. I shake my head. My parents would kill me.

My mother walks down the hall and sees me sitting on the steps and I guess I don't look overjoyed.

"What's wrong?" she says.

"I got into Duke," I say.

She squeals and hugs me. "Francie, that's wonderful! Congratulations! I'm so proud of you! Are you proud of yourself?"

I shrug. "I guess," I say.

"Barry, Francie got into Duke!"

My dad comes down the hall from the kitchen and hugs me, too. "That's wonderful, Francie. What a relief."

I smile. I'm lucky. This is a good thing, this is a great thing. I go upstairs to call Sooz and AJ and Tammy and tell them. I would call Eitan, but he's already left to go camping in Joshua Tree with his family. We haven't spoken since Sooz's Christmas party, and I'm going crazy not knowing what he's thinking. Did I say or do something wrong or mean or hurtful? My friends don't know, Lola doesn't know, either, and we have rehashed the entire conversation a million times.

I don't love AJ's parents, but they are very generous, and they let AJ invite us up to Vermont for part of Christmas week. In the car, AJ, Sooz, and I whisper among ourselves while AJ's dad blasts the heat in the car and plays conservative talk radio. Her mother is driving up separately with AJ's brother, Evan, so that us girls can drive back to New York together before New Year's. I always have to pee more often than AJ's dad thinks is acceptable, so I'm always holding it in for, like, half the trip.

It's good that Evan didn't drive up with us because he has been teasing AJ relentlessly about Alex since he got home from college, even though he hasn't met him yet. Once he does, he might have more to say. The more time Sooz and I spend with Alex, the less we like him. And Eitan can't stand him, either, which means he doesn't want to hang out with AJ. Which means I don't hang out with AJ as much on the weekends. It's making for some awkward conversations.

Alex likes to drink. Alex likes to fight. When she's with him, AJ acts like a different person, like she's OK with these things. Alex is, if not stupid, not smart, like AJ is. Is he cute? Enough. But is he cute enough to overlook all this other stuff?

I'm also pretty sure it's not any of my business if Alex is all of these things, if AJ acts differently with him, as long as she is happy with him.

When we get to the house, I have to check the pantry, because they always have the best, most sugary snacks and cereals, stuff my parents don't buy, which is ironic because AJ's dad is a dentist. I emerge with a s'mores granola bar, and Sooz says, "How can you eat that and stay so skinny? Both of you." Susannah is always worried about her weight, but I think she looks fine. She is, however, the only person I know who goes to exercise classes.

We wake up the next morning very early. Since it's the first time we're going out for the season and we've definitely forgotten everything we learned last winter, Sooz and I are taking a lesson. We borrow nearly all of our snowboarding clothing from AJ. AJ and her family get out on those black diamonds right away, while Sooz and I will be lucky to get down the bunny trail.

I hate using the chairlift because I have a hard time getting off it with that snowboard strapped to my foot. The back of the lift almost always whacks me in the head or the hip as I try to scoot away. Susannah glides off effortlessly. Years of ballet gave me no gracefulness or balance, apparently.

We meet up with our instructor, Bart. The rest of the class is mixed ages—some people are older, some are younger. Bart is probably 20, with blondish hair and bright blue eyes, and I can see that Susannah is instantly smitten. He's a really good instructor, too, reminding us of all the ways we should learn how to fall. Learning how to fall properly is probably the most important part of learning how to snowboard.

At the end of the lesson, Bart asks Susannah what we're doing the next night, and invites us to a party. It takes all of her self-control to wait until he is out of sight to squeal wildly.

That afternoon, Eitan calls me at AJ's parents' house and I take the phone into the pantry closet. I'd given him the phone number before Christmas break.

"Hey," I say. It's been nearly a week since we last spoke, which is the longest we've gone since we officially started dating. My heart feels like it's in my throat.

"Hey," he says.

"I miss you," I say, before he can say anything else. "I miss you very much. I've been thinking about you this whole vacation."

"Was that difficult for you to say?"

"What? No. Why would that be difficult for me to say? I miss you. I miss you. I miss you. I wish you were here. Or I wish I were there."

"I miss you, too, Francie. I'm sorry I was so weird after Sooz's party."

I start to cry.

"Are you crying?" he asks. I nod, but of course he can't see me, so I say, "Maybe."

"Why are you crying?"

"I don't know," I say, starting to laugh. I wipe my tears with the back of my hand. "I'm—maybe I'm relieved. That you called. That you're not mad at me for something."

"I can't get mad at you for—for being you. Or for not reacting the way I thought you would, or how I wanted you to. I mean, I guess I can, but that's stupid."

"How did you want me to react? To what?"

"Never mind. Tell me what you're doing in Vermont."

So I tell him about our first day of snowboarding, and he tells me about Joshua Tree and the hikes they're going to take and the shooting stars they hope to see.

"Oh, Eitan," I say, "I got into Duke."

He yells and I pull the phone away from my ear for a moment. "Francie! Why didn't you tell me that right away?"

"Because right away I had to tell you that I missed you like crazy! I thought that was more important."

"That's—yes, that was more important," he says, "but congratulations! Aren't you happy about it?"

"Yes," I say, although it feels like a half-truth.

"I'm so happy for you," Eitan says. He sounds like he's going to say something else, but then there's a beep on the line.

"I'm running out of quarters," he says. "Have fun with Sooz and AJ, Francie. I'll call you at New Year's."

I almost say, "I love you," as he hangs up the phone, like, of course I love him, of course it's the most natural thing to say, and then the line is dead, and I look at the phone and push the off button and lean against the shelves of the pantry and laugh. I love him.

Bart's party is in an old house that he shares with a few other guys. They play Dave Matthews Band on the stereo and have a keg and a fire pit and we sit around and talk with them and some of their girl friends. We can't tell if they are friends who are girls, or girlfriends. It doesn't matter to me, of course, but Susannah is very interested in learning the distinction.

When we have to leave, the party is still going. I don't know how they all get up so early in the morning to teach. Bart and Susannah exchange numbers, and he kisses her goodbye. She is so thrilled, she lights up the whole car.

That night, as we are in AJ's room going to sleep, AJ on the bottom bunk, Sooz on the top, and me on the trundle, we talk about boys. As usual. Sooz dissects her interaction with Bart and we eagerly participate with her. He is very cute, and was very attentive to her all night. I hope he calls her. I'm crossing my fingers that he does. Even if he lives in Vermont for the ski season, Sooz can go back up with AJ to see him.

AJ rolls over from her back to face me. "Tell us more about you and Eitan," she says. "You never share enough."

"What do you want to know?" I ask. "I'm an open book."

AJ and Sooz laugh for, like, five minutes at that. It's not like I'm not telling them stuff about Eitan and me because it's a secret. It's more like, I'm not good at talking about my feelings, or even about stuff like hooking up. It makes me uncomfortable.

"OK, OK, I get it. Um, things are good. We had a good talk. I think everything is OK. I've been missing him a lot this week."

"Things are good. I'm missing him a lot," AJ imitates me. She throws a stuffed animal at me. "I want to hear what you guys are doing, you know."

I blush even in the dark, I can tell, I feel my face turning pink.

"I'll start," AJ says. "Alex and I got to third base a few weeks ago, on both of us. I'm probably going to give him a blow job after New Year's, or maybe on New Year's Eve." Planning, planning, planning.

"Is he...you know..." Sooz leans over the top of the bunk and puts her hands a few inches apart.

"He's like..." AJ holds up her hands a few inches apart. "Bigger than Rob, for sure, but not like, I'm gonna choke on him or anything."

Sooz hasn't sex yet, either, but Sooz and AJ have done just about everything but. And now I guess I have, too.

"So?" AJ says to me. "I hope you've seen his dick, Francie. And, you know, touched it."

"I have," I say, defensively. "We got to third base, too. On both of us. Both ways."

"Both ways?" Sooz asks.

"You know—hands, mouths..." I say, so glad this conversation is taking place in the dark.

AJ and Sooz are quiet.

"He used his—I mean, he, like, down there?" AJ says.

"Yeah," I say.

"How was it?" Sooz says.

"Weird at first, but then, like, really good," I say. "After I did it to him, he was like, Why shouldn't I reciprocate?"

Silence again. None of us knows anyone whose boyfriend ever, like, went down there, with their mouths.

"Is he big?" AJ asks.

"I don't know," I say. I do not want to think about the size of Alex's hard-on every time I see him, thanks, AJ, for that visual, and don't really want my friends thinking about Eitan's, either. "I don't really have a basis for comparison."

"Hold out your hands," AJ says.

I hold them out a few inches apart, maybe six inches, I don't know, the last thing I'm going to do the next time I'm in close contact with my boyfriend's erect penis is measure it.

"Is it fun?" Sooz asks. "Like, are you having fun with him?"

"Yeah," I say. "It's so much fun. It's the best."

I think about all the time Eitan and I spend together, talking, doing things, anything, really, fooling around, just sitting and being in the same space together. Now would be the time to tell Sooz and AJ that I'm in love with him, but I want to tell him first. It seems like he should be the first to know, even if he doesn't love me back. When I think for a moment that he might not, that I might be alone in this love, my throat tightens and I feel hot tears come to my eyes. I take a deep breath and roll over and the tears drip into my pillow. Why should it feel like there's so much uncertainty when I've never been more certain of anything in my life?

We drive back to Long Island in the Jeep so that AJ can spend New Year's with Alex. Her parents think she's staying at Sooz's house with me. This is the first time AJ's parents have let her do this drive, and it is a little nerve-racking to drive nearly five hours with her. I force Sooz to give me shotgun so I don't get carsick in the back. "I want to prove to my parents that I can do it," AJ says.

For New Year's, I go with Susannah to a party at Jason's house. We're still not totally back to our usual friendship, but it's not like there are so many other options. His parents are out of town on a last trip before his brother is born. His half-brother, actually, there's that term again, because this is his mother's second husband. "That's nuts," I say. "When your brother is having his bar mitzvah, we will be 30."

"Thirty is ancient," Jason says, as we all sit outside on the patio furniture in our coats, shivering, because no one is allowed to smoke indoors and half of the people here are smoking, including Jason. He stubs out his cigarette into a special container for this purpose, his hands shivering.

"This is ridiculous," I say. "It's freezing. Let's go inside."

A few people who have already smoked a lot of pot loll about on the corduroy couches in the TV room. The TV is on, tuned to a Twilight Zone marathon. We end up sitting in the kitchen, which is empty. "Francie," Jason says, "are you gonna visit me in Providence?"

Jason found out right before Christmas break that he was accepted into Brown.

"Of course," I say. "Are you gonna visit me in Durham?"

"Yes. I'm definitely gonna visit you. I'll miss you," he says. I realize now that Jason is a little drunk, on top of being a little stoned.

"I'll miss you, too," I say, which is true. I've been missing him all year, not in the same way that I've been missing Eitan these past two weeks, but still. We used to spend so much time together, and now we mostly see each other in class. We haven't had a good talk about movies or music or anything in a long time.

Dave walks into the kitchen. "Hey, guys," he says, giving a large burp. Ugh, gross. "Sorry about that. It's almost midnight. Should we do a countdown?" Because I'm sleeping at Sooz's, I don't have to worry about being home by my curfew.

We all walk into the TV room, where someone has turned on Dick Clark's special. Susannah finds me and holds my hand as we count down into 1995. On the one, I give her a hug. "We're gonna graduate this year," she whispers. "I can't wait to get out of this town."

While I love Susannah and Jason and all my friends, and I'm happy to celebrate New Year's with them, I miss Eitan so much. My stomach flutters every time I think of him. I don't need a bracelet to remind me of him. When he called me from California earlier in the day to wish me a happy New Year, I thought I might burst with joy at hearing his voice.

I am not sure how to tell him that I have fallen in love with him. That every day I don't get to see him is a little bit sad for me, which is, like, nearly every day because we aren't at the same school. Not that I'm going around all depressed. It's more like, the days I do get to see him, I'm full of light and butterflies and anticipation. When we talk on the phone, about everything and nothing, I am so happy. I know it's not great, that it's probably not healthy, tying my happiness to another person like this, much less a boy, but it's how I feel. Maybe this is the real boy disease.

The next morning, Sooz and I decide to watch the video she's been recording all year, which is when we discover she filmed, like, 40 minutes of the camcorder bag because she forgot to turn off the camera. But the rest of it is not bad. It's fun to watch your friends goofing around and being silly. That first night at Dunkin' Donuts, before I started going out with Eitan, before AJ had met Alex—that was the best footage. It will be interesting to see how she puts it all together. I wonder what happened to my cute skater boy.

When Sooz tells AJ about having filmed so much of the inside of the bag, AJ is like, That's so typical, Sooz. It's mean, but Sooz just takes in stride.

When we go back to school after break, I am inspired by Sooz to spend a lunch period developing my film from the first few months of senior year and printing some photos. I hand out prints to everyone. It's like a second round of holiday gifts. The photo of Eitan from the Guggenheim goes in my locker.

When Jason sees it there, he's asks, "Do you kiss that photo every time you go to your locker?" Just to annoy him, I give the photo a kiss, and then I think, Why would I kiss a photo of my boyfriend in front of my friend and not my actual boyfriend? I need to get out of my head and care less about what other people think. I'm starting to be like AJ, thinking that people are paying attention to me when they are almost definitely not.

***

I am eleven years old and Lola is nine years old and Joseph is 15 years old. We are sitting at the table for dinner, all three of us reading books. My dad has made roast chicken and rice and my mother is adding dressing to the salad.

"Kids," she says, when they have sat down, "can you put your books away, please?"

Reluctantly, we pile them on the counter.

"Barry," she says to my father, "I forgot to ask you. Did you take that envelope with the cash in it, the one I got from the bank the other day?"

"No," my father says, also reluctantly putting away his magazine.

"Are you sure?" my mother asks, dishing out some rice to all of us, even Joseph, who is definitely old enough to take his own rice.

"Yes, I'm sure, Ellie. How much money was it?"

"It was $500, so I'd like to know where it went. It was in my drawer, and then it wasn't."

"Kids, did one of you take it?" my father asks, looking at the three of us.

Lola and I look at each other, like, What would we do with $500? Buy a ton of Swedish fish? We shake our heads.

"Joseph?" my father says.

Joseph doesn't look up from his plate, but he shakes his head.

"I can't hear you," my father says.

"No, we didn't take it," I say.

"I'm waiting to hear from your brother," my father says.

"What do you want me to say?" Joseph asks. "I just told you that I didn't take the money."

"Barry," my mother says.

"I don't believe you," my father says.

Joseph stands up suddenly, knocking over his chair. "I didn't take it, OK? Maybe Mom just forgot where she put it or, or she spent it or something." He's still not looking at either of my parents.

My father stands up and picks up Joseph's chair. He grabs Joseph by the arm and walks him out of the kitchen.

"We're going to find that money now, Joseph, whether it's in your room or not. It's strange how much money goes missing from this house nowadays," I can hear my father say as they walk up the stairs, my dad's tread heavy.

My mother has her head in her hands and I can see tears falling onto the table.

***

I don't get to see Eitan until the weekend after we get back from Christmas break, which feels like an eternity. When he opens the door, we stare at each other for a moment and then I practically jump into his arms. We kiss for like ten minutes just standing in the entrance to his house.

"I missed you so much," I whisper into his ear.

"I missed you, too," he whispers back.

His hair has some golden highlights and his nose is a little sunburnt from a week spent hiking, and it's ridiculous, because I did not think he could get cuter, but he has. Whereas I have windburn and a bruise on my hip because, once again, I could not get off the chairlift properly.

We meet up with AJ and Alex to go bowling. I don't really want to, but she wants me to get to know Alex better, and Eitan says he doesn't care, he just wants to spend time with me. Well, if you really want to spend time with someone, I cannot say that bowling is the way to do it. Every two seconds, someone is popping up from their seat to toss a ball down a lane.

AJ is terrible at bowling, but she is very willing to have Alex attempt to improve her stance. I think that is secretly what she wanted, an excuse to show him off a little and have him cozy up to her in public. The bowling lanes on a Saturday night are pretty crowded with other kids from Elmwood and Maplehurst. AJ has never dated anyone from Elmwood, either, although she hooked up with one or two guys from our school. I think she wants our classmates to see that she's got a boyfriend.

I am also not very good at bowling, but Eitan does not care at all. Every time either of us bowls, the other walks with them to the line and stands there, so that we can keep talking. I fill him in on Bart the snowboarder; on Jason's New Year's Eve party; on Lola's discovery of a new record store in the next town over. He tells me about his brothers, how great it was to see both of them, how he thought he was going to break his leg while climbing, but only twisted an ankle. Every so often, Eitan touches my hip or I touch his arm, and we look at each other and there is a lot of pent up need to make out.

After bowling, we go to the diner, where we also see tons of people we know. AJ introduces Alex around as her boyfriend. He's a little uncomfortable meeting so many people, but he takes it in stride. I almost feel a little bad for him, being sort of pranced around to different tables and booths. Eitan and I just sit really close to each other, his arm around my waist, his hand resting on my hip.

"I really missed you," I say, like I can't say it enough, and my stomach tightens as I think about how much I love him, and then, before I can think too much, I turn to him and kiss him, right there in the diner, in front of probably half of the juniors and seniors of Elmwood and Maplehurst High Schools. He's so surprised that he almost pulls away and then, realizing what's happening, puts his hands around my face and kisses me back.

At that moment, Alex and AJ plop back down in the booth. "Sorry to interrupt," AJ says, grinning.

"I wasn't sure you guys ever kissed. You never even touch each other in public," Alex says. He and AJ are constantly making out in public, it's awful.

I look at Eitan, who I can barely take my hands off right now, whose hands I want all over me right now, and he makes eyes at me, and we crack up. AJ just shakes her head.

The food arrives a minute later. AJ pours about a pound of sugar onto her pancakes as Eitan watches in horror.

"What?" she asks.

"Nothing, just—isn't your dad a dentist?" he says.

"Yeah. So?" She adds a few pats of butter.

"What did you do for Christmas?" I ask Alex.

"Went to visit my grandparents in Florida for a few days. Man, Florida is amazing. I can't wait to retire there."

"You can't wait to retire to Florida?"

"Yeah. We did spring training for baseball down there last April vacation, and I loved that, too."

"Do you know what you want to do?" I ask.

"I'm gonna get myself a boat and just cruise around that intracoastal waterway," he says.

"No, I mean, like, for a job. What will you be retiring from?"

"What is this? Are you my mother?" he says, kind of joking. "I'm hoping to get drafted, at least into the minors, and then I'll see what happens next."

I can't believe this is AJ's boyfriend, AJ who plans her outfits three days in advance, who's known she wants to be a lawyer since the seventh grade.

When the waitress brings the check, Eitan and I chip in some money and Alex goes up to the front to pay the tab. Eitan goes to the bathroom and AJ slides around the booth toward me. "We said 'I love you' for the first time. Like, just yesterday." She is very excited. I smile with her.

"That's amazing," I say, squeezing her hand, hoping she can't tell what I'm really thinking. Why can't I be happy for AJ and Alex, even if I don't like Alex? Why can't I scrounge up that lovingkindness for my best friend? And why can't I tell her how I feel about Eitan, that I've also fallen in love, that I don't know how to tell him, that I'm scared he doesn't love me back?

When the boys come back, we walk out of the diner, Eitan and me to my car, AJ and Alex to hers. "I'll call you tomorrow," I say to AJ.

Eitan and I get into my car and I drive toward his house. We are quiet for a few minutes, listening to the radio. He turns to me. "Man," he says. "Alex kind of sucks."

I take a quick glance at him. "I know," I say. "It's hard for me to, like, put my finger on exactly why I don't like him. I'm sorry I dragged you to hang out with him."

"It's OK," he says, "I just wanted to see you. Alex is, uh, a byproduct." He puts his hand on my knee.

I swat him off. "I'm too ticklish for that," I say. "I'll get us into a car accident." I look at him again when we are stopped at a light, and he is still looking at me.

"What?" I ask.

"Nothing," he says, smiling at me. "What got into you in the diner? I thought you hated kissing in public."

My stomach flutters, and I know I need to tell him how I feel. Instead, I say, "AJ said that they're in love," I say.

He snorts. "That's ridiculous," he says. "How could they be in love? Alex is such a goon, and AJ is so superficial." He pauses. "I'm in love with you, though," he says, and I think I'm going to have a heart attack. I pull the car off to the side of the road.

"Are you OK? I didn't mean to spring that on you," he says. "You don't have to say you love me back, I know you're hard to read...you play things so close to the vest. I'm not always sure how you feel about me, which isn't, uh, the best feeling all the time, so maybe this is too soon for us, but I've been in love with you for a while now, like, that's what I was hoping you'd say before Christmas, and maybe I was trying to see if I could get you to say it, so I would know something, anything, about how you were feeling, but I can't wait for you, I had to say something, but maybe you could say something, too, Francie, because you're freaking me out a little—"

And as he's talking, I unbuckle my seat belt and reach over the gear shift and kiss him. He pulls me closer, and I squirm my way across the car to sit on his lap, facing him. I reach under the seat and push it all the way back.

"I'm completely, totally, in love with you," I say. I laugh. He looks so relieved. "I love you." I laugh again and then I look at him and I start to cry. "Oh, Eitan," I say, crying and laughing at the same time. I push my glasses up onto my head.

"Francie," he says in a soft voice. "Why are you crying?" He wipes the tears away from my face, kissing my cheeks.

"I'm so sorry," I say. "I'm sorry you didn't know how I was feeling. I love you so much, it hurts my heart sometimes."

"It hurts my heart, too," he says. "But I think it'll hurt a lot less now that I know you love me back."

I kiss him again.

"How could you not know how I feel about you? Do you think I got naked with a whole bunch of other guys?" I ask him.

"No, but it's not the same thing..."

"No, it's not, but you know you're the first."

I kiss him.

"Hey," he whispers. "Tell me what you love about me."

I pull away so I can see his face better, leaning back onto the dashboard. He pulls me closer. "You don't have to get so far away. You can whisper in my ear."

So I whisper, "I love your seven little freckles, and your smile, and your incredible body, and the fact that you're so outgoing, you're smart, you love your family, you make me feel safe. I love to be with you. Like, when I'm with you, I just want to be as close to you as possible. I would, like, sit on your lap like this all the time if it weren't kind of weird, so we could be so close."

Eitan swallows. "It's not weird, and I wish you would." He kisses me. "Don't you want to know what I love about you?"

"If you want to tell me."

"I've been thinking about it for a while now, so... I love how your hair is always making that swoop across your eyes, because then I get to tuck it behind your ears." And he does. "I love your dimple." He kisses my cheek. "I love your incredible body." He slides his hands into my coat and pulls me closer. "I love that even when you're quiet, I know you're thinking interesting thoughts that you're gonna share with me. I love that we can laugh about things together."

And then we make out in the car until I have to take him home for my curfew. I thought those steamed up windows were just something that happened in the movies, but now I know they are for real.

***

I go to see Lola in the school play three times—once during school hours and twice in the evening performances. My parents come in the evenings, of course, and the first time I go, I sit with them, but the second time, I sit with Starr and Ari and Eitan. I bring her flowers every time because that is, like, a huge reason why she does plays—the attention and adoration and flowers. The second time, I bring some for Tammy, too, who is Juliet, of course.

We meet Lola backstage and she is thrilled to see us. Her fame has spread beyond Elmwood High. I hand her the flowers and she cradles them, and then Eitan takes my hand and I look up at him, and then I have to look away, I'm certain everything I'm feeling is written so plainly on my face.

Eitan has never been to my school before, so after the play, I show him around the building. I mean, it's just a high school, I'm sure it looks like Maplehurst, but I show him the darkroom, which is closed, and the cafeteria, which is not very exciting. I tell him there's a pool on the fourth floor, and he's like, Really? Elmwood has a pool? And then I say, No, it's what we tell the freshmen to mess with them. Elmwood only has three floors, and no pool.

We go up to the second floor and when we get to my locker, I open it up and there's the photo of him inside. He touches it.

"There's a photo of me in your locker," he says.

"I know," I say. "I put it there." I shut the locker and lean against it. There's no one on the hall because it's, like, nine o'clock. I pull Eitan closer and stand on my tiptoes and kiss him. We kiss in the hallway until we hear someone coming up the stairs.

"That's probably the only time I'll ever make out with someone in this high school," I say. "Unless you come back here for some reason."

"Is that why you took me up here?" Eitan asks, taking my hand, swinging it as we walk down the stairs. "To make out with me?"

"Well, yeah," I say. "I can't graduate from high school without kissing someone in a hallway at least once. And I wanted you to kiss me. That's the secret code, right? When I want you to kiss me, I kiss you?"

He laughs. "I might have to bring you to Maplehurst for the same reason."

I nod. "That would be OK."

That night, after I drop Eitan home, Lola comes into my room, flopping down on my bed. She still has makeup on from the performance.

"You were so good, Lo," I say, petting her curly hair. Sometimes, I stretch out a little piece just to watch it spring back.

"Stop messing with my hair," she says. "You're gonna make it frizzy." She sits up. "So," she says.

"So," I say.

"So, when were you going to tell me that Eitan is totally in love with you!" she asks. "Are you in love with him?"

Once again, I feel myself flush. I nod.

"You guys are like the best," she says.

"What about Ari?" I ask. "Is he dating Starr? Are you interested in him?"

"No, and no. And please don't change the subject. I'm very invested in this love story now, so tell me everything. But nothing too gross, please."

***

Tammy and I go to lunch together at the Italian sandwich shop once a week now, usually on Wednesdays, when AJ and Sooz go to the pizzeria. I'm not sure how she rigged it, maybe Mr. Whitman had a hand it in, but Tammy always has a spot in the student lot when truly it's supposed to rotate every month. Every time, AJ is like, "Oh, you're going to lunch with Tammy again?" AJ thinks Tammy is a little too weird, a little too slutty, a little too druggy. But I'm not doing drugs with her, and I'm not sleeping around, and I'm a little weird, too, so none of this bothers me. And Sooz has so many weird art class friends, she doesn't really care what people think of her.

"So, what's up with your super-hot boyfriend? Are you gonna break up with him when we graduate?" Tammy asks.

"I don't know," I say. "We haven't talked about it yet."

"There are gonna be so many hot guys at college, Francie. And you should, you know, fool around before college, too. That's what the summer after senior year is for."

I swallow, a lump forming in my throat as I even think about breaking up with Eitan.

"Sweetie," Tammy says, touching my arm. Only she could get away with calling one of her classmates sweetie.

"He's your first," Tammy says. "It's always hard to break up with your first." I'm not sure if she means the first person you fall in love with or the first person you have sex with. I mean, we haven't had sex yet, but I think about it all the time.

"Who was your first?" I ask.

"I'm not gonna kiss and tell. Or, you know, sleep around and tell."

"How many guys have you slept with?" I ask.

She pauses and thinks for a minute. "Five. But I wish it had only been three. Two of them were real assholes."

She leans into me. "I find myself regretting the guys I didn't sleep with more than the guys I did sleep with, though. Like, I would totally sleep with Dave. We hooked up a few times. He's got that hot soccer boy thing going on, but I don't think he's interested in me."

I snort. "Dave would definitely be interested in you," I say. I want to ask her, how can she just sleep with someone without being in love with them? But that doesn't seem like a nice thing to ask a friend.

***

There are all these activities for seniors. AJ, Sooz, and I don't go on the senior class trip, because we don't think it will be that much fun. It turns out that it was, and we missed out, so that's something we'll have to live with forever.

I invite Eitan to come to senior ice skating. I'm sure the point is to hang out with your fellow seniors, but that doesn't really matter to me. I pick him up and we get to the rink with everyone else. I can tell that my classmates are like, Who is that guy with Francie? Maybe I am like AJ, maybe I want to show him off a little, too. This is our first time ice skating for the season and it feels almost strange not to have Ross and his Maplehurst friends here, too, like the rink is missing someone. I wonder if AJ is thinking about him, too, but before I can ask her, she has laced up her skates and dragged Sooz out onto the ice.

Even after all that ice skating, every winter weekend for a few years, I'm not a very good skater. Ross always skated circles around me, sometimes literally. Sooz is a decent skater, and AJ does this weird thing where she kind of walks on the ice in her skates, and somehow does not fall.

Eitan, though, is like an ice skating hustler. Like, he is amazing and was keeping it from me this whole time. Usually, I don't want to hold hands with anyone while I'm skating because I'm afraid I'll bring us both down, but I take his hands as he skates backwards to "More Than Words," which I usually find super-cheesy, but now it seems just fine, perfect, even. He pulls me along slowly, and then he pulls me closer to him and kisses me on the ice, wrapping his arms around my absurd layers of clothing. And I do not care at all who is watching.

***

Sooz and I go to hang out with Ari and Eitan, not like a double date, just the four of us going to the movies. Eitan wants to see "The Lion King" again, which is nuts because I just don't think it's that good, but also, I can't believe it's still in the theatres. Sooz wants to see "Little Women," but we know our audience. We end up seeing this movie called "Before Sunrise," which I convinced the guys they would like because Julie Delpy is really pretty. Sooz didn't need any convincing because she loves Ethan Hawke.

After the movie, we go to this restaurant near the theatre that serves the best Belgian waffles with gelato. Sooz and I are, like, practically swooning about how romantic the movie was, and wondering whether Julie and Ethan's characters meet up a year later. We think they did, for sure, but Eitan and Ari think they did not. They were like, He's gonna come all the way back to Europe, on a whim? What if she's not there? And we were like, Then he's in Paris! It's not such a bad thing!

"I guess I could see how it's romantic," Eitan says, "but is that the kind of romance that you want? It's basically a one-night stand."

"Only if you think they don't meet up again!" says Sooz.

Eitan drapes his arm around the back of my chair. "I'm much more interested in a relationship that grows, uh, normally, over time." He looks at me as he says this and we look at each other for maybe a moment too long and then I turn away, and I can feel myself blushing, blushing, blushing.

"Susannah, are you gonna finish that ice cream?" Ari asks. She pushes her plate over to him. "I think the French chick was really hot, but I'm not sure I'd trust her to show up."

"Because she's French?" I ask, sort of offended because I study French and because Aunt Darla is my favorite aunt and so I have an affinity toward French people because of this.

"No, because maybe she doesn't trust him, either. And then there's this mutual distrust, of course she's not going to try to meet him."

"Even though she lives in Paris?"

This conversation continues as we walk down the block to Sooz's car. I'm spending the night at her house, so she drops Eitan and Ari off at Ari's house before heading home.

When we are at a red light, she turns to look at me.

"Francie," she says. "What is up with you two?"

"What do you mean?" I ask.

"You are sharing these very meaningful looks all night. You guys haven't had sex yet, right?"

"No!" I pause. "But we did tell each other that we love each other."

"What?" she screeches. "Why didn't you tell me?"

"I don't know!" I say. "It was just a few weeks ago."

"That is so exciting, Francie," Sooz says. "I'm so happy for you."

And I think about my reaction when AJ told me that she was in love with Alex, the sinking feeling I had that she was making a mistake, and I can tell that Sooz doesn't feel that way at all about my news about Eitan, that she is really, truly happy for me. And I feel like an even worse friend to AJ for it.

***

Somehow, we have discovered the best pizzeria in this town full of pizzerias. Maybe it took so long because it's technically in the next town over. Down the block is an old-time ice cream parlor. There's an outdoor section that's really indoors, because it's covered and has Christmas lights up year-round, and that's where we are sitting after having pizza. Sooz is drinking cappuccino, because she is on a diet, again.

"My parents are going to Vermont this weekend, and I think this is when I'm going to do it, when we're going to do it," AJ says. She and Alex want to sleep together. Her mother has taken her to get birth control, which is much more than my mother would ever do. If I told her that Eitan and I were planning to sleep together, she and my father would lock me up, even though every week they send Lola to work at Planned Parenthood, literally. AJ keeps the pills in her purse, and seems very proud of taking them.

"Where are you going to do it?" asks Sooz. "In your room?"

"I don't know," says AJ. "Maybe in my parents' room." She squeals, sounding excited about this potential option.

"We're going out to dinner, then we'll come back to my house. Evan got me some vodka last time he was home, so we'll drink that, too." She squeals again. "It feels like I'm planning a wedding."

Before I can even stop myself, I say, "It won't be a white wedding."

AJ looks at me, completely taken aback. "I'm sorry," I say. "I just mean, are you sure you want to do this? With Alex?"

She narrows her lips and eyes. "Who else would I sleep with, Francie? What's wrong with Alex?"

"Nothing, but—I don't know. I don't know," I say. I should be happy for her, I know, but in my heart of hearts, I can't be.

"Just because you and Eitan aren't in love yet, and you don't want to sleep with him, doesn't mean no one else is going to sleep with their boyfriends," AJ says.

Sooz and I exchange a glance. I never told AJ that Eitan and I have fallen in love with each other. And I do want to sleep with him, just not yet. I also don't want it to be a production—I don't think it's such a big deal, losing your virginity, but everyone else does, obviously, so I'm not sure what to say.

"I think what Francie means is, is Alex good enough for you?" Susannah says, looking at me. "He'll always be your first."

"Yes, he is. We are in love, and we're going to have sex this weekend," AJ says, stabbing her chocolate ice cream with a spoon.

***

It has taken me absolutely forever, but I finally finish *Zen and the Art of Motorcycle Maintenance*. I bring it to Eitan's when I go to his house on Wednesday after school.

"Eitan," I say. "Please tell me what you loved so much about this book." I put it down on his desk.

"You finished it!" he says.

"Oh my God," I say, "it was such slow going!"

He sits down on the floor and I sit next to him, leaning against the bed.

"Oh, I didn't read all of the stuff about philosophy and quality. I skimmed a lot of that."

"What? That's, like, the whole point of the book!"

"No, it's not! Well, what did you think?"

I say, "I didn't really like that he was, like, pitting country living against city living, as if living in a city was bad. Like, he wrote something about people living in cities looking angry and sad and people living in the country, or outside the city, looking happy and more welcoming. It seemed, I don't know, racist or something."

"Racist?" Eitan says.

"Yeah. I mean, who lives in cities? People of all races, right? I don't mean, like, the inner city, necessarily, just, like, cities in general. They're much less homogenous than the suburbs or countryside. And they're more environmentally friendly, too, which seems like it would be something he'd be into."

"How are cities more environmentally friendly?" Eitan asks.

I look at him like he's crazy. "Well, you don't need a car in the city."

"That's New York City," he says. "In lots of other cities, you need a car. In Los Angeles, you need a car."

"OK, but people live closer together, there is public transportation, usually, like a bus or a train. There's, like, more stuff to do all in one place, so you don't have to drive all around to access it." I pause. "What did you like about it?"

Eitan says, "I like the idea that you should do everything with your whole self. That, to me, was the idea of quality. If you do things wholeheartedly, that's quality. And it's really important when you're hiking or mountain climbing. Like, don't half-ass things or you'll get hurt, or hurt someone else. Take care of things, take care of people, and they will take care of you."

Is this book actually about acts of lovingkindness and I missed it? I am not going to read it again to find out.

"I'm sorry you didn't like it that much," Eitan says, "but I'm glad that you read it. It means a lot to me."

***

I get a call from Dr. Simon and, for the next few weeks, instead of going to the soup kitchen, he'd like me to help some of the seventh and eighth graders practice their prayers for their upcoming bar and bat mitzvahs. Adam is still the seventh and eighth grade teacher, so I make my way to his classroom at 9 AM on Sunday morning. It's weird being back in here after four years. I mean, I am not really any taller than I was when I was 13, but everything looks a little bit smaller. As the kids trickle in, I stay in the corner of the classroom as they all glance at me like, Who is this older person?

Adam introduces me and then has me pull a few of the kids out one at a time to help them practice their prayers before and after the Torah and the Haftarah readings and any other reading they need help with. I don't know all of the Torah portions, I'm not, like, studying to be a rabbi, obviously, but I can help with reading the Hebrew, even if I don't know the correct way to chant everything. It's also cool to recognize a lot of the words from my Hebrew class, like, this ancient language is not so foreign to me anymore.

After class, I help Adam prepare the food donations for his visit to the soup kitchen that afternoon.

"You don't have to stay," he says as he tallies up the number of loaves of bread we already have in the synagogue pantry.

"It's fine," I say. "I'm not going to be there tonight, so..."

"You could still come, even though you were here this morning. You don't have to limit your volunteering to what you're getting school credit for."

"I know," I say, "but when Dr. Simon asked me to come in during Hebrew school, I made other plans for tonight."

"Oh," Adam says. "That's cool. What are you up to?"

I hesitate for a moment. "Just hanging out with my boyfriend," I say.

"Right," he says. "The *Zen and the Art of Motorcycle Maintenance* guy. Did you finish the book?"

"I did," I say. "I did not really like it."

"Maybe you need to read it again in a few years," he says.

"I don't think I'm ever going to read it again," I say.

He laughs. "Never say never. We read the Torah every year, right? And every year, I get something different from each portion, because I'm different. If you read it again, you'll be different, and it'll mean something different to you, even if it only reminds you of your high school boyfriend."

I nearly take a step back when he says that. Of course it's true, of course each time I reread a book, I have a different appreciation for it. But will it only remind me of my high school boyfriend? Will that be what Eitan becomes in a few years?

***

I am eleven years old and Lola is nine years old and Joseph is 15 years old. My parents sit the three of us down in the living room, the two of them on one couch, and the Lola and me on the other, and Joseph by himself in the big armchair.

My dad clears his throat, but it's my mother who speaks. "Look, kids, we know there's been a lot of yelling and anger and uncertainty in the house over the past..." she looks at my dad. "Over the past couple of years. Your father and I aren't sure how much you girls know about what's been going on with Joseph, but we wanted to talk to you about it together."

Lola and I look over at Joseph, who looks off into the distance.

"Joseph is going to live somewhere else for a little while," my father says. "Joseph, do you want to tell them about it?"

Joseph gives a half laugh. "No, not really, Dad." The way he says "Dad" is full of anger.

"Where is he going?" Lola asks.

"He's going to a rehab facility," my mother says. "In upstate New York. Well, only about two hours away, so we can visit him."

"After two weeks, we can visit him," my father clarifies.

"How long will he be there?" Lola asks.

"I'm right here, Lola," Joseph says.

"A month," my mother says.

"Will he—will you come home afterwards?" I ask Joseph.

Joseph shrugs.

"We hope so," my mother says, reaching out to take Joseph's hand. He pulls it away.

"When are you leaving?" I ask.

"Tomorrow," my dad says.

***

Eitan and I meet at the train station in Maplehurst. We're going into the city for Valentine's Day, but first we are going to visit my Aunt Darla. We take the train in and the subway downtown—I have to lead Eitan around, too—and we go up to my aunt's apartment. My uncle is traveling for work.

"Eitan!" she exclaims. She is very exuberant. "It is so wonderful to meet you." She gives him a big hug.

"Would you like something to eat? I got some pâtisserie." Of course, something French.

I am always interested in pastries, so we take off our coats and sit down at the dining table.

"I know you're going to dinner nearby, so I thought we could go to a gallery here first, if you're interested."

Eitan looks at me, and shrugs a little. I know he's not super into art, but he's game.

"That sounds great, Aunt Darla," I say.

We walk outside into SoHo and as we do, Aunt Darla tells us about how the neighborhood has changed so much. It used to be only artists and galleries, and now there are fancy shops moving in, boutiques and things. I guess it's OK with her if the fancy shops are, like, Dean & DeLuca, which is maybe the most expensive coffee shop ever, but not shops selling expensive shoes.

We walk into a gallery and I understand immediately why my aunt likes this place. It is enormous, like maybe the ceilings are 40 feet tall. The art is almost incidental, but we walk around and Aunt Darla peppers Eitan with questions.

"So, you have another year of high school after Francine, right? And then you'll be going to college, too?" Higher education is very important to my aunt.

"Eventually. I'm going to take a year off between high school and college," Eitan says. This is the first I've heard of this.

"Really?" I ask. "Why?"

"If we were in Israel, I'd have gone into the army for two years. My parents did that. So instead of the army, they want us to do a year of service. My brothers did it, too."

"In Israel?" I ask.

"No," Eitan says. "If I went to Israel, they'd probably just draft me. Jonathan and Ori worked for this non-profit that helps resettle Russian Jews in the US. I'm thinking of, uh, the Sierra Club or something. Maybe over the summer, I can lead an adventure tour out west, like the one I went on with Ari last summer."

"That's fascinating," Aunt Darla says.

Meanwhile, my mind is reeling. Why didn't he tell me this before? Like, I can't even think about breaking up when I go to college, it's so many months away, but that would mean he'd be two years behind me.

"Yeah. They just mean, don't go work for, like, the Gap or something."

"What's the Gap?" Aunt Darla says. Sometimes she is completely clueless. Eitan and I look at each other and laugh.

We walk my aunt back to her apartment so I can use the bathroom. Truly, I always have to pee. When we are back in the hallway, waiting for the elevator, Eitan looks at me and says, "Your aunt doesn't know what the Gap is?"

When we get to the street, Eitan leads me to our destination. I don't know where we're going for dinner. It's a surprise, which is very difficult for me, but I know Eitan really likes surprises, both receiving them and planning them, so I'm trying to be more chill about it.

We end up at a small French restaurant in the Village, the theme of the day is France, I guess. The waiter gives me a rose when we sit down. I raise my eyebrows at Eitan, and he raises his back at me. We are, of course, the youngest people in the place. However, when we order Champagne, the waiter does not bat an eye.

While we're waiting for our food, Eitan gives me a card. We agreed not to give each other anything big. I smile at him, and pull a little wrapped gift out of my bag. He takes it, shakes it, and grins like crazy. "You made me a mix tape?" he says. "I was hoping for one! I was starting to get jealous of everyone else."

"Good things come to those who wait," I say, as he unwraps it and examines the track listing.

"Should I open your card now?" I ask.

"If you want. Or maybe wait till you get home. I don't want to watch you read it. What if you think it's, like, really sappy?"

"It's really sappy? I can't wait to read it!" I say. But I put it in my bag and it sits there, practically pulsing at me.

After dinner, we are both a little tipsy. This is, like, the second or third time I've had any alcohol aside from a sip of my parents' wine or a shot of whatever random bottle of alcohol we might find at AJ's.

After dinner, we walk around the Village a little and sit on a bench in a public square with a fountain, although the fountain isn't on because it's February. Eitan pulls me closer and pushes down the hood of my jacket.

"There," he says. "Now I can see your face." He kisses me and I unzip his coat and slide my hands inside so we are even closer. Our noses touch and our breath comes out in little puffs between us.

"Why didn't you tell me about not going right to college?" I ask.

"I don't know. It never came up," Eitan says.

"It seems pretty important."

"I guess so. But you won't be here anyway. You'll already be in college, so, it wouldn't really matter whether you're in college and I'm in Maplehurst, in high school, or you're in college and I'm in Oakland or Washington or whatever, working for some not-for-profit."

"You might not even be in Maplehurst? You might live somewhere else?" I take a sharp breath.

He pulls me to sit sideways on his lap, wrapping his arms around me. We sit like this for a minute, and I think about the future.

"We should go soon," I whisper, leaning my head into his chest as he wraps his coat around me. "We have to get the train."

Goddamn Long Island Railroad. Goddamn change at Jamaica. Goddamn feeling annoyed at your best friend for no good reason, goddamn missing your brother, and goddamn graduating in four months, and leaving your boyfriend behind. My breath catches in my throat again, and I know I'm going to cry if I don't snap out of it.

Eitan picks me up around the waist and sets me down and takes my hand and we walk toward the 1/9 train to head back to Penn Station.

We get off at the Maplehurst station and share a taxi. Eitan drops me off at my house, and I kiss him goodbye in the cab. My parents are out to dinner, and Lola is out with her friends, so the house is all mine. I love to be home alone. It's so rare.

In my room, I put on my pajamas and brush my teeth and take out my contact lenses and do everything I need to do before I can finally get into bed and read Eitan's Valentine's Day card. I know it's a stupid, manufactured holiday, but this is the first year I have a real boyfriend to spend it with.

I open up the white envelope and pull out the card and I burst out laughing. He's drawn a picture of the two of us sleeping under bright stars, snuggled in a Care Bears sleeping bag. I did not even know that he could draw.

The card reads:

Dear Francie,

It's been almost six months since we first met. I remember everything about our time together: our first movie, playing cards at your house, dinner at my house (memorable for more than one reason), sleeping over at AJ's, being the youngest people everywhere, our first trip into the city to look at weird art, hanging out with your friends, "homework" Wednesdays, parties at Ari's house, driving around aimlessly and singing, sneaking looks at you when you're driving, talking to you for hours on the phone and never running out of things to say, laughing at nothing and everything with you.

I'm so lucky you were with your sister that night at the diner, because otherwise, I wouldn't have met you, and now I can't imagine my life without you.

I love you.

Please be my Valentine.

Love, Eitan

I close the card and hold it to my heart. It is perfect.

VALENTINE'S MIX TAPE FOR EITAN
What You Do to Me, by Teenage Fanclub
Ice Cream, by Sarah McLachlan
Fade Into You, by Mazzy Star
Don't Go Away, by Toad the Wet Sprocket
Nightswimming, by REM
The Promise, by When in Rome
Sometimes, by James
Into Your Arms, by The Lemonheads
In Your Room, by the Bangles
Something So Strong, by Crowded House

***

Eitan and I are out to dinner at this Italian restaurant in our town, and once again, we are the youngest people in this place. We have both ordered pasta and when the waiter brings our food over, he offers us Parmesan cheese, like, four times.

"What do you want to do after dinner?" Eitan asks. "We could go back to my house, but my parents have a bunch of their friends over."

"We could go back to my house," I say. "My parents are in the city and Lola is staying over at Penny's."

Eitan looks up from his pasta, mid-swirl. "Yes, we should go back to your house."

I'm not sure I'm ready to have sex, although the line between sex and everything but seems thinner and less important every week.

When we get back to my house, the lights are off, but still, I call out to make sure no one is home. I shut the door and turn the alarm back on and lead Eitan up the stairs to my room and shut the door, wishing, not for the first time, that it had a lock.

He turns on the lamp on my bedside table and takes off his watch. We start to kiss, and we get under the covers. I unbutton Eitan's shirt and he pulls it off, tossing it across the bed. He pulls off my sweater and tank top. We roll onto our sides and touch each other all across our chests and backs, kissing. He reaches behind me to unclasp my bra, tossing that across my bed, too. He cups my breasts, kissing them, and I arch my back, it feels so good. He peels off his jeans and I shimmy out of mine. I feel Eitan hard against my leg. I roll over to sit on top of him, rubbing against him. He puts his hands around my waist.

"Francie," he whispers. "I'm gonna come like this."

I kiss down his chest, touching him as I go.

"I'm serious," he says.

"Would that be a bad thing?" I ask. I make my way down until my mouth is poised right above him, and I'm about to pull his underwear down. He moans.

And then I hear the alarm go off downstairs, someone has opened the front door, and it's so quiet in the house even with our heavy breathing that both of us hear it. "Shit, shit, shit," Eitan whispers. "That's your parents?" I hear my mom opening the closet door downstairs to hang up her coat.

"Quick," I whisper, "go get dressed in the bathroom." I put on my sweater, no bra, and hustle into my jeans. It's a good thing I never make my bed. No one would think messed up sheets are weird. I open the door quietly as I pull my hair into a ponytail and call down the stairs, "Hi! It's Francie! Eitan and I came home for a minute, but I'm going to drive him back to his house."

My mother walks up the stairs as Eitan comes out of the bathroom, his shirt untucked. He picks up his coat from my desk chair and runs his hands through his hair. "Hi, Mrs. Baum," he says, as smooth as he can be under the circumstances. I'm not even sure how he got his jeans to zip. I spot his watch on my nightstand and hope that my mother does not.

My mom looks at me, then down the hall. "Is Lola home?" she asks.

I shake my head. "She's staying at Penny's," I say.

She looks at me again, as I cross my arms underneath my breasts to prop them up, then walks back down the stairs. "Please drive safely, Francie. It's starting to snow a little bit."

Eitan and I look at each other and exhale. He puts on his watch and we walk down the stairs, Eitan moving slowly and adjusting himself under his shirt.

"This is really uncomfortable," he whispers.

"I'll be back soon," I call out to my parents.

I drive the back roads to Eitan's house and pull off to the side on a dark stretch. "What are you doing?" he asks. I climb into the back seat and pull him after me.

"We need to finish what we started," I say, so we do.

When I get back home, my parents are like, We really don't want you home alone with Eitan, who knows what could happen? As if it's only Eitan who wants it.

***

My parents drop me at the synagogue for a bat mitzvah of one the eighth graders I've been helping with prayers. I'm sitting in the congregation waiting for services to start when I see AJ and her parents come into the synagogue. She looks surprised to see me and she says something to her parents and then slides down the bench to sit next to me while her parents sit down in front of us.

"I didn't know you'd be here," I whisper to AJ.

"Why are you here?" she whispers back. How did AJ and I not communicate what our Saturday morning plans were? Had I not talked to AJ in that long? We see each other in school every day, but she does most of the talking. She talks and talks and talks about Alex.

"I've been doing my community service here, so I'm going to some of the kids' bar mitzvahs."

"Are you going to the party, too?" AJ asks me.

"No," I say.

"That's too bad. It's going to be so boring, and I can't even bring Alex with me." Alex, Alex, Alex. AJ's mother turns around and shushes us.

Then, halfway through services, Eitan shows up. It's like Grand Central Station in here all of a sudden. He just slides down the wooden bench and snuggles up next to me, totally cool. I look up at him with surprise and happiness—I am just so glad to see him. "Eitan! You're here!" I whisper.

"You said you'd be here for this bat mitzvah, so I thought I'd surprise you," he whispers, nuzzling my ear. Shivers. He looks around me.

"Hey, AJ," he whispers.

"Hey, Eitan," she whispers back.

AJ nudges me. "You should get out of here with him," she whispers. "Go down to the kids gym or something. He does not give one shit about this bat mitzvah."

"C'mon," I say to Eitan. I get up and walk out of the main sanctuary. I pause at the back of the room, and turn around for a moment to make sure Eitan is behind me. He gets up, buttons his suit jacket, and follows me down the aisle.

I continue down another hallway and down the stairs, through the ballroom, into the gym that the little kids use. He's a few feet behind me, and then we shut the door and I push a few mats in front of it. I look at him. He's always wearing jeans and sneakers and cozy boy sweaters, but in a suit, Jesus Christ.

"C'mere," I say. I unbutton the suit jacket and drape it over the kiddie basketball hoop. I pull him a little closer by his tie and try to unknot it. "How do you do this, anyway?" I ask. He undoes the tie and lays it across the suit jacket.

"What about you?" he asks. He unbuttons my cardigan.

"We are not going to get naked in here, Eitan," I say.

"Oh, I know," he says. "I just want to make it a little easier to touch you." And then he does—he pulls me close and we kiss. We stand there kissing and, I don't know, kind of exploring with our hands.

"I like you in these heels," he says.

"I didn't think you cared about shoes," I say, looking down at my feet.

"I like that your mouth is a little closer to mine. And this dress..." he runs his hands down the back of my dress, which is, I think, called a sheath, and cups his hands under my ass, squeezing a little.

"I like you in your suit," I say. "You look really hot."

Eitan laughs. "Really hot?"

"Yeah," I say. "I mean, I think you always look great, obviously—"

"It's not obvious," Eitan says.

"Oh," I say. "Well, Eitan, I think you're incredibly good looking. Like, really attractive. Like, super hot. Like—"

"OK, OK," he says, laughing again. "Thank you. I mean, it's nice to hear it from you every once in a while."

We sit down in the corner on some of the gym mats. I kick off my shoes and tuck my feet underneath me, and fold myself into his arms.

"I haven't been in a synagogue in a long time," Eitan says.

"Your family doesn't go for the high holidays, even?" I ask.

"No, not really. It's not, uh, really an Israeli thing," Eitan says.

"What?"

"Yeah, I mean, we're Jewish, obviously, but not very observant."

"I guess we aren't, either, but every so often, my mom gets struck with some religious fervor. I'm just here for the bat mitzvah this week."

"Which you are now missing."

"I saw the important part," I say, turning around to kiss him.

"What do your parents think about me?" Eitan asks.

"I don't know," I say, surprised by the question. "Why do you ask?"

"Well, my mom dropped me off here. She sees you every week, pretty much. She likes you a lot. I was just wondering what they think of me."

"They don't really say anything about stuff like that. They don't really tell us very much of anything, like, what they're thinking about or feeling. My dad was like, Eitan seems OK, which probably means he thinks you're amazing. And my mom was like, Don't have sex with him."

He laughs. "What?"

"Yeah, before our first date, even, she was like, Don't do too much, Francie..."

"That is so weird. My parents tell us everything. Like, they overshare. I don't need to know it all. My oldest brother, Jon, says he thinks it's because they're Israeli, but also, German. Like, their families left Germany right before the Holocaust and ended up in Palestine, and then it was Israel, and then they left to come to the US, so they have no roots. They're, like, wandering Jews."

We laugh.

"So they don't feel like they should keep secrets, because life is short, and who knows when you're going to be forced to leave your country."

"Oh, that is not what I expected you to say."

"Yeah, it's a little dark." He kisses the top of my head. "That's why I know about my mom's miscarriage, they tell us everything." I nod. "She was so sad about it. But if I get married one day, and that happens to my wife, I'll have some idea of what to do."

This is the first time either of us has ever mentioned marriage. I mean, we are only in high school, and I certainly never thought, Hey, we are going to be together forever, but to hear him say it, I don't know, it's weird. Like, if we aren't going to get married, it means we're going to break up.

"Eitan," I say, "Let's not break up."

"What?" he says, pulling me up to look at him.

"I don't want to break up with you when I go to college."

"Jesus, Francie, I thought you were breaking up with me right now. Don't do that to me. Please."

"I'm sorry. It's just, I know Duke isn't around the corner, but I can come home, like, probably once a month, and you can come visit me on vacations and stuff. It's not that far. I don't want to break up when I go away."

"I don't want to break up, either, but I don't think we have to talk about it now. That's months away, you leaving for college."

"Right, but I can't imagine my life without you. Why would that change when I go to college?"

He shakes his head. "I don't think you can know how things will change. Ori had a girlfriend in high school and they broke up over Thanksgiving his freshman year—it was too hard for them to be apart."

He pulls me to sit on top of him and my dress slides up and Eitan runs his hands down my thighs. I kiss him. I want to be as close to him as possible.

"Eitan," I say.

"Francie," he says.

"I think we should ignore my mom's advice."

"What advice?" he asks.

"We should sleep together," I say.

He laughs. "I thought we weren't going to get naked in here."

"Not here! Eew. Little kids play here." I look at him. "Do you want to sleep with me?"

"Oh my God, Francie, of course."

"Good," I say.

***

AJ and Sooz come over to take photos for a page in the yearbook. It's something we planned a long time ago, taking out a page. Everybody does it—all the friend groups. Does it matter that our friend group is hanging by a thread?

When they arrive, we put on some lipstick and AJ puts on face powder, and asks us, like, 45 times if she should keep her hair down or put it half up as she makes her mirror face. We have to pause for a few minutes to mock her for this. This is the first time in a while we've all hung out outside of school and it feels both totally normal and totally strange. Finally, we are all ready, and Lola comes in and we organize ourselves.

Lola snaps some photos of us posed on the bed. "Do you want to go somewhere else? This looks a little weird that you're all on Francie's bed."

We walk down the stairs and arrange ourselves on the staircase as Lola takes some photos from below. She gets on a stepstool so that she's not shooting straight up our noses. We take some photos on the living room couch and also perched on our butcher block counters in the kitchen. Who knows which ones will be good? I hope there are at least a few where all of us look somewhat decent.

"Hey, Lola," AJ says when we head back upstairs. "Do you still work for Planned Parenthood?"

"Yeah," Lola says.

"Do you, like, have stuff at home? Like, condoms and stuff?"

"Yeaaahhh," Lola says. "Do you need some?"

We follow Lola into her room and she opens her closet and there is a literal shopping bag full of condoms on the floor. She pulls it out into the center of her room and then, almost as an afterthought, shuts her door.

"I guess you're having sex with Alex," she says. "Or you're thinking about it?"

"No, we're having sex," AJ says, totally proud of this. "But condoms are expensive!"

"You can get them for free from the school nurse," Lola says. We all shudder at that thought. "I mean, it's an option."

"Take what you need," she says. "I'm not using them for anything." There are all different sizes and kinds and some with lube and some that glow in the dark (!).

"What about you, Francie?" Lola asks. "When are you and Eitan going to sleep together?"

I blush bright pink, but before I can say anything, AJ says, "Francie is not ready to sleep with Eitan. They're not even in love, right? I mean, I don't know how you can be dating him for so long if you're not in love with him. Do you think you're going to break up?"

I look at Susannah and Lola, who both know exactly how I feel about Eitan. They look a little confused, like, How does AJ not know, too? I just never told her.

I clear my throat. "I do love him. I mean, we love each other. We're just, like, not all over each other all the time."

AJ pauses for a moment. "Oh," she says. "Well, that's great, France."

"And we might sleep together. We've talked about it. It's not like I'm saving myself for marriage. I just don't know when it would happen."

"Well, I don't want to be the only one who's doing it!" AJ says. "You should take some of these, so you're ready."

She scoops up a bunch of condoms and drops them in my lap.

The next day during lunchtime, AJ, Sooz, and I go to the darkroom to develop the film and print some photos. The photography teacher loves Sooz and me, so she doesn't care that we're not in her class anymore, although she's not thrilled to see AJ, who has never taken any art classes. I take extra special care with the negatives and after I squeegee them dry with my fingers, we hold them up to the light to see which ones we should print. Sooz and I end up printing nearly half of them and we choose one for the yearbook ad. In that picture, the three of us are on my bed, arms around each other. We think about using one of the more "outtake" type of photos, where we're all making faces and smacking each other with pillows and stuffed animals, but AJ vetoes it—she wants something where she looks really good.

***

I have just a few more hours of volunteer time for my community service. Forty hours is forever, it turns out. I'm still the youngest volunteer, but no one treats me like a kid. I like seeing the same guests each week at the soup kitchen, hearing about what's going on in their lives. I might keep volunteering even after I finish my hours.

My dad drops me at the synagogue early on Sunday afternoon to make sandwiches, but somehow, I must've gotten the wrong information, because I'm the only one there besides Dr. Simon, who lets me into the building.

"I think Adam is going to make the sandwiches at the Mission today, because they got a big donation of cold cuts," he says. "He didn't let you know?"

"Oh," I say. "I guess he forgot. Is there anything I can do while I'm here now?"

"Well, Francie, would you be up for helping to organize the supply closet? It's got everything for Adam's class and the nursery school."

"OK," I say, and follow him into Adam's classroom.

Dr. Simon opens the door to the closet in the classroom and pulls the string for the light. I walk over to stand next to him.

"Wow," I say. It is a total disgrace in there.

"Wow, indeed. I don't expect you to make it perfect, but see what you can do. If you don't know where something goes, or whether or not we should keep it, just put it on the windowsill. I'll be in my office if you need anything."

"All right," I say.

I start by taking everything off the shelves and organizing all the loose papers and art supplies and prayerbooks. I'm sitting on the floor of the closet, getting into a bit of a groove with the bottom shelves, when I hear someone come into the classroom.

Adam pokes his head into the closet.

"Hey, Francie," he says, smiling down at me. "How's my favorite volunteer? Dr. Simon told me about the mix-up—sorry about that—but thanks for staying anyway."

He walks into the closet and pulls the string and the dim light gets brighter.

"It's a little tricky," he says, "but now we can see better."

I look up at him and realize that maybe AJ was right, maybe this Duke tank top is too tight. I stand up and take my cardigan from around my waist and try to put it on, but the closet is small, too small for two people.

"Let me help you with that," Adam says, and he reaches over and around me and fixes the right sleeve. He pulls my hair out of the back of the cardigan as I pull the sweater around my front, even though it's hot in this room, in this closet, and I can feel my cheeks starting to flush.

He stares at me for a moment too long and looks away and swallows and takes a step back, out of the closet.

My heart is racing. What is going on?

"Jeez, Francie," Adam says, "if only you were a little older."

As fast as I can, I push past him and grab my bag and coat and run out of the classroom and up the steps and out of the synagogue.

I am so out of sorts that I feel like I'm going to faint. Nothing happened, so why do I feel so awful? I walk home as fast as I can, I'm practically running by the time I get there, and when I go inside, the house is empty, and for the first time ever, I don't want to be in the house by myself. I wish Eitan had his license and could come over and pick me up, but he's not even home, he's at his cousin's house in New Jersey.

I call Susannah, but she's not home. I call AJ, but she must be at Alex's. I call Tammy, but she's at work. Finally, I call Jason.

He picks up on the first ring. "Hello?" he says.

"Jason, it's Francie."

I hear him shuffling around a little and I can picture him settling in on the corduroy couch in his living room.

"Francie! To what do I owe this phone call?"

I'm about to tell him and then I just burst into tears.

"Francie! What's going on? Are you OK?"

"I don't know," I sob.

"You're home, right? I'm coming over." I hear a click as he hangs up the phone and then I hang up the phone and I put my coat back on and walk outside to meet Jason on the front porch. He jogs up a few minutes later, Roxie on the leash behind him.

"What's wrong?" he asks, coming up the steps. He looks like he's not sure if he can hug me, and I'm suddenly so sad about the whole weird thing between us, which was maybe just a misunderstanding, like whatever happened or didn't happen with Adam. Instead, I hug Jason.

"What's wrong, Francie?" he asks again. "Is it—did something happen with Eitan?"

I shake my head and we walk around our neighborhood as I tell him what went on with Adam, but nothing went on, right? Jason went to Hebrew school with me, he knows Adam, too. They would sometimes run into each other on the beach over the summer, where Jason was a lifeguard at one of the beach club pools. Everyone thought Adam was so cool.

"So did he kiss you?" Jason asks.

I shake my head again. "He didn't even touch me, really."

"Did you tell your parents or Lola?"

"No," I say. "No one was home."

"Was I, like, your last phone call?" he says, smiling a little.

I swallow and smile a little, too, and nod. We look at each other and start to laugh.

"I know it's not a big deal, but I thought it was weird, and it made me feel weird, and he knows I'm 17 and he knows I have a boyfriend, anyway. If I were 18 or 19 or 20, would he have kissed me?"

"It is weird," Jason says. We pause while Roxie makes a poo on the side of the road and Jason has to bend down to clean it up.

"There is absolutely no way to look cool while you're picking up your dog's shit," he says. "I have definitely tried."

"Do you think I should, like, tell Dr. Simon? He is the principal of the Hebrew school. Wouldn't he want to know something like this?"

Jason looks uncertain. "Do you want Adam to get fired?"

"I— I don't know. I mean, I thought he was a good teacher. But what if he's actually going to try to make out with some student?"

"Maybe it was just you, Francie. Maybe you're just irresistible." He looks directly at me as he says this, and I have to turn away.

"Thanks for coming over, Jay," I say. "It was good to talk to you. Please don't tell anyone about this."

"Of course. It'll be our secret," he says. "Next time, maybe I'll be the second or third person you try."

"Yeah, next time one of my teachers maybe makes a pass at me, I'll call you first."

"You know what I mean," he says. "I'm here for you, Francie."

I can't tell my parents about this. They will freak out, and they will make sure that Adam gets fired, and for what? Because he helped me put on my sweater and said he wished I were older? I try to put it to the back of my mind.

***

That Wednesday, I go to Eitan's after school and he opens the door as soon as he sees me pull into the driveway.

He kisses me when I walk into the house. "My parents are in the city all night," he says. "They're going to see a play. My mom told me this morning, and I've been thinking about it all day."

"You've been thinking all day about your parents going see a play?"

We walk up to his room and I drop my things.

"Yeah. We have the whole house to ourselves for, like, hours. They won't be back till nearly midnight." He locks the door, just in case, I guess.

"I was thinking about you all day," he says. "About, like, this moment, right now. I actually had to jerk off when I got home from school."

"What? Why?" This is a really weird conversation.

"Because you were in my head."

He takes off my coat and puts it on the back of the desk chair and takes off my glasses and kisses me again.

"Don't you think about me?" he asks.

"I think about you all the time," I say, truthfully.

"No, I mean, don't you think about me and, you know, play with yourself?"

I turn bright pink and he laughs.

"The reason for, uh, jerking off, was that I was thinking about you coming over, and I was hoping we could take advantage of this completely uninterrupted time to, you know...what we were talking about a few weeks ago..."

I nod even as I shiver with anticipation.

"Are you cold?" he asks, and puts his arms around me to literally warm me with his body.

I shake my head, even as I continue to shiver.

"You're shivering."

"I'm just nervous. Like, excited nervous," I say.

He tilts up my chin and I stand on my tiptoes and kiss him.

"I'm excited nervous, too," he says.

We get into his bed, still in all of our clothing, and keep kissing and touching until I finally stop shivering, and suddenly, I'm really hot, and Eitan's really hot, and we start to take each other's clothing off. My body is ready for his, and I can feel that his is ready for mine, and he reaches over into the drawer of his nightstand and pulls out a condom.

The next part is awkward and sweaty and fast and, to be honest, a little painful. It is also, to be honest, not that amazing. We try to make it slower, but suddenly, we are both no longer virgins. Eitan kisses me and I pull him closer and then he rolls off of me so that we are both lying on our sides and I kiss him. We are still breathing quickly. I run my hands through his hair. "What did you think?" he whispers.

I pause, measuring my words. "What did I think?" I pause again. "I love you, and I'm glad my first time was with you. But also, I want my second time, and my third time, and my fourth time—"

He kisses me. "Yeah, me, too," he says. He rolls over onto his back. "Just give me, like, thirty minutes." He turns his head to look at me, and we laugh. I'm glad we can laugh together about everything. "In the meantime, though..." His warm hands explore their way down my body.

After, we get out of bed and he opens the door to his room. We dart across the hall into the bathroom.

Even though we just had sex, and even though he's seen me naked a bunch of times already, it's usually in low lighting or under the covers. I'm a little shy about standing around naked in front of him in the bright bathroom. He absolutely does not care about being naked in front of me, though, and he's quite happy for me to remain unclothed as well. He turns on the shower and tests the water, and we both get in, and this part is probably the most fun.

***

AJ's parents only wanted her to apply to state schools, like her older brother, although not necessarily New York state schools, which seems weird to me. They were like, Why should we pay private school tuition? Then, she took the SAT and got, like, a 1400, and they were suddenly like, Oh, OK, maybe you should apply to some private schools. So, when she found out she got into Middlebury, she was thrilled. College and skiing? Perfect for AJ.

Susannah has wanted to go to NYU and study art forever. She's been wearing an old ratty NYU t-shirt to sleep for five years. She is both surprised and excited to have been admitted.

I already know where I'm going, I've known for four months now, but I listen to my friends and get excited with them. They've been listening to me blather on about Duke forever, so I figure it's only fair. Plus, I am excited with them, and for them, even though I wish I'd seen a prediction in one of Sooz's tarot readings about falling in love with a younger guy and not wanting to go to college so far away from home. Maybe I could take a gap year? My parents would literally not even understand what I was talking about if I brought up the idea with them, and certainly would not let me postpone college for a boy.

We are out to lunch at the pizzeria one day in the spring, after all the college acceptances have come through.

"My parents are going to let me take the Jeep up to school. Oh, Francie, you have to come and pick out your bedding while I'm working—it'll be fun!"

I'm not sure how much fun shopping for bedding is, but before I can respond, Susannah starts to cry.

AJ and I are like, Sooz! What is wrong? "You guys are all accepted to college, and you're talking about stuff like buying new sheets and bringing cars to school and I'm worried about how I'm going to afford it! I didn't get the financial aid I need. My dad owns his own business, but it's not like he makes so much money." She blows her nose on a tiny napkin.

"Sooz, I'm sure it will work out," says AJ.

"No, you're not," yells Sooz. Everyone in the pizzeria turns to look at her. "It'll work out for you, AJ, because you have money. I don't know what I'm gonna do," Sooz says.

"Sooz, you'll take out loans, and you'll have a work-study job, and if you really need to, you can live at home and commute to NYU. You can take the LIRR and the subway by yourself, I swear. I'll teach you how to do it," I say, smoothing down Susannah's hair. "Soon, you'll be teaching me." She laughs a little.

"Or, what if I don't go to NYU at all, and I go to FIT and live at home and commute," Sooz says. AJ and I look at each other.

"FIT?" AJ says.

"The Fashion Institute of Technology," Sooz says.

"I know what FIT is, Susannah," AJ says, "I just didn't know you wanted to go there."

"Our guidance counselor made me apply." She wipes her eyes again with another napkin. "My mom thinks I should go to NYU, but my dad thinks I should go to FIT. It's so much cheaper, it's not even funny." She looks at both of us.

"That sounds great, Sooz," I say. "Why didn't you tell us you applied to FIT?"

"You guys applied to fancy schools. I just felt like, I don't know, losers go to FIT. It's like a step up from Nassau Community College."

"Sooz, FIT would be a great place for you. I bet everyone wears weird clothing all the time," AJ says.

Sooz smiles through her tears. "It's true," she says. "They do."

***

I'm supposed to have two more hours of volunteering at the synagogue, like how is this possible, why does 40 hours feel interminable? There's obviously no way I'm going to finish my time with Adam. I'm dreading running into him in the hallway or something, and at least I won't be at High Holiday services this fall. I tell Dr. Simon that I'd rather spend the last two hours working with him or with the younger kids or on Saturday mornings in the synagogue or anything else, really.

Instead, he asks me to write something about the acts of lovingkindness that Adam was teaching about. It can be short, but he's interested in understanding my perspective. My current perspective is that Adam is the last person to be teaching kids how to be better people in the world, but I agree to the assignment.

This is part of what I turn in to Dr. Simon:

Ruth is a Moabite who marries into a Jewish family. When her husband dies, she follows her mother-in-law, Naomi, back to Bethlehem and finds work there to support both of them. Naomi helps her find a new husband, Boaz, who is a cousin of Ruth's deceased husband.

To me, this story embodies the notion of g'milut chasadim because of the actions of Ruth, Naomi, and Boaz.

Everyone in this story seems to act only out of lovingkindness. Some rabbis think this story is like a parable, like it was written only to show how to perform acts of lovingkindness. Ruth could have stayed in Moab, but she went with Naomi and took care of her. Boaz did not have to be kind to Ruth, or kinder than he was to anyone else, but he had heard of her own act of lovingkindness toward Naomi, and that made him kinder toward her.

That's one of the things I took away, that these acts aren't selfless, everyone is doing what they want to do anyway, what will be better for them, but there is a side effect that these are also the right things to do.

I also think this story is about choices that we make. It probably would have been easier for Ruth not to go with Naomi, especially because she wasn't Jewish. But her kind heart pushed her to go. And this first choice, this first act, made all of the other acts of lovingkindness easier.

I've been thinking about choices a lot lately. Some choices are really easy, like what to have for breakfast. Some are more difficult, like should I study for an exam or should I go out with my friends. And some are really complicated, like who should I be dating, what should I do with my life, what kind of person do I want to be in the world. And all the choices we've made to get to the current choice at hand will influence that decision.

It's made me think more about the choices I'm making, and how each choice influences the choices and decisions I make next, and how to think of not only what's best for me, but what's the kindest choice.

***

I am twelve years old and Lola is ten years old and Joseph is 16 years old. Joseph is at a second rehab facility. I guess the first one was only for one month, and this one can be longer. Also, the first one didn't allow visitors, but this one does, so we go up to visit him. This is the longest amount of time that I've gone without seeing him, except maybe for the one summer he went to soccer camp.

When we get to the rehab facility, it's a few big brick buildings, kind of like a school. We park the car and we sign in at the front desk and they check my mom's bag and they check all our pockets to make sure we aren't bringing in anything we're not supposed to. It's not a prison or anything, but they're just being careful, I guess.

Joseph meets us on the other side of the lobby. He looks a little thinner and his hair is too long, but he seems happy to see us, especially Lola and me. He takes us to his room, which he shares with another guy, but the other guy isn't there. It looks kind of like a dorm room, from what I've seen of dorm rooms in movies and TV shows.

"You can sit on the bed," Joseph says, so Lola and my mom and my dad sit on the bed while I look out the window. There's a can of Coke on the windowsill and a Styrofoam cup next to it.

"You should never drink Coke," Joseph says to Lola and me. "It's been eating a hole through that cup for the past three days."

"That might have more to do with the Styrofoam than the Coke," my father says.

Joseph sighs.

There's a group therapy session that he has to attend after lunch, so we have lunch in the cafeteria. It's not a special visiting day or anything, people can visit whenever they want, so there are only a few other families there. Most of the other patients are kids or maybe in their early 20s.

Joseph is like the prom king here. He knows everyone, waves to everyone, smiles at everyone, says hello to everyone, as we walk down the hallway to the cafeteria. My parents exchange worried glances at this.

When we leave, I hug Joseph goodbye very hard. I'm not sure when I'll see him again. We can't talk to him on the phone very much, so I tell him that I'll write him a letter. Of course, Lola immediately says that she'll write him, too.

In the car on the way home, I ask my parents why they seemed to think it was weird that Joseph knew everyone at the rehab. My mother turns around to address Lola and me in the back seat.

"Joseph is very charming," she says. "He can bend anyone to his way of thinking, and that's part of what got him here in the first place. So it's not great to see it happening again in a rehab facility, of all places, where you'd hope they'd be immune."

***

We have the first Passover seder at our house, with my Aunt Darla and Uncle Gerald and some of my parents' friends. My parents let us go to our friends for the second seder, which is unusual, but they're going to New Jersey, and Lola and I really don't want to shlep all the way out there. I drop Lola at Starr's house, and head to Susannah's.

Sooz's mother has set an extra place for me next to Sooz. Her older brother, Jeremy, who just got married, is there with his wife, and her older sister, Linda, is there with her husband. I am the youngest person there and must say the Four Questions.

"Francie, I had no idea you had such a nice voice. I'm glad you're here, so we didn't have to listen to Susannah's singing," Linda says. Sooz and I exchange glances. Her sister really is the worst.

After the seder, we sit on the floor in Sooz's room and play Tetris. I call Eitan to see what he's up to, if he wants to hang out. He didn't do a second seder, it's not an Israeli thing, but he can't get together—he's having some family time with his brothers. I hear him walk into a quieter room with the phone.

"Hey," he says, "my parents are going to Florida tomorrow for a few days and Jon is supposed to stay with me, but he really couldn't care less what I do."

"Oh," I say.

"Like, he's mostly going to be in the city...," he says.

"Ohhhh," I say.

"Yeah," Eitan says. "So...do you want to come over?" he asks.

"Yes," I say.

When I get to Eitan's the next day, he's alone in his house. He's in a white t-shirt and jeans and his hair is a little rumpled and he has a bit of scruff from not shaving for a few days, and it's all I can do to keep it together. We kiss for like fifteen minutes, me on the counter in his kitchen. Then, we raid his fridge for snacks and watch "The Shining," which is basically me sitting in his lap, peeking out through my fingers. Even though I've read the book, the movie is pretty scary. Throughout the movie, we kiss and whisper into each other's ears and, like, pet each other, and the whole movie is like two and a half hours of foreplay for us, why is it so damn long. As soon as it's over, we go up to Eitan's room and I'm kind of impressed at our self-restraint so far.

I walk into the room and he shuts and locks the door and we look at each other, like, how does this work the second time around? And then, in like two strides, Eitan is next to me and he picks me up and carries me to the bed and we take each other's clothing off and get under the covers and the second time is much better than the first.

As it turns out, Eitan's parents want him to go to Florida with them after all, so they send him a ticket through a travel agency and he and his brother go to meet them in Miami for a few days. They are going to explore the Everglades.

One night over break, Lola invites me to come hang out with her and Starr at Ari's house. We get there and it's much smaller than the last party, maybe only ten people. We all hang out in Ari's room, listening to music and talking, while a couple of people smoke up.

"Hey," Starr says, as Ari takes a hit from a bong shaped like Snoopy, "is that pot kosher for Passover?" Everyone laughs. I guess whatever animosity Lola had toward Ari faded at some point this year, because they hang out all the time now.

"Hey," Ari says to me, "how's everything with Eitan?"

"It's good," I say. Understatement of the year. I'm glad Ari can't really see me, because I know my cheeks must be pink, pink, pink. We are lying on the floor of his bedroom on the rug, looking at the glow-in-the-dark stars.

"Are you sure you don't want to smoke?" he asks.

"I'm sure," I say. For the same reason I don't like surprises, I don't want to smoke pot—I like to at least pretend I'm in control.

"That's cool," Ari says.

"Yeah, it is," I say.

He laughs. "You're very sure of yourself, Francie," he says. He looks over at me, and I feel it again, like Ari is flirting with me. It's unsettling, but, who are we kidding, it's kind of flattering.

Lola is on the bed above us and she pokes her head over the edge. "What're you guys talking about?" she asks.

"Your sister is very sure of herself, Lola," Ari says, sitting up.

"She sure is," Lola says, but when she says it, it doesn't sound quite as much like a compliment.

Eitan calls me once he's back from Florida. In a quiet voice, he's like, I had a really great time with you, you know...when we... And I'm like, Yeah, me, too. And then I hear his voice crack a bit, and he tells me that his parents are making him go to Israel for the summer and my heart plummets so far, so fast, that I have to lie down, I think I'm going to faint.

"What?" I ask.

"They want me to see my family there and I'm going to go on this, like, adventure teen tour."

"You're going on a teen tour of Israel. A country you've been to, like, thirty times."

"Yeah," he says. "I could probably lead the fucking teen tour," he says, and he never curses either, he must be so angry.

"Do you really have to go?" I ask.

"I do," he says.

"It's just—I thought we'd have the whole summer," I say.

"Me, too. I don't want to go." And then he has to hang up the phone. I thought we had four more months together before I went to college, four months to figure out how we could stay together, but now it's only two. I never went on a teen tour, but AJ did, the summer after our sophomore year, out West, and I heard about what goes on—all the random hooking up.

I call Susannah. "What's up?" she says when she picks up the phone. I tell her what Eitan just told me, and my voice catches, and I start to cry.

"Oh, Francie," she says. "You really love him."

I nod, even though she can't see me.

After we hang up, I lie on my bed, running the scenarios in my head about breaking up with Eitan or not breaking up with him, and what each might look like, and they all end with me in North Carolina, heartbroken because of my own stupid decisions.

AJ has to go a doctor's appointment in the middle of the day, so on Wednesday, Sooz comes to lunch with Tammy and me. We go to the sandwich shop again, it's kind of our thing now, and this time, we sing along very loudly to the mix tape that I made for Tammy. It's very heavy on the Andrew Lloyd Weber.

When we sit down with our lunch, Tammy keeps giving me the once-over. She's like, Something about you looks different. She looks at me really closely and then gasps. "Oh, my God, Francie, you two totally fucked. You are fucking. You are having sex with Eitan."

Susannah looks at me like, This can't be true, as I turn bright pink. Meanwhile, Tammy grabs my hands and jumps up and down in excitement as much as you can jump up and down when you're sitting in a chair.

"You did? You are?" Susannah says.

"Just twice," I say.

"How was it? Tell us everything," Tammy says.

I haven't told my friends that I slept with Eitan. On the one hand, I want to tell them, because it's exciting news to share. But on the other, I don't really want to share it, I want to keep it for myself, or really, for the two of us. And the longer I wait to tell my friends, the weirder it will be, like, Why didn't you tell us right away? I don't think it's a big deal in the way AJ was making it out to be, but that doesn't mean it's not important to me, because Eitan is important to me. And then, leave it to Tammy to guess.

"Can you lower your voice, please? I really don't need this whole sub shop to know."

"So? How was it?" Tammy whispers.

"Um, the first time was OK. I mean, I don't know if you can expect the first time to be great."

Tammy nods, knowingly. "But it got better, right?"

I nod, still blushing furiously.

"I think this is the right thing for you two," Susannah says. "You are so in love with him." She pauses. "Did you tell AJ?"

"No," I say.

"OK," she says. Maybe Susannah feels in the middle between AJ and me. I don't want her to feel torn between us. "Are you going to tell her?"

"I don't know," I say.

Tammy nods. "I can understand that."

"You can?" I ask.

"Yeah. You and Sooz are so much nicer to be around without AJ. Everybody thinks so."

Sooz and I look at each other. I never realized that I might be different with or without AJ in the same way that AJ is different when she's with Alex.

BROADWAY MIX TAPE FOR TAMMY
I Dreamed a Dream, from Les Misérables
Try to Remember, from The Fantasticks
Anything Goes, from Anything Goes
Any Dream Will Do, from Joseph and the Amazing Technicolor Dreamcoat
I Know Him So Well, from Chess
Putting it Together, from Sunday in the Park with George
What I Did for Love, from A Chorus Line
As If We Never Said Goodbye, from Sunset Boulevard

***

In math class, Jason tells me that his friend Stacey from Maplehurst is going to Duke, too. He met her at the diner and they became friends because they kept running into each other all the time, kind of like how we became friends with Ross at the ice skating rink. He gives me her number.

I am shooting some hoops one afternoon after work when Starr drops Lola off after school. Starr just got her license and she and Lola stayed late for Spanish club. Lola drops her bag and I pass the ball to her and we take turns just trying to make baskets. I can't play a real game against her because I'm better than she is, but she's taller, so she ends up just holding the ball over my head and we don't get anywhere.

"Lo," I say, "I found some journals in Joseph's room a while ago."

Lola takes a shot and then bounces the ball to me. I hold it.

"What kind of journals?"

"Like, his journals. Like, diaries."

"Oh. Did you read them? I'd've read them."

I nod.

"What did you do with them?" she asks.

"They're still there. Lo, did you know that Joseph tried to kill himself?"

"What? That's what it says in the journals?" Lola sits down on the driveway. I sit down next to her, the basketball in my lap.

"Yeah. I mean, he doesn't go into details... It was the summer he was home for a few weeks, like, five years ago."

"I barely remember that. I just remember him leaving again, fast." Lola shakes her head. "I can't believe the parents would still use this tough love bullshit with him after they know he tried to kill himself." She turns to look at me. "Why didn't you tell me this when you first read them?"

I shake my head. "I don't know. It took me some time to process it, I guess."

Lola nods. "I wrote him some letters, a while ago. He never wrote me back."

"Same," I say.

"Did you tell Eitan?"

"Of course not!"

"I figured you tell him everything. You guys are like joined at the hip. Even more than you and AJ were."

"I don't want to tell him this. It feels, like, too private. It's not my story to tell." I look at her and then I look away.

"Eitan and I slept together," I say.

She gasps.

"Wow. I mean, I thought you would, after that conversation with AJ. I know you used a condom," she says, poking me in the ribs.

"Of course, Lola."

"Was it a glow-in-the-dark one?"

"Oh my God, no. Eew. Please stop."

She grabs the ball from my lap. "I'm still going to beat you," she says, standing up and taking a shot.

***

This whole year, since January, Sooz has been talking with Bart the snowboarder, and she went to Vermont with AJ in February and hung out with him, and even saw him once when he came into New York City for a few days. Turns out, he's from New Jersey. But she decides she cannot ask a 20-year-old snowboarder to prom and expect him to want to go with her. So, she asks Mark, a 20-year-old college student, who jumps at the chance to escort her. She went to his prom two years ago, so it's almost like she's returning the favor.

AJ asks Alex, of course. And I ask Eitan, of course.

AJ makes the limo arrangements, and we buy the prom tickets, and we think about what we want to do after prom. Some people go into the city, some people go to the beach. Some parents let their kids have co-ed sleepovers, but I don't think AJ's parents would let that happen if they were home. They seem to have a don't ask, don't tell policy, I guess. Sooz's mother says we can all stay over at her house, so that's our tentative plan. Definitely no co-ed sleepovers, but we can wake up in the morning together.

***

One day when I'm working at the photo developing shop after school, Adam comes in to pick up photos. I haven't seen him since that day in his classroom at the synagogue, and I was hoping I would never have to see him again.

"Francie," he says, giving me a tentative smile. I do not smile back at him. I turn around and rifle through the envelopes of photos and pull out two packets for Fox, Adam, and drop them on the counter.

He picks them up and passes them from one hand to another nervously. He clears his throat.

"How are you?" he asks. "We miss you at the Mission."

"I'm fine," I say, and I ring up his photos. "That's twenty-one thirty-five."

He pulls out his wallet and takes out the cash and puts it on the counter.

Michelle looks up from her seat at the photo processor and catches my eye. She must hear something in my voice because she gives me a questioning look, but I shake my head at her.

"Can I—" Adam starts, then stops. He clears his throat again. "I wanted to say—"

"I'm not going to tell anyone, Adam. I mean, nothing happened, but I'm not going to tell anyone, if that's what you're worried about."

He swallows, and looks relieved.

I lean across the counter, glad that for once I'm not wearing a goddamned tank top, and I say in a quiet voice, "I liked you, and I trusted you, and what did you do with that?"

He nods and sighs and takes his photos and walks out of the shop, the bell on the door jingling as he goes.

"Who was that?" Michelle asks.

"Nobody important," I say.

***

I am standing in the gym hallway between seventh and eighth periods, talking to Lola about the lit mag, when all of a sudden, I can't see anything in front of me, I have only blurry peripheral vision. I grab her arm.

"Lo," I say, "I'm going to have a migraine."

"Shit," she says.

"I need to go now. Can you tell the office I had to leave, that I got sick?"

"Francie! You can't see! You can't drive home!"

"What am I supposed to do, Lola? I can't stay here."

"Let me come with you, at least."

And so I drive home with Lola, very slowly and when we get there, she walks me upstairs to my room and shuts the shades and puts the trash bin next to my bed in case I need to throw up and I climb into bed and she gets me a wet washcloth and then I take three Advil and she kisses me on the forehead and quietly closes the door to my room and I fall asleep.

The next thing I know, I feel someone sit down at the foot of my bed. "Francie?" It's my mother.

I sit up, my hair matted and my mouth dry, my headache gone.

"Francie, are you feeling better?"

I nod. My mom gives me a glass of water and I take a sip.

"You have a visitor," she whispers.

The door opens and I wince a little at the light that comes in from the hallway. It's Eitan. I look like crap and I am probably smelly and I still feel nauseous. I am so glad to see him.

"Hey," I croak.

My mom gets up and Eitan sits down on my bed, closer to me than my mother was. She closes the door a little on her way out and then turns out the light in the hallway.

"It only took a debilitating headache for my mom to shut the door on us in here," I whisper, smiling at him. Eitan does not think this is funny.

"I called to talk to you, to see why you hadn't come over, and Lola said you weren't feeling well. She was like, Francie gets these headaches. Why didn't you tell me?"

"I don't know. It's not a secret. Every few months, I get a migraine. I never know when it's gonna happen."

He takes my hand. "Can't migraines cause aneurysms? Or brain damage?"

I shake my head very slowly. "No." He exhales.

"Francie." He looks like he's going to cry. "I was so worried about you." I pull him into my arms. "You have to tell me about stuff like this, Francie. I want to know."

***

AJ's parents go away for another weekend without her and she decides to throw a little party. Sooz, Jason, Dave, and a few other people all come, along with Eitan, Alex, and me. Eitan and I are planning to stay over again.

We're hanging out in the den downstairs, some people drinking the wine coolers that Evan left behind in the garage fridge for AJ when he was home for spring break, when AJ brings down the Ouija board. The boys groan, like, don't be ridiculous, and I wonder if they have ever used a Ouija board before. Like, what do boys do on sleepovers? Do boys even have sleepovers? I can remember my brother having friends stay over a few times, but not, like, a whole bunch of them at once.

Anyway, it's not possible to get all of our hands on the little planchette, so it's just the girls, and then Alex is like, Hey, I want to try, so I sit back down next to Eitan. He puts his arm around my waist, his hand resting on my hip, and I lean into him and he kisses the top of my head and I wish it were just the two of us. We've had sex three times so far. I really have to stop counting stuff like that. I want it to be so many times that I lose count.

Sooz says, in that same very low, serious tone, "Spirits, are you here with us tonight?"

Alex says, "What's up with your voice, Sooz?" AJ shushes him.

"Spirits, we have some disbelievers—"

"I think it might be unbelievers," says Jason.

"Shut up!" says AJ.

Susannah continues, "We have some skeptics here tonight, but please don't let that deter you. I will start with the first question. Will I get the financial aid I need from NYU?"

The planchette veers around the board, and lands on the number 4. We all lean in to look at the board.

"What the hell does that mean?" asks Mike.

AJ looks at Alex. "You can't put your fingers on the thingy if you're not going to really participate," she says.

"I can't believe you're taking this seriously," he says. "OK, OK, I'll be more serious." He settles his face into a very serious expression while obviously trying not to laugh.

AJ accepts this, and Sooz repeats her question. The planchette moves to "Yes." Sooz opens her eyes, and squeals.

"Are you really taking this seriously, Sooz?" Alex asks.

"Of course," she says. "The spirits know things."

"All right, I'm out," he says. "Anyone else want a turn?" None of the guys are interested in participating, but they seem interested in watching. I swap with Alex and put my fingers lightly on the planchette.

"I'm sure you know, Sooz, that the Office of Financial Aid determines your package, not the spirits," Jason says.

"All right, it's my turn," AJ says. She clears her throat. "OK. This is a very serious question, because I think someone has been holding out on us." She pauses dramatically. "Are Francie and Eitan having sex?"

I stand up, knocking over the board. "What are you doing?" I ask, looking first at her, then at Eitan.

She looks up at me. "What?" she asks, all innocent.

"What are you doing?" I repeat. Eitan stands up, too, looking uncomfortable. "Well, I guess we have our answer, and we didn't even need the spirits' help," she says.

"AJ, you're supposed . to ask questions about yourself," Sooz says, looking at me.

I turn around and my eyes catch Jason's, and he looks away. Did he think I'd be saving myself for him?

I take Eitan's hand and pull him out of the den, up five stairs to the main floor, down five stairs to the foyer, and Jesus Christ, who invented a split-level house, what is this nonsense? I grab our coats from the closet and walk out the front door. I am so angry at AJ that I am shaking.

"Hey," Eitan says, pulling me close, smoothing down my hair and my flushed cheeks. "Can you, uh, pause for a second and tell me what's going on?"

I swallow. I am not angry at Eitan, how could I be angry at Eitan, and I don't want my voice to sound like

I am. I take a deep breath. "I didn't tell AJ that we had sex," I say. "Did you tell your friends?" I ask.

He shakes his head. "No, but I thought maybe girls talked about that stuff."

"I thought guys talked about that stuff!"

"Oh, yeah, we'll be like, Hey, I totally nailed this girl—Oh, God, that sounds awful." He shakes his head. "I never say stuff like that." I look at him and we laugh.

AJ opens the door to her house and walks outside.

"Francie," she says. "It was just a joke. I wasn't sure you guys had done it—" she looks at Eitan.

"Why does it matter to you?" I say.

"Why didn't you want to tell me? Did you tell Sooz? Or... Tammy?" And from my face she can see that I did. "Oh. So, you just didn't want me to know."

"It's not about you. It's about Eitan and me. Why does me sleeping with my boyfriend have to be about how I didn't tell you about it?"

"But why didn't you want to tell me?" she says, in a small voice. "I told you about Alex and me—" again, she looks at Eitan, and I can tell she really doesn't want to have this conversation in front of him.

"I don't know," I say.

"But I love you, and I think you guys are so good together, and it makes me happy that you're so happy. I wish you felt like you could share that with me."

I shake my head. I don't know why I didn't tell AJ, only that I didn't, and it seemed like the right thing at the time. Now, AJ looks like she's going to cry. I do not want to comfort her.

"I'm sorry, AJ. If you wanted to know, you should have just asked me."

"I didn't want to have to ask you. I wanted you to tell me."

I shake my head. "I can't talk about this now," I say.

I open the door to my car and Eitan gets in on the passenger side and we drive away. It's still early, and I'm so keyed up. We drive around a little bit with the windows down and I even crank open the sunroof, because it's a nice night. We drive out to the next beach town over and park by the arcade.

"I guess what AJ did, what she was trying to do, was what I tried to do before Christmas break," Eitan says.

"What do you mean?"

"She was trying to get you to tell her something you didn't want to tell her, or you weren't ready to tell her."

I look at him, and of course he is right.

"C'mon," Eitan says. "Let me win you something." I laugh, and he takes my hand as we walk up the steps to the boardwalk. I proceed to accumulate, like, 200 tickets at skee ball and win myself a small stuffed creature, possibly a dog, which I give to Eitan.

He snuggles it. "I'll cherish it forever," he says. We hold hands and walk down the boardwalk a ways, turning around after a few blocks.

We sit down on one of the benches and look at the ocean. Eitan puts his arm around me and I swing my legs over his lap and he pulls me closer.

When we get back into the car, he says, "I know this place..."

"What kind of place?"

"Uh, a place. At the end of this road. It's a parking lot. It's usually empty. I've actually never been there."

"Why are you telling me this?" I ask.

"Ori told me about it, when I first started dating you."

"Your brother told you about a parking lot when you first started dating me."

"It's, uh, you know, usually empty."

"Ohhh," I say.

"Like, the docks are always full of people and cops, but this one is empty," Eitan says. "We can't go back to my house because my parents and both of my brothers are home."

"And why did Ori tell you about this place?" I ask, joking with him.

"You know," he says.

"Did you tell your brothers we had sex?" I ask.

"God, no," he says. "I don't need them teasing me about you anymore than they already do."

"They tease you about me?" I ask.

"Yeah, it's pretty constant," he says. "Like, Ooh, baby Eitan has a girlfriend, and then you gave me that photo of the two of us, from when we went to the Guggenheim, and Ori was like, Not only does baby Eitan have a girlfriend, but she's super hot, so..." He looks at me. "Anyway. Just keep driving till you can't drive anymore, and then make a left."

I follow his directions, and sure enough, we are at a deserted parking lot. If I were by myself, this would be scary, but I am not by myself.

Driving a station wagon does come in handy sometimes. There are a few sheets and blankets in the back because my mother is paranoid that someone will break into the car, so she drapes things in the trunk with the sheets and blankets. I unlatch the back seats so they lie flat, and use the sheets to make a kind of curtain over the back windows. We lie down on the sheets and while it's not the most comfortable environment, I forget all about that once we get going.

Afterwards, we pull the sheet over ourselves and cuddle in it.

"I wish I could wake up next to you," Eitan whispers to me. "I wasn't kidding about being jealous of your stuffed animals." He swallows. "Francie," he whispers.

"Eitan," I whisper.

"Why didn't you want to tell AJ about us sleeping together? Are you embarrassed? Of me?" His voice gets very quiet.

My heart jumps into my throat when I hear this. How could Eitan think that I'd be embarrassed of him?

"No," I whisper. I run my hands through his hair. "I love you. Just because I don't, like, make out with you in public..." I kiss him. "Obviously, I want to make out with you in private."

"But, then, why didn't you tell her? You told Susannah."

I take a deep breath. "My friendship with AJ is...I don't know. It's complicated. It's like, she always has to be in charge, and she has to know everything, and we usually do the things that she wants to do. And, like, after we met you at the diner, I thought you were so cute, and I figured it was a lost cause, because you'd met her, too. Almost every guy I've ever had a crush on has chosen AJ over me. It just, I don't know, sometimes I don't love her the way I think I should."

Eitan nods.

"And, maybe I didn't want to tell her because I knew it would hurt her feelings once she found out, once she knew I'd already told Sooz and Tammy. Like, I wanted her to feel what I felt all those times someone didn't choose me. Except, obviously, I'm not a boy not choosing her. Just her best friend."

Eitan shakes his head. "I can't imagine anyone choosing AJ over you. You're so different, and you're so much—better."

"I don't need to feel like I'm better. But I don't think I'm being a very good friend all the time, and that makes me feel kind of crappy," I say.

"You thought I was cute when you first met me at the diner?" he says, smiling.

I laugh. "That was the most important part of all of that for you?"

He laughs.

"So cute," I say.

If it's even possible, Eitan pulls me closer. If we were any closer, we'd be having sex again, which it seems we are almost ready to do.

***

That Sunday, Sooz and I try to buy tickets to see the Beastie Boys. They're playing in two weeks, and we thought they were sold out, but Starr said that sometimes, there are extra seats released a few weeks before the shows, so we decide to try our luck. The radio station can't help me out for this show, but there's this, like, secret Ticketmaster outlet in the Burlington Coat Factory down the street from our high school, next to the layaway counter. When we get there, there are already a few other kids that we recognize loitering about in the entryway. The store doesn't open till 10, and we are early.

"Look," says Sooz, and I know she's going to bring up something serious. "I know you're angry with AJ, but I was thinking, if there are tickets, we should get her a ticket to this concert as a birthday present."

"I'm not getting her anything," I say. Sooz even mentioning it makes me angry again.

"It's her 18th birthday," Susannah says.

"She doesn't. Even. Like. The Beastie Boys," I say.

"Francie," she says, "that's not the point."

"If you want to get her a ticket, that's fine, but I can't. I wouldn't want to go with her," I say. Aside from the fact that I'm angry with her, AJ is the worst person to go to a concert with. She never knows the song lyrics, she can't dance, and she's so worried that people are looking at her, dancing badly, incorrectly mouthing the words, that she spends the whole time posing for people who are absolutely not paying her any attention.

Susannah sighs, but when we get to the ticket window, we only buy two tickets.

When I am back home after getting concert tickets, I call Ross. We haven't spoken in a long time. I want to know why he stopped speaking to AJ, and if she doesn't know, maybe he'll tell me. Maybe talking to someone else who was so close to her and then just couldn't deal with her anymore will be helpful. Someone answers after, like, five rings. By that point, I was expecting to get an answering machine, but what kind of message could I have left? "Hey, Ross, it's Francie, can you tell me why you didn't want to be friends with AJ anymore because I am considering that, too? Thanks! Bye!"

"Hello?" says the guy who answers the phone.

"Ross?" I ask.

A pause. "Francie?" I smile. "Hi, Francie! How the hell are you?"

"I'm good! How are you? How's NC Squared?" That is what we call Nassau Community College.

"I'm not really sure it's for me. I just spent 12 years in school. I don't know if I want more school, you know?"

I mean, I don't really know, but I guess I've been thinking about it, what with Tammy going to LA and Eitan planning to do a gap year. It certainly sounds appropriate for Ross.

"What's up? I haven't heard from you in ages," he says. "How's it going?"

I lie down on the floor in my room, twisting the phone cord. "It's going all right," I say. "Honestly, I'm—I was wondering what happened with you and AJ."

There is silence on the phone. "Is she with you now?" he asks.

"No!" I say. "I've just—I've been finding myself less able to deal with her ... I don't know, her whole thing, her smugness and her constant posing and self-consciousness and sometimes she's just mean!"

Ross laughs. "Oh my God, Francie, what took you so long? You were friends with her a lot longer than I was."

I laugh. "I don't know. She started dating this new guy and he's the worst, and he makes her worse, too. I guess I never noticed a lot of this stuff before."

Ross sighs. "I loved AJ, really, I did. Not, like, I was in love with her, but we really got each other on, like, a deep level. I mean, you and I were really good friends, too, but with Alison... and then I started noticing all this shit about her. Like you said, she's so self-conscious, it makes her need constant attention and constant, like, validation. She needs to look perfect all the time. You know what? People aren't looking at you all the time!"

I nod, even though obviously he can't see me. "Yeah," I say.

"And she always has to be right. Like, it's fine not to be a pushover, but you don't have to bully everyone into your way of thinking or your way of doing things every single time!" Ross is getting very heated, like he's been waiting for months to talk about this with someone. "Sometimes, I miss her, and I miss you, too, and Sooz—like, that's an unfortunate side effect of me not talking to AJ anymore, that it might be weird for us to hang out."

"Yeah, I get it. I miss you, too," I say.

"I don't want to talk about AJ anymore. Tell me something you've been doing," Ross says. I tell him about school and my job at the photo shop and getting into college and Eitan.

"I know that kid," Ross says. "I knew his older brother, too—he was a year ahead of me at Maplehurst. His family is really rich."

"Yeah, that's totally why I'm dating him," I say. There's a pause on the line, and we both laugh.

When I see AJ in school on Monday, things are still really awkward. I don't know how to tell her why I didn't want to share this about Eitan and me. I only just told her that we were in love, so maybe she thinks I slept with him on a whim, like maybe it wasn't a big deal, when in fact, it is. But it also seemed like the most natural thing ever, like, of course we would sleep together, we are in love, why wouldn't we?

"You were so judgmental when I told you I was going to sleep with Alex," AJ says at the pizzeria at lunchtime. Sooz has stayed at school for extra tennis practice, so it's just the two of us. I can't tell her that I was judgmental because I don't like Alex.

"But now that you've done it, we can talk about how awesome it is," she says. It's not like I'm some kind of expert, having had sex only a handful of times, but who knows, maybe AJ can teach me something. I try to find my lovingkindness to understand why she felt she needed to learn about it in this way, but also why I didn't want to share it with her.

I buy her a book for her birthday, and make her a mix tape, and bake her her favorite chocolate cookies, but I know she is sad and hurt that Sooz and I didn't get her a ticket to see the Beastie Boys.

BIRTHDAY MIX TAPE FOR AJ
Closer to Fine, by the Indigo Girls
32 Flavors, by Ani DiFranco
Conversation, by Joni Mitchell
The Ballad of El Goodo, by Big Star
Box of Rain, by The Grateful Dead
Bad Reputation, by Freedy Johnston
Moonshadow, by Cat Stevens

***

Senior picnic is always held at some secret location. They don't want anyone to plant drugs or alcohol there ahead of time, so they don't tell us where we're heading.

AJ and Sooz sit next to each other on the bus and I sit across the aisle with Tammy. AJ has kind of come to terms with Tammy, in that she has stopped asking me why I hang out with her so much. We have bathing suits on underneath our clothing in case we are going somewhere with a body of water, which is good because we end up at a state park on the North Shore of Long Island with a little rocky beach.

There is a BBQ set up and a volleyball net and a bunch of other sporty activities. AJ rolls out her blanket and the four of us sit down. We take off our tee shirts and lie around on the blanket until Dave comes over and forces us to play some volleyball, which we only do because we know Tammy has a crush on Dave.

I am terrible at volleyball. My wrists are really skinny and apparently weak and I can never hit the ball hard enough, but I stand in the front row and give it a try for like ten minutes until I give up and go sit down with Jason under a shady tree.

"Do you want to go see Toad the Wet Sprocket over the summer? I know you really like them, and they're playing at Jones Beach."

"Sure," I say. "Let me know when it is."

"You don't need to make sure you don't have something going on with Eitan?"

"Eitan's going to Israel for the summer."

"Fuck, Francie. That sucks."

"Yeah," I say. "It really does."

***

Eitan invites me to go on a little hike with his brothers about an hour and a half north of the city. Of course, I have no hiking gear at all, so I've borrowed a pair of AJ's hiking boots. I've been wearing them all around the house, trying to make sure they're comfortable. Eitan and his brothers pick me up in their dad's old station wagon. Jonathan is driving, at least, I guess it's Jonathan, because he looks the oldest. Eitan is hands down the hottest of the three of them.

Eitan introduces me to his brothers as we settle into the backseat. Ori and Jonathan mostly talk to each other in the front seat, flipping through radio stations, while Eitan and I talk quietly to each to each other in the back.

"It's a really easy hike," Eitan says, tracing his fingers on my palm.

Ori turns around and looks at Eitan, who drops my hand, and then at me. "You ever been up to Bear Mountain before?" he asks.

I shake my head. "I've never been hiking before."

Ori and Jonathan groan. "Eitan," Ori says. To me, he says, "I hope your boots are comfortable. We're not gonna wait for you."

Great. Eitan takes my hand again. "I'll wait for you, Francie," he says.

Ori and Jonathan groan again. Eitan makes eyes at me and we giggle.

When we get to the trailhead, each of us takes a small backpack with food and water and a map. They have walkie talkies or radios or something, they are very serious about this, and Eitan and I take a radio and Ori and Jonathan take one.

The morning is cool and misty. I'm wearing a knit hat because even though it's practically the end of May, my ears get very cold. Eitan lent me a sweatshirt, which is too big on me, but which I don't think I'm ever giving back. I also have my camera and I'm taking photos of everything—the scenery, Eitan and his brothers, Eitan and me.

We are doing a moderate trail, but it's not so moderate for me. Jonathan and Ori walk ahead of us and then pause every few minutes for us to catch up, even though Eitan keeps telling them it's not necessary. They're like, What if we lose baby Eitan? Eema will kill us.

We hold hands as we walk on the paths, except where we have to go single file and Eitan has me go first. He points out the different trees and birds we see on the trail. I can understand why he loves this so much. It's quiet and peaceful.

We pause at the top to eat lunch, which means we are halfway done. The mist has cleared and it's warm and we can see the lake down below. There are bathrooms here, but only I have to go, of course. Then, maybe ten minutes later, back down the trail, Eitan and Ori have to pee. They head into the bushes, and Jonathan and I walk down the trail without them.

Jonathan clears his throat. "I know about your brother," he says. "I mean, I heard about it, everything, years ago."

I don't know how to respond to this, so I say nothing and just keep walking.

"It was kind of a big deal, the star goalie dropping out of soccer, dropping out of high school, to go to rehab. Everyone knew about it." Why is he telling me this?

"We were friends. I don't know—I didn't know anything about it, though. I mean, if I had..."

Oh, that's why. "You couldn't have done anything, Jonathan," I say.

"Did you tell Eitan?"

"Of course."

Jonathan nods. "You guys are really into each other, aren't you."

I blush as, again, I don't know how to respond to this. Jonathan looks at me and stops walking. He reaches out as if to touch my cheek, then pulls away.

"Are you all right?" he asks.

"Yeah, just, I blush really easily."

"Why are you—you're in love with Eitan." And I blush even more furiously as he laughs. "Baby Eitan!"

"He's not a baby," I say, annoyed.

"But you're going to college in August. Aren't you gonna have to break up?"

Where the hell are Eitan and Ori? I turn around and see them a few yards behind us.

"I don't know what we're gonna do."

"Well, don't break his heart," Jonathan says, suddenly very serious as they catch up to us. Jonathan then gives Eitan a noogie because they are brothers, I guess.

He and Ori walk ahead of us again and I take Eitan's hand.

"What were you guys talking about?" Eitan asks.

"Nothing," I say.

In the car on the way back, Ori turns around. He says, "Eitan, you ever go to that parking lot I told you about?"

I blush again, oh my God, is my head going to explode?

"You told him about that?" Jonathan says, catching my eye in the rear-view mirror. He grins as he sees my pink cheeks.

"I hope you're using protection. Don't need any actual baby Eitans crawling around."

"Could you guys just shut the fuck up, please?" Eitan says. He moves into the middle seat to be right next to me and puts his arm around me and kisses me and of course I kiss him back, even though it's weird and awkward. His brothers groan again.

That afternoon, we sit on the little dock behind Eitan's house and we finally talk about what's going to happen over the summer, and after I go to college.

Eitan says, "What if you get to Duke and you are surrounded by all these really smart older guys and you're like, Ugh, now I have to call Eitan and break up with him. Or worse, send him an email and break up with him. Everyone at college uses email, that's what Ori said."

"Everyone at college uses email to break up with their boyfriends?" I say, teasing him.

"Francie. I'm being serious."

"OK, OK." I put on my most serious expression. "Are you saying we should break up?" I can barely say the words.

"Just—what if you want to be with other people?"

"Eew, other people, no thank you," I say. And then I realize—what if he wants to be with other people?

"Do you want to be with someone else?" I whisper, my heart all of a sudden in my throat.

He puts his arms around me and kisses me and tucks the hair behind my ear and it's hard to think about breaking up with someone you love, who's sitting right next to you, who loves you back, who's kissing you as you try to interject something about kissing other people, making you realize you don't think you ever want to kiss another person, just him.

***

I am about to turn thirteen years old, Lola is about to turn eleven years old, Joseph is almost seventeen years old. After he left the second rehab center, he went to a halfway house in Minnesota, where he lives with other guys who are also in some kind of drug treatment. He goes to high school there, too. He ran away last summer, but they took him back after he spent a month at a different drug rehab center in Minnesota.

I've mostly avoided having my friends come to my house for the past year or so, since Joseph started rehab. When they did, I just said that Joseph wasn't around. No one really thought about it too much, I'm sure—older brothers are never around and sometimes, when they are, like Evan, you don't want them around. The only person I told was Jason. He spends so much time at my house that there's no way he wouldn't realize it right away.

My bat mitzvah is the first Saturday of September and my parents asked the halfway house if Joseph could come home for it, and they said yes. He'll only be home for, like, 48 hours, but I'm so excited to see him and have him at the bat mitzvah. My father went to the halfway house to pick Joseph up and when they got home from the airport, Lola and I hugged Joseph forever and he hugged us back.

But dinnertime is weird and awkward. Lola asks too many questions, and Joseph doesn't want to answer any of them. By the time we go to bed, everyone is exhausted.

The morning of my bat mitzvah, I get up very early and my mother blow dries my hair so that it looks neat and straight. I have a navy blue and white checked suit to wear for the services, and Lola has a navy blue dress and my mother has gotten Joseph has a navy blue suit that doesn't fit him quite right. My mother used to dress Lola and me in the same outfits, even though we are two years apart, even though we look nothing alike, so I'm not surprised that somehow, on this day, we are all three of us wearing navy blue.

My whole family and all of my friends show up at the synagogue. My mom's parents and her brother Leo are there, with his wife Jenny and my cousins Georgia and Iris. My dad's sister Darla and my Uncle Gerald and my older cousins Jack and Matt. My parents' friends and their kids. And a whole bunch of strangers who just happen to be at Saturday morning services.

I'm not nervous, though. My Hebrew school teacher, Adam, made me a tape of my Torah portion and my Haftarah so that I could practice over the summer, so I feel prepared. And the reading goes off smoothly, and everyone compliments me afterward.

After the bat mitzvah, my family and my parents' friends come back to our house for lunch, except for

*Uncle Leo and Aunt Jenny, who have to go home for Iris'
naptime. Joseph disappears with Matt and Jack—Jack is
a year older than he is and Matt is a year younger, so
they are pretty close. When they come downstairs an
hour or so later, Joseph seems different, like, he is
giggling and bouncing around the living room. Matt and
Jack look upset and worried and they walk over to my
father and Jack whispers something into his ear.*

*My father gets to his feet, reaching out for Joseph.
He pulls Joseph outside onto the back patio, but we can
see them through the sliding glass door. He's not yelling,
but he is very angry.*

*When he comes back inside, he takes his sister aside
and then she whispers something to my uncle Gerald,
who gets up very quickly.*

*"Francine," Aunt Darla says, "you were so wonderful
today, and you look so beautiful. We have to get going
to catch the train, but we will see you tomorrow at your
party."*

*She kisses me goodbye on both cheeks, like she is an
actual French person.*

*Meanwhile, my parents' friends start to realize that
something is going on, and they start to make their way
over to me to say versions of the same thing, and they
kiss me goodbye and they walk through the house to the
front door and then it's just Lola and me and our parents
and Joseph and my grandparents.*

*"Your parents are handling this all wrong," my
grandmother says to me as she grabs my arm a little too
tightly. "It's good that he's back."*

*"He's only here for the weekend, Grandma," I say.
"He's going back tomorrow night."*

*"He should be here for good," she says. "What is this,
sending kids away for this kind of thing? In my day, no
one was sent away. You dealt with it at home."*

My father comes back inside, leaving my mother outside with Joseph. He sighs deeply, running his hands through his hair.

"Francie," he says, "Joseph has to go back tonight. I'm not sure they'll take him, but if they don't, we'll find another place for him."

"What do you mean, he has to go back tonight?" I ask, looking outside. "What about the party tomorrow?"

"Joseph can't stay for the party. I don't think he should stay here tonight. I'm going to take him back to the airport and fly with him back to Minnesota."

I look at my father like he's crazy. "You're not going to be at my bat mitzvah?" I ask. I start to cry.

"Sweetie, I was at your bat mitzvah. The important part was today," he says, kneeling down to be closer to my height. Next to me, I can practically feel the judgment from my grandmother.

I can't help it, I let loose with a huge sob and I run out of the living room and up the stairs to my room and I slam the door shut, which is definitely not allowed in our house, and I flop down onto my bed in my stupid synagogue suit and cry into my pillow until I hear someone open the door to my room and I feel someone sit on the edge of my bed. I roll over.

"Francie, honey. Your brother has a problem, you know that." My mother pets my hair.

"He couldn't, like, for one weekend, not have a problem?" I say, knowing how ridiculous it sounds. "Why is he so selfish?"

"It seems selfish, but it's just part of who he is. It will always be there. He has to learn how to control it, but he hasn't yet. He needs more time."

Time away from us, is what she doesn't say.

***

We get our yearbooks the second to last week of school and we trade them around furiously. There is only so much real estate for your good friends to write something meaningful, so I make sure to leave the back pages for AJ, Sooz, and Jason. I'm not reading what other people have written until everyone has signed.

Jason gives me Stacey's phone number and I call her. I am oddly nervous, like I'm calling someone to go on a date. "Hello?" says a girl's voice on the other end.

"Hi," I say, "this is Francie Baum. Is Stacey there?"

"This is Stacey," she says.

"Hey," I say. "Jason gave me your number." Oh, my, God, duh.

We talk for a little bit, and decide to hang out so we will know at least one person when we get to Duke.

In the meantime, we are second-semester seniors. Everyone who is going to college has gotten their acceptances. We are coasting through most of our classes, even me, even though I'm taking, like, four AP tests at the end of May.

There's prom to deal with, too. Everyone is wearing a black dress, but I want to find something different. I go to the mall in Garden City with my mother. We are not looking to spend tons of money, so maybe this is not the right place, because it's pretty fancy, but my mom wants me to get some ideas. I find a few dresses to try on and when I emerge from the dressing room in each of them, there is something not quite right.

As we are about to leave, I see one more dress. It is pale blue, like ice blue, and has a halter top with strips of fabric over the back, so it's kind of open, but not entirely. I try it on, and my mom and I both love it. "Do you think it's too weird?" I ask. "Everyone else will be wearing black."

"Francie, you are not everyone else," my mother says. "You should wear what you want to wear. This dress is beautiful," my mother says. "You look beautiful."

"AJ showed me her dress. It's very classic," I say.

"You don't need to compare yourself to Alison," my mother says. I look at her. "Francie," she says, "you are always going to have girls in your life like AJ, and you have to decide how much of yourself you want to give to them. Not everything is a competition, even though some people seem to think it is."

We buy the dress.

Stacey comes over to my house. She lives nearby, right near the docks, in fact. When I tell my parents who she is, and that she's going to Duke, my dad is like, Oh, I did medical training with her uncle. This town is not that small, but Jesus Christ, you'd think my father knew everyone.

She drives a red Volkswagen Cabrio convertible, which is incredibly adorable, as is Stacey. We go to my new favorite pizza place in the next town over, and then we go to see a French film from the 1960s where, yes, we are the youngest people in the theatre. It is almost exactly like a date, but we do not make out. By the end of the night, we've decided we should be roommates at Duke.

My mother is not sure this is a great idea. "Don't you want to meet new people?" she says.

"She is a new person," I say. "And I will meet new people. She is going to be the only person I know on campus, besides Amelia. That's, like, nearly six thousand new people to meet."

***

Our prom is at some fancy party place in Queens, which has a view of Manhattan. It's where Sooz had her bat mitzvah, although I don't remember her bat mitzvah all that well because somehow, I got sick while I was there and by the time my parents took me home, I had a fever of, like, 103.

Everyone arrives at my house to take photos beforehand. And I mean, everyone. All of us, obviously, with our dates, and everyone's parents, including our dates' parents. Lola is here, obviously, because she lives here, but also Starr is here. Eitan's brother Ori is here, and I can barely look at him without blushing, knowing that he knows Eitan and I have slept together. Sooz's brother is here, too, in a suit, having just come from work. One of the dads—Alex's? I can't keep track—asks Sooz's brother if he's going to prom, too. One of my mom's friends from when she used to teach English is here, and all of our neighbors and their kids, who I used to babysit. The kids are very excited to sit inside the limo.

I go inside my house and Eitan follows me into the little TV room. He stands leaning in the doorframe as I pick up my bag and a shawl from the couch. Never in my life did I think I would need to wear a shawl, but here we are.

"You look amazing," he says in a low voice.

"Thank you," I say. "You look pretty hot yourself. You should be, like, James Bond for a living, so you can always be wearing a tuxedo." It is true that now I've seen Eitan in all states of dress and undress, and this is definitely the hottest he's ever looked clothed.

"It's a shame we're going to prom, because I can think of a lot of better ways to spend the night," he says in the same quiet voice, making eyes at me. I laugh.

We've been sleeping together at least once a week for, like, three months and I don't know what I'm going to do when he leaves for Israel in a few days. Having sex has been fun, yeah, like it feels amazing, but it also makes me feel so much closer to Eitan. We have this, like, secret with each other, this special knowledge of what the other person is like when they are literally naked. We aren't hiding anything. I can't imagine sleeping with someone I'm not in love with, or who I don't at least love.

I shut the door and we are out of sight of the front window, hidden behind a bookshelf filled with back copies of *The New England Journal of Medicine*, and I push him against the door and smooth down his lapels and kiss him.

"Yeah, that's what I'm talking about," he says.

Once we're in the limo and on the way to prom, we relax a little bit. Alex takes this as a license to open up the bottle of vodka he stored in the inside pocket of his tuxedo jacket. He downs about one-third of it before we even get to the venue.

The prom is extremely well-attended. It seems as though almost everyone from high school is there. My school is not some 1980s movie type of high school, where there are jocks and brains and popular kids and no one talks to each other. The food is terrible, but we eat it anyway, and then we dance. Some of the guys in my class think they are DJs, and so they attempt to DJ for a few songs, but then the professionals take over. The class president makes a little speech, thanking everyone for coming.

The prom ends at about 11 PM, and we do not go to any after-parties with anyone else from school. We head into the city to go to Limelight, where a girl from the class ahead of us who Susannah knew from her advanced painting class has put us on the list. In the limo, Alex drinks another third of the bottle, and when we get to the club, he is very drunk, almost belligerent. The bouncer nearly doesn't let us in, but we are all in tuxes and fancy dresses, it's almost punk rock to be dressed up so much, although of course Limelight isn't very punk rock. Inside, the club is dark, obviously, and it's hard for us to find Sooz's friend, but once we do, she hooks us up with a round of drinks. I only take a few sips of mine—it's a vodka and soda, and tastes like nothing, but also, disgusting.

Dancing at prom was a little awkward. People form an idea of you over the years, and it's hard to change that. They don't know me as someone who dances, who wears cleavage-baring dresses, who has a boyfriend, much less a boyfriend she wants to make out with on a dance floor. That was another interesting thing I got from *Zen and the Art of Motorcycle Maintenance*—that you need to be able to change your values as you move through life, or you won't be able to grow at all. Most of the kids at our high school haven't grown all that much in the time I've known them.

Eitan and I dance at Limelight, and it's very freeing to dance with him where we know almost no one else. We haven't danced together since the disco concert, when we barely knew each other, when we hadn't even kissed, when everything was just anticipation. I dance with my friends a lot, but not with him. We should have done more of that, just dancing and being silly, but here we are now, club music thumping, his hands sneaking up the back of my dress where it's bare and pulling me close.

I lean into him, whisper-yelling into his ear, "Thank you for being my prom date!"

He leans into me and says, "Thank you for inviting me!"

I dance around with my hands in the air, and he kisses my neck, and I can't believe he is leaving for Israel in five days.

In the limo on the way back to Long Island, at, like two in the morning, Alex finally loses it and throws up all over. Some of it makes it into the Champagne bucket, which is empty. I'm glad that I am sitting as far away from him as possible, but I feel bad for AJ. The driver pulls over and gets out of the car and smokes a cigarette while he watches AJ try to help Alex clean himself up. I'm sure Alex is not the first person to puke all over his limo, but man, what a sucky job to have to clean it up.

Instead of going to the beach, which we wanted to do, if only to dip our feet in the ocean for a minute, the driver drops AJ and Alex back at her house. He drops the rest of us back at Sooz's house. Sooz and I are going to sleep in her room, while Eitan and Mark, Sooz's prom date, will sleep in her brother's old room. It's nearly 3 AM by the time we get there, but we are so overtired that first we have to eat some of the junk food that Sooz's dad brings home against her mother's wishes.

We say goodnight to the boys and shut the door to Sooz's room. Once we are in bed, we talk for a little while to recap the evening—who looked good, who did not, who was a surprise couple, and so on. We do not talk about the fact that Alex spent the whole night getting more and more drunk. Sooz falls asleep and of course I have to pee one more time, so I tiptoe out of the room and into the bathroom in the hall. As I'm coming back into the hall in a pair of old flannel boxer shorts and Eitan's sweatshirt that I never returned, Eitan opens the door to Sooz's brother's room, wearing only his boxer briefs. I put my finger to my lips and motion him into the bathroom. We lock the door. There's a little night light, so we are not completely in the dark.

Eitan picks me up and puts me up on the countertop next to the sink, kissing me. "I wanted to do this all night," he whispers.

"I wish you had," I whisper.

He stands in between my knees and I wrap my legs around him, pulling him closer. He quickly realizes I'm not wearing a bra, and I quickly realize he's very turned on by this, and we do not have sex in the bathroom of Sooz's house, but we come pretty damn close. We wash our hands as quietly as possible and open the bathroom door as quietly as possible and sneak back into our respective rooms as quietly as possible.

The next morning, we are all so tired. AJ and Alex come over to eat breakfast. Sooz's mom has gotten us bagels. Alex looks about 100 times worse than all of us. He apologizes for getting so drunk and throwing up and ruining the last part of the night. At least he realizes it wasn't very considerate. Eitan does not roll into breakfast in just his underwear, of course. He's put on some sweatpants and a tee shirt, and his hair is messy and I realize I've only seen him in the morning like this once, when we slept over at AJ's. I'm sitting across the table from him and we just keep sneaking sneaky, dirty glances at each other. If one of us had had a condom, there definitely would have been prom sex on the floor of that bathroom last night.

I drive Eitan home after breakfast. We are still in our pajamas. When he gets out of the car, I roll down the window and he leans in and I kiss him.

***

Graduation is the Monday after prom. I am the first of my parents' children to graduate from high school, although not, like, the first in my family to graduate or anything like that. The graduation is held on the CW Post campus further out on Long Island because our high school auditorium isn't large enough to hold everyone and their families. Most people have grandparents at graduation, maybe even aunts and uncles. I just have my parents and Lola and Eitan. They are enough.

The graduates have to be there early, so Sooz and I ride over together. We take the top down on her Mustang and sing really loudly to Long Island's "alternative" radio station. By the time we get to CW Post, our hair is a huge mess and we have to comb it out in the bathroom for, like, ten minutes before we can get our caps on.

We line up alphabetically in the wings of the auditorium, so I'm after this girl Rachel Ballance and in front of Jason, whose last name is Bell. Jason is giving a speech because he's the salutatorian.

Jason and I talk smack about everyone else while we wait for people to arrive and line up. I tell him about what I did after prom—going to Limelight and Alex throwing up in the limo, not what happened with Eitan and me in the bathroom at Sooz's, obviously. He tells me about this after-party he went to. Some of the kids in our school live practically right on the beach, so the after-party was at one of the houses, with a pool overlooking the bay that separates the little barrier beach island from the rest of Long Island. Everyone got really drunk and half the girls jumped into the pool in their underwear. I cannot imagine doing either of those things—getting so drunk, or jumping in a pool in my underwear with people from high school.

Finally, we are lined up, the audience is settled, and we are about to walk out. I grab Jason's hand and give it a squeeze. "Good luck with your speech," I say. He squeezes my hand back and then we walk out across the stage to accept our diplomas.

After graduation, my parents take tons of photos of my friends and me in all different combinations. We go out to dinner at some place in Port Washington with Sooz and her parents. Sooz, Lola, and I gossip about everyone and Sooz asks Lola and Eitan if they know any other cute guys from Maplehurst or any other neighboring high schools—Long Beach, Oceanside, Valley Stream, she'll travel. Lola sighs. She does not.

My parents have a little graduation party for me at our house the next day. All of my friends come, and some of Lola's. Toward the very end, after most of the guests have already left, Eitan arrives. He's been busy packing for the summer and getting last-minute things he needs.

We go into the den to get away from everyone for a minute and he gives me two graduation presents: a mix tape—I'm so excited; I'm always the one making mix tapes for everyone else—and a necklace of red stones interspersed with little pearls. I pick up my hair and he fastens the necklace, kissing the back of my neck.

MIX TAPE FROM EITAN
You're My Home, by Billy Joel
Winterwood, by Don McLean
If Not for You, by George Harrison
I've Been Waiting, by Matthew Sweet
So Far Away, by Dire Straits
Handle With Care, by The Traveling Wilburys
Cinnamon Girl, by Neil Young
I Will Follow, by U2

***

The next day, Eitan and I go to see REM as an early birthday celebration. His actual birthday will be the second day he's in Israel. The tickets are behind the stage, but the band plays to all sides of the stadium. It's fun and we sing along and dance around, as much as you can dance around to REM, and I forget for at least five minutes that Eitan is leaving for Israel in 24 hours.

We take the train home from Madison Square Garden and run into a few other people we know, but I don't want to talk to anyone. These are last precious hours together, and I want it to be just the two of us. I fall asleep on his shoulder briefly after we change at Jamaica and when the train jostles me awake, I am annoyed that I lost even those minutes. Eitan is watching me.

"I'm really going to miss you," he says. I nod, a lump in my throat.

We get off the train in Maplehurst and I drive Eitan home. "Stop here," he says, right outside the driveway to his house on his deserted street. "I'm going to need to kiss you for a long time, and I don't want to do it where anyone can just walk out the door and see."

We climb into the back and make out for, like, half an hour. Then I unbuckle the belt on his jeans and slide my hands into his pants and he undoes my jean shorts and we have sex right there, me on his lap, my legs pushing into the leather seats of the Volvo.

"I wasn't expecting this kind of goodbye," he whispers into my ear as I lay my head on his shoulder.

"I don't want to give you any kind of goodbye," I say, "I don't want you to leave."

I push myself off of him and he puts the condom into a tissue and we zip ourselves up and try to look sort of presentable even though we have just had sex in my mom's car.

We get out of the car, and I walk him up the driveway and then he walks me back to my car, and I walk him back up the driveway, and he walks me back to my car, and this could go on all night, and I wish it would, so I wouldn't have to say goodbye, but finally, I give him one more kiss and he walks up the driveway and I get in the car and drive home, trying not to crash as I maneuver through my tears. And the next day, Eitan gets on a plane to Israel for six and a half weeks.

A week later, I feel almost settled into a routine. I'm working five days a week, six hours a day, so I have plenty of time to see my friends at night. My summer job is at the same photo shop, just more hours. I come home every day smelling like chemicals and cigarettes so I don't even shower in the morning anymore. Lola got a job at a restaurant nearby, waiting tables. Sooz is working at a day camp. She worked there last summer, too. They are constantly saying things to her like, Susannah, you are on playground duty—say it out loud—and she can barely keep it together not to laugh her head off at that.

Tammy is working at a day camp at one of the beach clubs, which is great, because she gets a pass to the beach club to use on the weekends, and she can bring her friends with her, although of course, we have to pay. AJ is still working at the housewares store. She helped me out when I went in to buy all of my bedding and towels and stuff for school, which was kind of weird. Also weird is that, independently, we chose the same bedspread.

I've written two letters to Eitan already.

Tammy, Sooz, and I go to some 16 and over club in Long Beach that Tammy knows about from one of her co-counselors. We wear outfits we can dance in, and wait on line to get in with a bunch of other teenagers. Inside, it's kind of like we are still outside, because there's a big tent set up in a parking lot off the beach. We have yellow wristbands because we are not 21. The first person we run into there is Dave. He's with a girl we don't know, so we just wave hello and go get sodas and scope out the situation. Well, Sooz and Tammy scope out the situation, while I help them.

"Damn, I was hoping to hook up with Dave this summer," Tammy says. She points her chin in a somewhat subtle fashion toward a tall, blondish muscly guy. "I think he's checking you out," she says to me.

I take a fast look, then look back at her. "He's definitely not my type. And I have a boyfriend."

"Francie, Eitan has been gone for three weeks and he hasn't called or written you."

"Thanks for reminding me," I say.

"My point is, he's probably hooking up with some girl from, like, Cherry Hill or something. You should do the same! Not, like, hook up with a girl, unless that's your thing. You know what I mean."

I shake my head.

"I don't know," says Susannah. "You didn't really spend any time with them. Eitan really loves her. There has to be some kind of explanation." Sooz, always in my corner.

"It doesn't matter," I say. "Maybe we should have broken up before he left, because we're probably gonna have to do it when he comes back. But we didn't. I'd feel like I was cheating. And ..." I take a deep sigh. "I really miss him." I swallow, and Jesus Christ, Francie, don't cry in this cheesy club.

"It's OK, Francie," Tammy says. "I'll take the blond with the crew cut." We look over at him—he is now dancing, badly, with a few of his friends. "Or maybe not." We make our way to the dance floor and dance for the next two hours, just for us.

***

Eitan's mother calls me, which is a shock. She says she has some photos from prom and wants to know if I'd like to come by to pick them up. At this point, I've written Eitan six or seven letters. They aren't mushy love letters or anything, just letters telling him about what's going on in my life here, what I've been up to, asking what he's doing in Israel, that kind of thing. He hasn't written me back yet, hasn't called, although he said he would do both. Every day I check the mail with my heart in my throat, and every day, I'm disappointed.

His mother welcomes me to the house and we sit at the kitchen counter and I flip through the photos. There are some really nice ones, and there's a funny one of Eitan and me, flanked by Lola on one side and Ori on the other, both of whom are making silly faces. And there's one of Eitan and me, where I'm looking off at something in the distance, and Eitan is, like, gazing at me adoringly, there's no other word for that look. I swallow hard when I see it. This was just over four weeks ago. Could he have made me a mix tape with goddamn "If Not for You" on it and then forgotten me in four measly weeks?

I know that if I don't get out of there, I'm going to lose it. His mother looks at me and she says, "I think he must be very busy in Israel. He'll be home in two weeks." I nod.

I back out of his driveway for what's probably the last time, and when I get onto the street, I pull the car over in the same spot where we had sex right before Eitan left for Israel and I sob, sob, sob.

Tammy invites me to hang out at her house so I drive over one afternoon. We walk from her place to the deli to pick up some snacks and when some guys catcall us, Tammy yells back at them and gives them the finger. At the deli, we run into Dave and Jason, so they come back to her house with us. Her new swimming pool hasn't been filled yet for some reason, even though it's July, so we climb down into it, sitting on the empty bottom, eating Swedish fish and cheddar Combos.

Tammy is leaving for LA in a few weeks. She's got an apartment lined up with some roommates and her parents are going to help her buy her a used car out there. She can't wait, but I guess she's still interested in hooking up with Dave, because she's really fawning all over him.

When it gets dark, we walk down onto the beach. Jason convinces Tammy that they should break into some of the cabanas and look for beer, and when Dave joins in, she really can't resist. She and Dave creep back a few minutes later with a six pack.

"A six pack? You don't think that's gonna be missed?" Jason asks, grabbing one anyway.

I pass, since beer tastes gross to me and I have to drive home anyway.

"These families have so much money, they will definitely not notice a few beers missing," Tammy says. She pops open her can and takes a long swig. After their little caper, she sits very close to Dave on one of the benches. I look at the two of them, and I can feel Jason next to me, wondering, and I'm just so goddamn heartsick for Eitan and so angry at him for not writing me.

I stand up. "I'm gonna leave," I say.

Jason stands up. "You're gonna walk back to Tammy's by yourself?"

"Yeah."

He shakes his head. "I'll walk you. Can you give me a ride home?"

Tammy says, "We'll go, too."

As we walk off the beach and back toward Tammy's house, Tammy grabs my hand.

"Come visit me in LA," she whispers. I smile at her. She's gonna be a big star, I'm sure.

***

Jason and I drive to Jones Beach for the Toad the Wet Sprocket show. I'm a huge Toad fan, so I'm very excited. Jason doesn't know them so well, but he knows I love them.

We get some popcorn at the concessions and look around for anyone else we know as we wait for the opening act to start. I lick the salt off my fingers.

"Oh my God, stop that," Jason says, and gives me a napkin. "This place is filthy."

Sometimes, I forget how germophobic and anal Jason can be. He is so neat, like, his room is neat, his clothing is always neat, even his kisses were neat.

I know most of the songs, even stuff from their first two albums. I watch Jason enjoying the show, and I make a plan in my head for a mix tape to give him before the end of the summer.

Toward the end of the set, the band plays "Don't Go Away," which is the song I put on my mix tape for Eitan and I have to sit down and take a deep breath. Jason leans in to whisper in my ear, and suddenly, I feel it down my spine—a shiver I thought was reserved only for Eitan, a shiver I never experienced with anyone else, certainly not Jason. What is going on? "That was a really good song," Jason whisper-yells into my ear, and when I turn to look at him, he's watching the band.

The last song they play is "All I Want," which, sure, is a crowd-pleaser, but it's also a great song and it's loud and everyone gets up and is singing and dancing. Jason grabs my hand and we shimmy a little together and we're laughing and then he leans in as if to kiss me and at the last minute, I pull away.

We look at each other for a moment while the song is winding down and everyone around us is dancing and singing and clapping for more. He leans into me—another shiver, what the hell?—and says, "I'm sorry, Francie. I forgot about Eitan."

The crazy thing is, for a second, I did, too.

"It's OK," I say, and we look at each other and we smile and then the song ends.

My parents drive all the way out to Huntington to have dinner with friends of theirs and Sooz and I go with them because there's a theater out there that's still playing "Dazed and Confused" for some reason and we are so excited to see it in on the big screen again.

Tammy and I go into the city to see "Kids" at the Angelika and we walk outside when it's over and it's a beautiful day and we look at each other like, What are we supposed to do after seeing this movie? Go shopping?

AJ and I go to see "Clueless" and we love it so much that we see it again the next day with Sooz and Lola and Starr.

Jason and I go to see "The Brothers McMullen" and we spend the rest of the afternoon talking about it and how we would make a movie about growing up on Long Island and who we would cast to play movie versions of ourselves and our friends. He did not write his movie yet, but I'm pretty sure he will.

AJ finally gives me back my yearbook. She took it at the end of June and said that she was waiting for the right time to sign it. All my teachers have already signed my yearbook, obviously, and all of my friends from school, except for AJ.

Here are some things other people wrote, not in their entirety, of course:

Tammy: I'm so glad we became friends this year. Our Wednesday lunches were the best part of my week. I can't remember any time with you that I haven't enjoyed. Be careful with your heart at Duke—boys are going to be all over you and your hot bod next year. I know we'll have an amazing summer, and can't wait for you to visit me in LA.

Dr. Choi: I guess Mr. O'Connor doesn't love you as much as I do because he only signed his picture. Sorry you're not going to major in math—we could use a sweet, bright, hardworking person like you.

Susannah: Well, the school year has come to an end. I don't know what to say except that I am going to miss you like I'd miss my own sister, if I loved my own sister. Let's not think about all we're going to miss, and look forward to an awesome summer together, filled with trips in the Mustang, listening to your amazing mixes. I can't fit our whole friendship onto this one page. I know that you were always at my side when it really counted, and I love you for that. I wish you every ounce of luck in the world, but with a body and mind like yours, who needs luck. I know you will succeed at whatever you do, and when I see "Soundtrack by Francine Elizabeth Baum" at the end of a movie, I can say that I knew you when you were young and silly.

I only read these after AJ gives me back my yearbook, because I didn't want to read anything until I could read everything. Here is what AJ wrote, at least part of it:

AJ: I'm finally writing in this, I've only had it in my room for three weeks or so. I remember doing "bad deeds" with you in the elementary school playground and putting old leaves in the mailbox and playing creative Barbies where we would design our own fashions out of our old socks. We've drooled over so many boys with so many nicknames, it's hard to keep track, but let's always remember that they weren't very bright. I think we're better off with our current boys. You're the most intelligent and motivated person I know who still appears to have a life. You're cute and amusing and obnoxious and fun, and also hard to read sometimes. I can only guess what you're feeling, so it's hard to know that you're upset and not have you share—

that must be hard for you, too. Always remember that I love you, and you can come to me no matter what.

I nearly cry as I read this entry, because it's so true. I should have just told AJ how I was feeling, about everything—about her and me and how I felt our friendship unravelling, and about how I was falling in love with Eitan, and my anger at Joseph—and maybe it's not too late, even if we are all leaving for college in a few weeks. I can make that choice, too, to be someone who changes, whose values can expand or change when they learn something new about someone. I don't have to see AJ the way I've always seen her, just because that's how I've always seen her. She's allowed to change, too.

As I read through everyone's entries, I realize that Jason didn't sign my yearbook. But he also said that he didn't want anyone to sign his yearbook, so maybe he isn't signing anyone else's.

I call AJ. "Hey," she says. "What's up?"

"I read what you wrote in my yearbook," I say.

"Uh huh," she says.

I can hear her crunching on something. I take a breath. "And...I just wanted to say...I'm sorry."

Her crunching pauses. "What are you sorry about?" she asks.

"I've been a bad friend this year," I say. "I was so caught up in Eitan that I didn't, like, pause, to have time with you. I know you were caught up in Alex..." I trail off.

"And you don't like Alex," AJ says.

I don't know how to respond to that.

"It's OK," AJ says. "I know you don't like him."

"You know what, AJ, I have come around. He's been there for you this whole year, and I haven't been. He's been calling you from North Carolina..."

She interrupts me. "Just because Eitan's not calling you, or writing you, it doesn't mean he's forgotten about you, Francie."

"I know," I say. "But it doesn't look good."

She sighs. "No, it doesn't."

"Anyway," I say. "I wanted to say that I was sorry for being a sub-par friend."

"You're not a sub-par friend," AJ says. "But thank you for—thank you for this."

***

My parents decide they should go to France for two weeks. My aunt and uncle will be in Paris, so they will visit them and then go to some wine region. As nice as it would be to go to France with my parents, it will also be nice to be home without them. Lola and I drop them off at JFK and then we turn to each other and practically squeal with glee. Not that we are going to throw wild parties, but just that we can do our own thing a little bit. I can't imagine our parents would have left us alone like this if Eitan were not in Israel, but maybe I am thinking about it too much.

They have left us some money for two weeks, but not enough that we will be able to order takeout every day, so Lola and I go to the grocery store and buy things we can cook easily, or just reheat. My parents don't believe in microwave ovens, so we are somewhat limited. I remind myself to get invited to friends' houses for meals over the next two weeks.

I also take this time to clean out some stuff in my bedroom, since, after all, I will be going to college at the end of the summer. I find so many old letters and journals that cleaning out my room is very slow going, because I have to reread everything and remember who I was when I was writing this stuff.

I read a journal entry from around my bat mitzvah, and there's a letter inside that I wrote to Joseph, which I obviously did not send. It's a long angry letter. My thirteen-year-old self was very angry with Joseph for abandoning Lola and me, for not doing what our parents wanted him to do. I read it a few times and I bring it down the hall to Lola's room. She is listening to music, reading a book, and polishing her toenails all at the same time.

"Lola," I say. "We should go visit Joseph."

She looks up. "What?"

"We should go visit Joseph," I repeat.

"No, I heard you. Why would we go visit him? The parents would freak—Oh," she says. The parents would freak, but they are in France for two weeks. "How do we know where he'll be?"

"He's been living with Uncle Leo," I say. "We just go to his house and wait." Lola sighs. "OK," she says. "Like, right now?"

"No, it's too late. We can go tomorrow," I say, wondering if I'll lose my nerve.

The next morning, I consult a map to figure out how to drive to Uncle Leo's house. Lola and I get in the car and drive past JFK and get on the Belt Parkway. Forty-five minutes later, we pull up in front of my uncle's house. It looks exactly the same as it did five years ago, the last time I saw it. Lola and I get out of the car and look at each other—what should we do now? I walk up the front steps and ring the bell and ... nothing. I look at her and she shrugs, reaching out to ring the bell again. We did not expect that everyone would be out, and then I realize it's Saturday morning, and they are probably all at synagogue.

"Should we wait?" Lola asks. We decide to wait till 1 o'clock. Since Lola slept till, like 11, and then took her sweet time getting ready, that's only about 20 minutes.

Then I see my Aunt Jenny, Uncle Leo, and Joseph walking down the street. Behind them are Iris and Georgia. Iris is maybe 11 now and Georgia is 16. Lola and I stand up. Iris sees us first and points and Uncle Leo and Aunt Jenny exchange glances. We can't hear what Iris is saying, but I'm guessing she's like, Who is on our porch? Last time we saw her, she was seven, and we had barely hit puberty, so it's understandable that she doesn't remember or recognize us.

Seeing Joseph for the first time in all these years feels like a punch to the gut. He's a little taller, and his hair is in a buzz cut and you can see the edge of one of his tattoos peeking out from underneath his polo shirt. I can't believe he's wearing a polo shirt. He's been here all along, less than an hour from our house, living his life, and I think this visit was a mistake, but it's too late now.

We walk down off the porch and wait for them on the sidewalk.

"Girls! It's so great to see you! What a nice surprise!" Uncle Leo says, reaching out to hug us. It would be incredibly rude to take a step back, so we allow ourselves to be hugged.

Our Aunt Jenny says, "Yes, such a nice surprise! Iris, Georgia, you remember your cousins Francie and Lola, right?" Iris obviously does not, but Georgia does, and she looks happy to see us, but also confused. She's taller than I am and has the same curly dark brown hair as Lola. Lola looks like my father, but her hair is from my mother's side, whereas I look like my mother, but my hair is from my father's side.

"Hey," Joseph says.

"Hi," I say.

"What are you guys doing here?" he asks. "Do Mom and Dad know you're here?"

"They're in France, with Aunt Darla and Uncle Gerald," Lola says.

He laughs. "Of course they are," he says.

"Well, come on in. We're just getting back from shul, we're going to have lunch. You'll stay for lunch?" Aunt Jenny asks. Lola and I look at each other—we had not planned this far. We follow them inside.

The front of the house is dark, but it looks the same inside, too, down to the nearly life-sized portraits of Iris and Georgia hanging in the living room. Aunt Jenny walks to the kitchen at the back of the house while our cousins go upstairs. We stand in the foyer awkwardly with Uncle Leo and Joseph.

Uncle Leo clears his throat. "Well, don't just stand around, come sit down." He gestures into the living room, and pulls open the shades, letting some light in. We sit down on the couch, Lola and I, and Joseph sits on the piano bench.

"What are you doing here?" Joseph asks again.

"We wanted to see you," Lola says in a small voice. She looks at me.

"After four years?" he asks.

"We wanted to see you the whole time," I say. "But I only got my license last year."

I am seized by anger. Why is he asking the questions? Why does it seem like he doesn't want to see us? I remember all the other letters that I wrote, the ones I did send, which went unanswered. And here he is, going to synagogue with my aunt and uncle, acting like a brother to my cousins instead of to Lola and me, his actual sisters.

I stand up abruptly. "I don't think we should have come," I say to Joseph and Uncle Leo. "Lola, c'mon."

"No," Lola says. "I want to stay."

Lunch is weird and awkward as my family members try to get to know Lola and me. We tell them about our lives, and they tell us about theirs, except for Joseph, who barely speaks the whole meal. He goes outside halfway through lunch to smoke a cigarette.

After lunch, the three of us sit on the back porch and Joseph smokes another cigarette.

"Well," he says.

"Well," I say.

"So you're going to college, huh," Joseph says. "The parents must be really proud." I shrug.

"They are," says Lola.

"And what about you, Lo? Are you going to go to college, too?"

"I mean, probably," she says. "I'm only going to be a junior, so..."

Joseph lights another cigarette with the butt of his current cigarette.

"Are you gonna go to college?" I ask Joseph.

He laughs. "No, I can't see that happening."

"You're just gonna live with Aunt Jenny and Uncle Leo for, like, the foreseeable future?"

Joseph stands up to walk around the little porch. He puts out his cigarette in an old paint bucket. "I have no idea what I'm gonna do, Francie. I'm just taking things one day at a time."

"Doesn't everyone just take things one day at a time?" I ask.

Joseph laughs. "It's from AA," he says. "You decide not to drink, or use, or whatever, and you finish that day, and you haven't used drugs. You made that choice for that day. And then you wake up the next day, and you choose again. Like, one day, I decided I didn't care what Mom and Dad thought about me living here, not being in treatment, not doing what they wanted. They kicked me out, then they wouldn't take me back in. Everything has to be on their terms. There's no compromise with them. And once I made that choice, not to care so much about what they thought, it was a lot easier for me to care about other things, like not using."

Lola nods. "I wish I could do that, care less about what Mom and Dad think."

I turn to her. "You don't care what they think!"

"Of course I do! But I just feel like I'm never going to live up to it, so I just, like, stop trying."

I think back to the book of Ruth that two-faced Adam made me read. It's been more than five months, and I'm still thinking about it. What kind of choices do I make? How do I make the choice of lovingkindness? I decide, right then, that's what I'm going to do. I don't know why Joseph's body is the way it is, why he can't drink or use drugs without becoming addicted, but he's making his way in the world, choice by choice, one day at a time. I can decide not to be angry with Joseph anymore. He's not the same person he was six years ago, or four years ago, and neither am I.

I can also decide that I don't want to wake up every morning wondering if Eitan is going to call me today or if I'll have gotten a letter from him in the mail. What a waste of my time. If he can forget me so easily, then I can try, every day, to forget him, and to live my life, this last summer before I go to college, while I'm still with all my friends, like every choice matters, because it does.

I stand up suddenly. "Joseph," I say, "Lola and I have to go. I have to drive her to work. But I don't want it to be another four years before we see you again." I give Joseph a fierce hug and he hugs me back, then Lola. We say goodbye to our aunt and uncle and cousins.

Joseph walks us over to the Volvo. "I can't believe you're driving, Francie," he says. I turn on the car and the tape in the tape deck is "In Through the Out Door."

"Is that mine?" he asks.

"It was," I say.

My parents return from France and seem a little relieved that the house is still standing, the car hasn't been totaled, everything seems OK. They have brought gifts for us, including chocolates and handbags. My mom has, like, 47 handbags. I have maybe three. But I thank her anyway and she says, "Thank your father, too," so I thank them both. Maybe I will need more handbags in college.

Lola and I have decided we will not mention our visit to see Joseph, but then she blurts it out over dinner anyway. My parents look at each other, then at us.

"Girls, we never said you couldn't see your brother," my mother says. "I know it's been hard on you. We can't have him living here, and I don't think we can visit him, or see him, because that's part of the tough love program."

"How is Leo, that asshole?" my father asks.

"Barry," my mother says.

"They're fine, everyone is fine," I say. "Joseph is staying in their basement, working with Uncle Leo. It's fine." I don't really want to get into the details, and I am a little annoyed at Lola for mentioning it, but I guess it's better. The last thing we need is for my grandmother to call my mother and tell her about it. I

239

know they still talk, even though my father thinks they don't.

***

Sooz invites us over to hang out at her pool. I haven't seen AJ for a few weeks because she's been off doing stuff with Alex. He left for baseball training in North Carolina at the beginning of August. He didn't get drafted, but he's still trying, I guess. I don't know the whole story, but I feel like there must be something sketchy going on, because it's Alex.

Sooz's parents would never allow her to have her friends over to use the pool if they weren't home, no unsupervised pool parties for her, and even her sister has come over from her house on the North Shore of Long Island. Sooz's sister is now pregnant, was probably pregnant at Passover and not telling anyone, and her pregnancy has made her even more insufferable. She keeps asking people to fetch things for her—a towel, iced tea, snacks, sunscreen, the list goes on. At least she knows not to ask AJ or me for this stuff.

The three of us laze about on the pool floats. There are only two, so AJ and I double up. AJ eyes me in my bathing suit.

"Did your chest get even bigger, Francie?" she asks. I look down at my black bikini top and shrug. It still fits, even if I look a little bustier.

"Wait till you get pregnant, girls," Linda calls from her lounge chair in the shade. "Then your boobs really get big."

AJ and I look at each other and burst out laughing.

***

Lola asks if I want to go to a party with her at Starr's house. I'm not too excited about it, but I have nothing else to do. Plus, I'm sure part of it is that Lola needs me to drive her.

Starr lives kind of in between Sooz and AJ, on the other side of town. When we get there, it's not clear that anyone is home, but Lola leads me around the side of the house and through the gate, and that's where everyone is hanging out, next to the pool. Everyone has a pool, it seems, Jesus Christ.

Because Starr is only a year younger than I am, I know a few of the people at this party, but not many. As I help myself to a can of Sprite, I wonder how Starr knows all these people. I feel someone put their hands on my glasses and before I turn around, I know it's Ari. "Hey," I say.

"What's up, Francie?" he says. "Congratulations on graduating! I knew you could do it."

"Very funny," I say.

"What've you been up to?" he asks, as we settle onto one of those long pool loungers.

"The usual," I say. "Going to work, hanging out with friends."

"What do you hear from Eitan? I got another postcard from him this week," Ari says.

My heart nearly stops beating. "What?"

"He's sent me, like, three postcards. I figured you must be getting one every other day. It seems like he's having a good time."

I say, very, very slowly so that I don't freak out, "He hasn't written me at all."

"Oh," Ari says. "Did you guys break up?"

I shake my head. "No. At least, I don't think we did. I thought maybe he wasn't writing anyone, but I guess that's not the case."

"I'm sorry, Francie. That's really shitty," Ari says.

I nod. "Yeah," I say. "It is really shitty."

"What are you gonna say to him when he gets back?" he asks.

I shrug. "I don't know. I mean, I'm going to college anyway, right? But if he wanted to break up with me, he could've done it before going to Israel."

"I would never do that, just not write, or call," Ari says.

"I know. I'm sure you're a great boyfriend," I say.

"No, I'm not," Ari says, laughing a little, turning to look at me. "I meant, I would never do that to you, Francie."

I don't know what to say to that, it's the most blatant flirting yet, but also, we are talking about his best friend, who I'm still, maybe, dating and definitely still in love with.

"Let's do something else," Ari says. "Let's get in the pool."

"I don't have a swimsuit," I say.

"Borrow one from Starr," he says.

Lola is already in the pool, why she didn't tell me to bring a swimsuit, I don't know. Starr lends me some tiny triangle top bikini that normally I would not have the guts to wear, but I don't have any other options. I am a total wuss about getting into water unless it's really warm, so I just sit on the side of the pool on a towel, dipping my feet.

Ari hops out of the water to sit next to me on the towel. He shakes his hair out of its ponytail, and then shakes it like a dog, getting me all wet. "The point is to get into the pool, Francie," he says, and then he slides back in, pulling me with him.

Everyone plays Marco Polo and Starr turns on the pool lights and we dive for little batons and stuff and obviously I don't have my glasses on so I can't really see anything, everything is blurry, but the blurriness and the lights make it seem almost magical.

When I get out of the pool, I wrap myself in a towel and go into Starr's house to get dressed. It feels freezing inside because the air conditioning is on. When I get out of the bathroom, I ask Lola if she wants to leave. She says she's going to stay over, and can I tell the parents. I say goodbye to Starr, and I look around to say goodbye to Ari. He's coming out of the house, too, also dressed. "Can you give me a ride home?" he asks.

When I pull up to his house, I realize this might be the last time I see Ari before I leave for Duke. I get out of the car to say goodbye.

Ari gives me a hug, and as I'm pulling away, he kisses me. It's really fast, but it definitely happens, and it's over before I can even react.

"Goodbye, Francie," he says. "Good luck in college. Don't forget me." He turns to go into the house, and I put my hand to my mouth, and get back into the car.

When Lola gets home from Starr's the next day, I'm sitting on my bed, wearing the sweatshirt I never gave back to Eitan, flipping through photos from the past year, rereading Eitan's Valentine's Day card to me, and listening to the mix tape he made me.

"Oh, Francie pants," she says, dropping her bag and sitting on the bed next to me.

I bury my head against her shoulder and cry.

***

Eitan comes home from Israel and calls me. I barely know what to say on the phone, I'm so hurt and angry and still love him so much that my heart aches. Boy disease in the end, I guess. He asks if he can come over and I say yes. He got his driver's license just before leaving for Israel, and he pulls up in front of my house in his dad's station wagon.

I walk outside to greet him. He is a little thinner, a little tanner, a little more adorable. It's all I can do not to bound down the steps and into his arms, but I don't know how he would react to that, and I also have to think about my own self and what little pride I might have left.

"Hey," I say.

"Hey," he says. He looks like he wants to say more. He looks, in fact, like it's all he can do not to grab me and kiss me.

I sit down on the little couch on the front porch of my house where no one ever sits, and Eitan sits down next to me.

"My mom said you came over to pick up some prom photos," Eitan says. Jesus Christ, he wants to talk about his mother?

"Eitan," I say, turning to look at him, my heart pounding in my throat. I can't not ask. "Why didn't you write me? Or call me? Did you forget about me as soon as you got on that plane?"

He looks at me like I'm nuts. "Of course not. I thought about you all the time, every day. But I thought it would be easier this way, Francie. That I would go away for six weeks and we could, like, get used to being away from each other and then it would be easier for you to go to college."

I laugh, but it's a hard laugh. "You did this—you didn't write me or call me—because you thought it would be easier for me?"

"It wasn't easy for me! I got all your letters, and then you stopped writing—"

"Are you joking with me? I stopped writing because I felt like a fool! I sent, like, three letters a week for four weeks, and you never wrote me back. You could have written just once, to break up with me, at the very least." I take a breath.

"Francie. I didn't want to break up with you. I'm still in love with you." Eitan swallows. "Ori was like—"

I nearly choke. "Ori? Your brother advised you on this?"

"He was like, She's gonna get to college and want to break up with you anyway, so you might as well break up beforehand..."

"But you didn't break up with me. You just— ignored me. If you'd wanted to break up, you should have told me. This whole year, you were like, tell me what's going on, tell me more, Francie, you should tell me everything. And I did! I told you everything, and I gave you everything. Or I tried to, anyway." I take a breath. "Look," I say, feeling like my mother. "I don't want to fight. I didn't want you to come over so we could have a fight. We never had a fight in a whole year."

"Why did you want me to come over?" Eitan asks.

"I wanted to know what happened," I say. "I was in love with you. I thought you were in love with me. We had sex the day before you left, for Lord's sake, and I wrote you all those letters, and when you didn't write me back, I thought my heart was actually breaking, like I could feel an actual pain in my chest. You broke my heart, Eitan." I take a breath.

Eitan's eyes look glassy, as if he's about to cry. "You <u>were</u> in love with me?" he says in a small voice. "You aren't anymore?"

I look at him, at his amazing body and his wavy hair that's in need of a cut and his adorable face and his golden brown eyes and I think about our year together and our conversations about everything and nothing and how he makes me feel, even now, sitting so close to him, and of course I'm still in love with him, but I shake my head, because I'm a few weeks into this heartbreak and I can't go backwards. "I—I don't know," I say. "But you accomplished what you wanted to, right? We aren't together anymore. I got used to not hearing from you. It was like a Band-Aid that you pulled off really, really slowly."

His tears spill over and he wipes at his face. "I'm so sorry, Francie," he says. He wipes at his eyes again.

I stand up. I know I told him he could come over, but I can't take this any longer, it's too difficult.

"Can I—can I give you a hug?" he asks.

He stands up and I stand up on my tiptoes and he hugs me and being here still feels so safe and he smells like Eitan and I would never mistake someone else for him. He pulls me closer, and I think about how easy it would be to tip my head back and kiss him, to forgive him, but I pull away instead, swallowing the lump in my throat.

"I can't do this," I say. "Goodbye, Eitan." I walk back into my house and I shut the door and lean against it and listen as he walks down the front path and gets into his car and drives away and then I allow the tears to come.

Tammy, Sooz, AJ, and I all go out to that same cheesy club on the beach. This is an attempt to cheer me up, although I insist I don't need it. I've been kind of mourning my relationship with Eitan for the past month at least. His coming home and making our breakup official is just that—making it official.

"But now that you're single, you should be making out with other people," Tammy says, as we jump around the crowded dance floor.

"Like, here?" I ask.

"Yes!" she says. I shake my head.

"I can't make out with a stranger on a dance floor," I say, even as we watch Sooz do that very thing ten feet away from us.

AJ and Alex haven't broken up. Despite everything I think about Alex, he turns out to be much better at being a long-distance boyfriend than Eitan was. I think about what Eitan would think about that, whether he'd still call it ridiculous that AJ and Alex are in love. They're going to stay together when she goes to college and see what happens. I wonder if Alex is drinking at baseball training. I wonder if he needs to take things one day at a time.

On my last day at the photo shop, I am filing the stack of photos that Michelle finished the night before. There are alphabetized bins and I take each of the packets of photos and organize them by last name. In the middle of the stack is a packet of Eitan's photos—I see his unique last name and his phone number and I am torn. Of course I shouldn't open them and look at his photos. What could I possibly gain by doing so? Why would he even drop them off here, knowing I work here? Maybe one of his parents did it, who knows.

Michelle sees me pause. "Did they forget to put a last name? You can just put it under first name."

I hesitate for a minute. "No, there's a last name," I say. "It's my ex-boyfriend."

Without missing a beat, she takes the packet from me, her cigarette dangling from her lips. She opens the outer envelope and pulls out the inner envelope, the one with the pictures. I stand next to her as we flip through Eitan's photos from his trip to Israel. Eitan in front of various ancient ruins, in front of various bodies of water, covered in mud at the Dead Sea, smiling and laughing.

I take a quick breath when I see him with his arm around some pretty girl in a bathing suit, maybe some girl from Cherry Hill, like Tammy said, I don't know. She's in a bunch of photos with him. Michelle looks at me as I pick up the bathing suit photo and they're not kissing, they're not even holding hands, but their faces are so close, and even though I'm not allowed to feel jealous anymore, I can't help it, I feel sick to my stomach with jealousy.

I put the photos back and file them away.

My father takes me to a camera store the week before I leave for Duke. I'm going to bring the SLR to college, but he wants to get me a slightly nicer point-and-shoot as a graduation present. The store is in a neighboring town and when we walk in, there are a few other people inside. My dad goes over to the counter and we look at a few models under the glass. A teenage boy comes up to us behind the counter.

"Do you need any help?" he asks.

I look up and our eyes meet, and it's my cute skater boy. He smiles at me.

"Hey," I say.

"Hey," he says. "Haven't seen you in a long time. It's Francie, right?"

I nod. My dad looks at him. "You two know each other?"

"Sort of," I say. I look at skater boy's shirt and see his name tag: Nick. Well, now I know.

***

After I stopped writing to Eitan, and certainly after he got home, I stopped checking the mail so obsessively. So it's a bit of a surprise when I pick up the mail from the mailbox at our front door and find a letter addressed to me. As I sort through the rest of the mail, I see there's a letter for Lola, too.

I flip the letter over as I walk up the stairs. There's no return address, and I can't read the postmark. I open it and it's two pages of loose-leaf paper and I can tell, without even looking at the signature, that it's from Joseph. His handwriting hasn't changed at all.

I sit on the floor, leaning against the bed, and read it a few times. He wrote that he's glad Lola and I came to visit, that he's sorry everything is such shit with the parents and our family, that he hopes I'll come see him again or maybe we can meet up in the city sometime, that he hopes I have a great time at college, and I should write him to tell him all about it. I tuck it back into the envelope and put it in the folder where I keep all of my letters.

***

Jason calls me and asks me if I want to come over.

"It's the last night I have before my mom and my step-dad come back from Florida and then I leave for Brown. I thought we could, you know, do our thing." Jason's mom had a baby boy in March. He didn't go with them to Florida because he's lifeguarding at the beach until the last minute to have money for college.

I walk over to his house and we pull out the old yearbooks and page through them, eating pigs in blankets that we made in the toaster oven.

When he goes to take Roxie for a quick walk, I stay behind because it's raining out and I don't want to get wet. I have ulterior motives, though, because I find our high school yearbook and true to his word, it has no autographs or signatures or anything. I crack it open and begin to write.

Dear Jason,

I am glad I'll be the only person to write in your yearbook. Our friendship has meant the world to me, and I know we will always be friends. That sounds like something cheesy that a person might write in a yearbook, but it's the truth. While you're off at Brown, eating chowder and doing New England things, and I'm off at Duke, eating biscuits and doing Southern things, we will be thinking of each other, I just know it.

I remember meeting you in kindergarten and it was clear from the first time I helped you with your phonics homework that we would be friends forever. I'll never forget our after-school walks, the time you called Mr. Everett's wife an old bag and got sent to the principal's office, when you asked Dr. Choi for a hall pass but really you went to the secret Ticketmaster to buy Allman Brothers tickets, watching TV together while talking on the phone. It's all burned into my memory.

I'll always love you, even if our timing as a couple didn't seem to work out right.

Dated till Niagara Falls,

Francie

I close the book and tuck it back on the shelf. When Jason comes back from walking the dog, he's nearly soaking wet.

"There are such things as umbrellas," I say.

"I know, I know," he says. "This is with an umbrella." He turns around and pulls off his wet t-shirt and puts on a clean white one, not knowing, of course, that a cute guy in a white t-shirt is like my Kryptonite.

"So," he says.

"So," I say.

"Do you want to watch the bar mitzvah video, or should we watch something else?" he asks. He walks over to his bookshelf next to the bed where he has, like, 50 VHS tapes. I kneel next to him, our heads almost touching, and that shiver runs down my spine.

I pull out "Ferris Bueller's Day Off," which I know is one of Jason's favorites. "Jay," I ask, turning to look at him, "are Jeannie and Ferris twins?"

"Oh my God, I can't believe I never thought to ask that question before," he says. He takes the tape, and we stand up.

All of a sudden, I know what's going to happen— we are going to start a movie, and then we are going to make out. This was not my intention when I came over to Jason's house. But if we're just going to make out, why even bother with the pretense of a movie? I am not interested in a movie, certainly not one I've seen a hundred times.

I turn to Jason, and then he turns to me, and then, this time, for the first time, I kiss a boy first. He drops the tape on the floor and kisses me back. This is easy to do because we're almost the same height. I think to myself, I should only date guys who are kind of short. Screw Eitan and his six feet of bullshit.

I take off my glasses and put them on the bookshelf and we move to the bed. "Why weren't we doing this all summer?" Jason asks in between kisses.

"Because I thought I had a boyfriend all summer," I say.

"Oh, yeah. You and your faithfulness to an absentee boyfriend," he says. I know I'm not going to sleep with Jason, but kissing him is fun, and I meant what I wrote in his yearbook, and there's no time like the present, right?

GRADUATION MIX TAPE FOR JASON
Accidents Will Happen, by Elvis Costello
Bittersweet, by Big Head Todd and the Monsters
Here Comes Your Man, by the Pixies
Labour of Love, by Frente!
Skyway, by the Replacements
Divorce Song, by Liz Phair
Is it for Me, by Toad the Wet Sprocket
After Hours, by the Velvet Underground

***

The night before our drive down to North Carolina, Lola sleeps in my room, in my bed with me. We talk for a long time.

"I can't believe you are really going. You're really leaving me alone with the parents," Lola whispers, even though obviously no one else can hear.

"I'm sorry, Lo," I say. "Maybe you can go to Duke in two years?"

Lola scoffs. "There's no way I'd get in."

I'm not sure if she's fishing for a compliment or something, but she is probably right. "I'll be home at Thanksgiving, and you'll come to visit me. It's not really that far. It's only, like, an hour and a half flight."

I think about Joseph's letter, and that his birthday is at Thanksgiving, and even though I shouldn't, I make a wish that he'll be at Aunt Darla and Uncle Gerald's in November.

"What are you most excited for?" she asks.

"I don't know...I don't even know what to be excited for, you know? Like, everything will be new."

"Yeah, I guess so."

We finally fall asleep and then it seems like only moments later that my father is waking us up so we can get on the road early.

We smoosh all of my bags into the trunk of the Volvo and cover them with the sheets and I try not to think about the last time I used those sheets. I mean, I washed them of course, but will everything always remind me of Eitan?

I have already said goodbye to Tammy, to AJ, to Sooz. They have already left. We promise to share our e-mail addresses once we have them. Everyone is very excited about e-mail.

Lola and I pile into the back seat, pushing aside my bedding, which does not match Stacey's bedding, despite AJ, at her job, urging Stacey to get something that would coordinate with mine. Stacey is driving down with her parents and her younger brother, and we're all going to have dinner together in North Carolina.

The drive is nearly ten hours, and as each hour passes, as we scan the radio for music we can all sing along to, as we stop for my mother and me to pee, I feel high school slipping away down the New Jersey Turnpike, down I-95, down I-85, and then we are off the highway and I watch the low houses go by slowly as we drive through town and pull into the red brick campus and I take Lola's hand and give it a squeeze.

I am seventeen years old and Lola is fifteen years old and Joseph is twenty-one years old. I don't know who we will be to each other in another four years, another six years, another eight years, but I can't wait to find out.

Acknowledgements

I would like to thank Halley Agnello, Nicole Cooksey, Mary Elder, Shawna Kaplan, Jocelyn Rick, and Pamela Winfrey for their thoughtful comments and time while reading drafts of this novel. Thank you to Brianne Kelleher, Jared Stern, and Cara Wulfsohn for their memories. Thank you to Reed Martin and Deborah Berry for their book marketing advice.

Thank you also to NaNoWriMo, for the platform and the push to get this novel started, and to The Girls Club, my online writing sorority.

This book would not have been possible without the support of my husband, Alex. My children, Asher and Phoebe, have also been very understanding when I couldn't do something with them because I was writing. I hope one day, they will read this book and not find it too cringe.

I also thank my siblings, Josh and Sarah, and my parents, Jane and Warren.

Books I read and music I listened to

The Life and Crimes of Hoodie Rosen, by Isaac Blum
Are You There God? It's Me, Margaret., by Judy Blume
Forever..., by Judy Blume
Emergency Contact, by Mary HK Choi
Saint Anything, by Sarah Dessen
You'd Be Home Now, by Kathleen Glasgow
Turtles All the Way Down, by John Green
Nantucket Blue, by Leila Howland
Nantucket Red, by Leila Howland
Jessica Darling Series, by Megan McCafferty
Fangirl, by Rainbow Rowell
The Catcher in the Rye, by JD Salinger
Today Tonight Tomorrow, by Rachel Lynn Solomon

And here is a QR code to a playlist of the mix tapes in
the book: